Bringing Forth Belial

Book 1

Riley Daemon

Riley Daemon Creations

To anyone society has deemed worthless.

Ave Belial.

Acknowledgements

Shout out to my friend Rhe, who also did the chapter header illustrations for this book. It probably wouldn't even exist if it wasn't for the two of us sitting at her kitchen table. I was browsing books about demons and mentioned that there were a lot about Lucifer and Asmodeus, but I hadn't seen any about Belial. So she suggested I write one with a plot that invoked his lawless nature. I really liked the idea and jumped right into planning.

Also to Cian who did the absolutely amazing book cover! I've loved Cian's art ever since I first saw their Ars Goetia reimagined illustrations. That being what made me reach out on a whim to see if they would be up for doing a book cover. It makes me *so* happy to include other people on this book who love demons just as much as I do!

Another thanks for my editor Quinton Li! I'm still nervous when it comes to showing people my works and having them pick it apart. But they made the process a fun one for me and I'm so happy that they liked this book, haha.

And, of course, a final thanks for the demons themselves. Ave~

Author's Note

Bringing Forth Belial has a positive outlook on topics such as the occult and theistic Satanism. If these are things that make you uncomfortable, then it might not be the book for you and that's okay.

This book also contains: Violence, Dark imagery involving skulls, death, out-of-body experiences, Religious themes and Religious persecution, oppressive and violent government systems.

Chapter 1

The sun began to set. Darkness befell the tiny apartment, as only the gentle flickers of candlelight remained to give a soft, warm glow. They created shadows that danced across the boarded up window and old sofa positioned beside it. A person sat there, hunched over and diligently working. Empty glass bottles and beeswax were strewn about her scuffed up coffee table as she carefully dipped another wick into her boiling pot. Furthest from her on the table were candles, completed, and not yet burned. She felt an ache in her back, but hardly paid any mind. Only when she heard a commotion from outside did she pause her work.

She sat up straight, an unsettled chill down her spine as she leaned towards the window. She carefully tugged one of the loose boards down and what little sunlight was left filtered into the room. The sudden light burned so she rubbed at her eyes to help them adjust. Just enough to catch a glance of the street below.

In front of her apartment complex was the back of a shop. Between the two buildings was an alleyway that few people used. However, at that moment, she could see someone lumbering about down there. They dressed all in black and paced nervously, looking towards the end of the alley. An upturned box of trash sat at their feet; the source of the noise. She felt a twist in her gut as she hoped they would continue on by. Then the person on the street bolted.

A moment later, a Paladin adorned to the brim with their usual tactical gear appeared. They rushed off in the direction the person in black had gone, vanishing from view. She wasted not a minute more to put the board back in place, casting her apartment into shadow once more. She wondered why someone would choose to wear such dark colors as they mulled about. They could have been too poor to have anything else, but it would be best to go naked in that case. Unless said person actually was... *nefarious*.

That was none of her business, she reassured herself as she turned back to her candle-making.

There was a knock on the door.

Her hands shook as a block of wax slipped from her fingers and clattered loudly to the floor. Damn it. She looked across the small living space to where the door sat next to the kitchenette. Was it the Paladin? What could they want with her? She had nothing to do with the person who had gone past her apartment window. Or could it have been... the person dressed in black? Her hands grew clammy as a million possibilities flew through her mind. A million painful ways she could find her end on the other-side of that door. Be it by fire or a ritual blade.

"Miss Alena Usher, are you home?" called a woman's voice from the other-side of the door. Unfortunately, Alena had to acknowledge that, yes, she was home. Alena, with the title of 'miss' feeling like poison to her ears, stood with stiff knees and hobbled to the door. She hesitated.

"I'm with the P.O.E. May I come in?" the woman asked.

Alena wanted to pretend she wasn't home. Instead, she calmed her shaking hands and opened the door. She had no other choice.

"Good afternoon, Miss. I'm Lady Chambers," the woman said with a large and almost fake smile plastered onto her sharp face. Alena wanted to say she didn't like such feminine titles as *'miss'*, but refrained. Instead, she gave Lady Chambers a once over, immediately noting how the woman wore a fanciful pantsuit. Human hands could have never crafted such an article of clothing, and so Alena knew it must have been a relic from the time when machines were still around to do menial tasks. Evidence of Lady Chambers' ranking and wealth. It made Alena feel out of place, even in her own apartment, with her handwoven clothes.

Alena brushed the feeling off as the woman looked at her expectantly.

"Is there a problem, my lady?" Alena asked, voice raspy from lack of use. She forwent introductions, as clearly this woman already knew who she was. A thought that made Alena sickened to her stomach. Lady Chambers was quick to wave her off.

"Oh no, nothing is wrong, in particular," she responded. Her tone was still chipper, and it grated against Alena's eardrums. Lady Chambers didn't wait for a response as she continued, "I'm actually here about your grandfather. A Mr. Rick Usher?"

Alena knew nothing of whatever trouble the man could have gotten into. He was practically a stranger. However, if the P.O.E. wanted him, then it must have involved something *nefarious*. A wall went up as Alena was quick to defend herself.

"I'm sorry," she said, "but I haven't had contact with any of my family in years. I don't know what he's done."

Lady Chambers let her own facade slip for a moment and looked surprised, but she was quick to bury it again. The woman's smile dripped down to display an air of sorrow.

"Mr. Usher hasn't gotten into any trouble, no." Lady Chambers sighed. "I'm sorry to be the bearer of bad news, but he's passed away recently."

"Oh," was all Alena got out. For how should one react to the passing of a family member they hardly knew? Perhaps she had met him once as a baby, but that would have been at least twenty-five years ago. Back when her parents still gave a damn.

"That being said," Lady Chambers went on, "you *are* his next of kin and so his house and other assets will go to you."

Alena gaped. That didn't sound right. What of her parents? Alena's brows pinched together as she gave the woman a confused look.

"Are you sure that's correct?" she asked. "Isn't there anyone else more qualified to get his stuff?"

Lady Chambers sighed, a long and drawn out melodramatic thing.

"Mr. Usher was born in the *Before Times,*" she explained, "so there's hardly any documentation on him. The man was a bit of a recluse."

Alena felt a hint of a smile on her face, foreign to her muscles. She and the old man had that in common, at least. It still didn't explain where her parents were, but for all Alena knew, they could have been banished or killed. She decided not to ask about them. They were no longer her business. Instead, she thought back to her grandfather. Maybe she could entertain the thought.

"You said I would get his house. Where'd he live?" Alena asked.

"It's nothing much." Lady Chambers looked around Alena's dust covered apartment. It consisted of the main living area, complete with kitchenette, a bathroom, and then a small closet-sized bedroom. There were several candles set around for light. All crafted by Alena's hands. "But it would definitely be an upgrade from what you have now. It's an old, outdated place up in the mountains, quite an annoying drive out there."

Alena had only ever seen the mountains from a distance, tall peaks that appeared green from the vast forest that covered them. She wasn't one for the outdoors, but the thought of inheriting her grandfather's reclusive lifestyle was tantalizing. Her mouth nearly watered at the thought. However, would that bring more attention to her from the government and P.O.E.? Not to mention her business. She had such a nice setup here and could easily barter and trade for whatever she needed. Perhaps it would be too much trouble. Lady Chambers cleared her throat to get Alena's attention once more.

"I understand if you don't want to uproot the life you already have here," she said. Her eyes sparkled as she went on, "If you don't want to leave, you can simply donate the house and its contents to the kingdom. We will be very thankful."

Alena didn't miss the part where she wouldn't get compensated, but that would be for the best. Greed was a demonic trait, after-all, and she didn't want the *Paladins of Exorcism* to doubt her motives. Alena was about to agree to Lady Chambers and just give the place to the kingdom when something stopped her.

The darkness within her tiny apartment felt thick and caressed her shoulders, as if expecting her answer. She turned to look around, nearly expecting someone to be behind her. There were only her supplies and the window, but no one could have possibly seen through that. Not with the boards and Alena being on the second floor.

She thought of the Paladin she had seen run by. And of the person dressed in black. Alena looked back towards Lady Chambers, who stared at her with expectation. Her smile never wavered. At that moment, something clenched in Alena's gut and she knew she couldn't give the house to the P.O.E.

Alena nodded and, as sure as she could be, said, "I'll take the house."

Only slightly did Lady Chambers' smile falter, but to Alena, it could have been a trick of the candlelight. Funny things, candles could be. In the distance, a blood-curdling scream echoed throughout the kingdom. The Paladin must have caught up to the person in black.

"Well then, Miss Alena Usher," Lady Chambers said, her smile reinstated. "Your life is about to change."

Chapter 2

Perhaps Alena had made a mistake.

She foolishly assumed inheriting her grandfather's property was as simple as packing her bags and leaving. That wasn't the case. Over the next couple of weeks, members of the P.O.E. frequently visited her. They showed up unannounced and flashed lights in her eyes, from technology she was unfamiliar with. Every person who visited would drill her with the same questions.

"Why are you moving?"

"What do you hope to accomplish?"

"What are your plans for the future?"

"Is anyone going to be living with you?"

Alena answered each one with the same answers every time. She answered honestly, to the best she could, void of any emotion. When the strangers were gone, she would curl up on her couch and hope it was finally over, only for a different agent to return the next day. The same questions.

They were trying to figure out if she had *nefarious* leanings, that much she knew. Alena didn't, of course, for the simple thought of being near those *nefarious* things brought her to tears. But the Paladins of Exorcism didn't know that, so she would have to appear as normal as she could. The last thing she wanted was for them to see her as strange.

Several times throughout those few weeks, she had nearly grown to regret her decision. Luckily for her, in the fourth week, she finally got approval for her move and ownership of the property.

That's how Alena found herself in the passenger seat of a *car*, of all things, Lady Chambers at the wheel as if she were an old pro. The vehicle slowly made its way up the old dirt road, bumping over roots and stray rocks that had fallen from the cliff sides. Alena wanted so desperately to look at the passing foliage as they went, but the blur of brown and green from the trees churned her stomach. She tried to get rid of the feeling by keeping her arms tightly wrapped around her flattened chest.

"So, how are you enjoying your first car ride?" Lady Chambers asked, to which Alena glanced up at her. The older woman had looked her way for only a second so she could focus mainly on the road. There was a slight smirk to her ever-present smile now. Alena didn't like the expression, but knew better than to call it out.

"It's fine," Alena lied. The conversation died down once more, the two obviously not having anything in common. Even if they did, Alena knew better than to associate with anyone from the P.O.E. The mere thought of being so close to a P.O.E. agent was enough to make Alena want to crawl under her blankets and stay there. At the thought, Alena turned her head to look out the back window towards the much larger truck that followed them. Emblazoned on its hood were the words *'Paladins of Exorcism'*, along with the government agency's emblem.

That was about all Alena could look at before she twisted back around, slightly dizzy. She would be happy when they got there and she would never have to set foot in another car again.

Alena glanced at the dashboard, full of dials and gauges that were foreign to her. She could hardly believe at one point in history, the average person used to drive such a thing. That was one perk of living in the city, Alena supposed. She didn't have to worry about borrowing a car from the government or buying a horse to get around.

Further the car went and eventually the trees thinned out. Alena could catch sight of the city that was once her home. The Kingdom of Lenoria. It looked small from several miles up in the mountains. The buildings of the most populated parts of the kingdom city were not super impressive, made of wood and stone from the local forests. They looked lived in and inviting, but Alena knew they were anything but. She could still see the kingdom's truths written by the enormous steel skeletons of buildings on the outskirts. Buildings that had once been populated in the Before Times. Lenoria had not always been a kingdom that existed. It was quite possibly the last remnant of a country that was once known as the United States. However, that was before Alena was born.

Soon, the city view vanished as they drove back into the cover of trees. Would she miss living there? She was unsure.

Eventually, the vehicle pulled into an overgrown clearing that doubled as a driveway. As they pulled to a stop, Alena threw herself forward as she snapped her gaze towards the house before them. It definitely was *old*, just like Lady Chambers said, the style of building far different from any down in the city. What exactly could it be called? It had at least two floors, the very top pointing towards the sky. In the building's front was a wrap-around porch with stairs that looked like they would fall in at any moment. Perhaps at one point the house was black or dark gray, but by now most of the paint had chipped off. That was for the best.

Alena still stared in awe as Lady Chambers turned the car off and got out. Alena, realizing she was being left behind, hurried after her. The mountain air flooded her lungs, crisp and clean. It was almost too much, especially after the jaunting ride. She glanced towards the trees in the direction the city had been in. There, through the foliage, she could catch sight of a few buildings. An ever looming presence, but she supposed she didn't mind. It would remind her of what was down there, just several miles away.

The truck that followed them pulled up just shortly behind Lady Chambers' vehicle. Alena decided it was best to not linger as a large man got out. He dressed in the tactical armor of a Paladin, a dagger at his side, the Paladins of Exorcism's emblem embroidered onto his vest, just like on the truck. The sight of a raven being knocked down from flight with three arrows in its chest was enough to make Alena scramble away.

She went over to where Lady Chambers awaited her on the porch by the front door.

"I want to apologize now for the state this place might be in," the older woman said as she held up a slightly rusted key. It matched the one from her car and dangled on the same keyring. "This place has been abandoned since Mr. Usher's passing and there's been some reports of squatters. You know how it is."

Alena nodded as she glanced back at the Paladin, his hand on his sheath. Lady Chambers cleared her throat.

"Oh, don't worry about him." She turned the key into the lock. "He's just here in case those people are still around and doing... nefarious things.

"Y-Yeah, that would be really scary to come across," Alena repressed a shudder. She knew something along those lines was what the P.O.E. agents would want to hear. She was right as Lady Chambers' smile widened. Alena would have breathed a sigh of relief if she weren't well aware of the Paladin that still stood behind her.

Alena was innocent. She did nothing "nefarious", which Alena and the rest of the Lenorian residents knew the true meaning of. The reason they even needed *'Paladins of Exorcism.'* Alena shuffled as the thought of dark claws and sharpened horns flashed through her mind. She didn't want to bring it up, but knew she had to keep an eye out for her own safety.

"Speaking of which," Alena said and hoped it wouldn't seem like she was too interested, "Am I safe out here without the Paladins to protect me?"

"Of course!" Lady Chambers was quick to say. "Because of the P.O.E. there are no *demons* in Lenoria. As long as you have faith in the Paladins, you shall be safe."

Lady Chambers threw open the door and a cloud of dust and cobwebs puffed out towards them. Alena peered into the darkness before her. Something moved. Alena nearly missed it as two tiny orbs flickered from deep within the house. The shadows burst forth and Lady Chambers screamed as something small and furry shot out of the building. Alena leaped out of the way as the creature vanished around the side of the porch. A second later, the Paladin's dagger soared through the air and embedded in the house's front.

Alena's chest constricted as if a snake had coiled its way around her. All she could do was grip at her shirt and wheeze. The dagger glinted threateningly in the sunlight, and the sight of it was too much to bear.

"What kind of vermin was that?!" Lady Chambers shrieked, her mask broken for the moment. Her voice snapped Alena out of it as she looked where the mysterious animal had run off to.

"Opossum, probably," the man said as he retrieved his dagger. Lady Chambers nodded as she sent the man off with a flick of the wrist. He followed the order and returned to the truck to gather up boxes. Alena's few belongings.

"Ah, well, I'm so sorry for that, Miss Usher," Lady Chambers went on as she finally entered the house. Alena followed and immediately the musty scent of dust and stale air slammed her sinuses. "Those ruffians must have let that thing in. Shouldn't be a problem now, though."

"So anyway, you won't have to worry about burning so many candles here," Lady Chambers said as she left Alena in the house's entryway. Alena frowned. What was wrong with candles? The woman went on from somewhere further in the house. "There's a lot of big windows with natural lighting."

Lady Chambers pulled open a curtain in the other room and light flooded through the house's interior. Alena winced and wondered if it would be okay to board up the windows. What if someone looked inside at her and thought of her actions as nefarious? Or what if there actually were monstrous demons in Lenoria? What if one passed by and saw her through the window? Alena could worry about that later, but for now, she looked around.

The staircase before her curled up to the second floor. Next to the first step was an archway, though the house beyond was still too dark to see. It was just like when the animal ran out of the front door. She could see the darkness rippling and nearly imagined movement. And if she stared longer, would she see eyes?

Alena forced herself away from the dark hall and followed where Lady Chambers had gone. The woman met her halfway as she entered the new room. It would have been large and expansive, had it not been for all the junk her grandfather had collected and never thrown out.

"This is the living room," Lady Chambers said as she gestured towards a rather nice looking sofa, all things considered. It sat facing a fireplace with a couple of other reclining chairs of varying quality. A coffee table similar to the one at Alena's apartment sat between them. She took a few steps forward to look at the fireplace, her thoughts on the cold winter nights in her apartment. Having a fire to keep warm sounded nice, but it was a fixer upper. It appeared her grandfather had used it as storage, several boxes and old newspapers shoved inside.

Alena turned back around and noticed something else shoved up against the opposing wall, shattered and long forgotten. She curiously approached it.

"What's this?" she asked, motioning to the strange box.

"Oh!" Lady Chambers exclaimed. "That's a TV! People used to watch those all the time."

"Why?"

"It was entertainment." Lady Chambers shrugged. "You never heard of TV?"

"I guess," Alena murmured, for she heard stories but never actually saw what they looked like. Interesting, it would appear her grandfather had even kept things from the Before Times. It made her curious, yet... weary. She was unsure about being around such archaic things.

"Well, never mind that. We need to hurry this along," Lady Chambers said, as she pulled Alena back into the foyer. She motioned to the stairs. "Up there is the main bedroom and bathroom. I'll allow you to check those out in your own time. You're lucky this place still has running water. It comes from the mountain stream."

The woman was quick to head over to the archway opposite of the living room, skipping the dark hallway by the stairs.

"And this is the kitchen and dining area," Lady Chambers went over. "The fridge no longer works, of course, but it'll be good extra storage."

Alena glanced over the room to see it was mostly tidy, unlike the living room. There was a long countertop that would put her apartment kitchenette to shame. Also appliances, like the fridge Lady Chambers mentioned, and even an oven and microwave, although they were of no use other than decor. To the left was a full dining table and chairs pushed up against even more windows. Beside those, there was another door that led out to the back porch. Alena had little time to take it all in as Lady Chambers ushered her back to the foyer.

"Well, that's about it," the woman said. "I've got some work to do back at the office so I'll let you get settled in. We'll be leaving your things on the porch."

Alena opened her mouth to question the dark hallway, but snapped it shut. Something made the back of her throat feel heavy, like she was close to a panic. It made her unsure if she wanted to mention it. Like she *shouldn't* mention it. And so she didn't.

Instead, Alena forced a smile and spoke in her broken tone, "Thanks so much for all your help."

She wasn't actually thankful, she just knew that's what the woman wanted to hear. Lady Chambers' grin brightened, if that were possible.

"Of course, now please don't be a stranger if you need help," she said. However, Alena already decided she wanted to be a stranger to this woman. Lady Chambers went on, "That being said, you *are* still in the kingdom's land, which means we need to keep tabs on you."

What? This was the first time anyone had mentioned it to Alena.

"We do this with all citizens that live outside the city limits," Lady Chambers explained, as if it were everyday business. "It's just to make sure nothing 'nefarious' takes place. So we'll be sending one of our Paladins once a month or so to do a wellness check on you."

'Wellness check, my ass,' Alena heard the thought before she could stop herself. She blinked, a little taken aback by herself. That wasn't like her, but she supposed she was just exhausted from what the P.O.E. had put her through during the past month. While she hadn't been checked on like that in the city, she supposed sacrificing a single day of comfort would suffice for the secludedness she would gain otherwise.

"That sounds good to me," Alena responded. The older woman's smile never faltered as she handed off her keys to Alena and turned to take her leave. Alena started as she now held both the house *and* car keys. She called after her, "Wait, you forgot your own key!"

"Oh, don't worry about that," Lady Chambers said as she stepped out onto the porch. Alena approached her, but hesitated by the door.

'*This is your home now,*' said her inner voice. Something about the words felt warm, like honey. Lady Chambers walked past Alena's boxes of belongings and headed towards where the Paladin waited inside his truck. She stopped only to motion towards the car she had driven there.

"It's a rental, you're going to need a way to get to the city," she said. "Instructions on how to drive it are in the glove-box. You'll be given your monthly ration of gasoline whenever the Paladin assigned to your wellness checks visits. Goodbye, for now, Miss Usher."

Alena wanted to argue, but found she could only stand there dumbfounded. And so Lady Chambers clambered her way up into the large truck and she and the Paladin took their leave. Alena stood there for a few minutes to watch as they vanished from view. She finally let out a breath as part of her didn't believe what was actually happening. She had escaped the city and now would reside all alone, far out from any prying eyes.

'*All alone...*'

Alena slid the door shut and turned around. The hallway by the stairs was still just as dark. And if she focused, maybe she really did see something move.

Chapter 3

Alena wasn't sure how to settle into her grandfather's old home. *Her* new home. She initially moved all her boxes into the foyer, where she would leave them for the time being. Perhaps eventually she would go through the old man's things and toss them out, but as of right now she felt weary. The whole move and interacting with the Paladins and agents of the P.O.E. had been far too stressful, and all she truly wanted was to get some rest.

However, she would keep herself busy as usual. Alena found it to be the best way to ignore the slight hollow feeling she got in her chest. Just as hollow as the emptied halls she now wandered by her lonesome.

Alena headed to the kitchen. She rustled through each of the cabinets and fridge to see what was already there. To no surprise, a majority was spoiled, aside from a few soup cans. She set those aside and tossed the rest away into a large cloth bag she found shoved in one of the cupboards. Once that was done, she left the bag by the back door and glanced over her handiwork. The place was now bare of food, aside from the few cans. Alena hadn't brought any herself.

She planned to go shopping for supplies once she settled in, after she saw what exactly she'd need in the new place. No deliveries went out this far, so Alena would still have to take trips to the city. Hopefully she could buy a few weeks' worth, if not a month, whenever she went out.

That also meant she would have to learn how to drive that confounded vehicle. She groaned at the thought. Alena turned to glance out the kitchen window where the sky turned shades of orange and pink. She'd get some rest for the night and leave in the morning.

As the forest around the house grew gray with shadow, Alena suddenly caught sight of movement in the bushes. She set her hand on the glass panes. Without the boards that covered up her old apartment's window, she felt exposed.

She stared where the movement had been, and there, the same two eyes she saw in the house's depths stared back. Alena fell still, her breath shallow, until there was a flourish and the strange animal vanished into the forest. It only left the leaves quivering in its wake. Alena sighed and left the window. Instead, she double checked to make sure the backdoor was locked up tight before heading back into the foyer towards the stairs.

She paused as she approached the dark hallway. Alena didn't understand the way the area made her legs quiver. It wasn't like there were demons hiding away in the shadows, ready to eat her soul. *There were no more demons in Lenoria.* It was just another part of the house. Alena shook off the feeling and wondered if it would be strange for her to board up the hall too. Though she supposed that wouldn't look too good in the eyes of the P.O.E. She was stumped.

It was something Alena would have to mull over as she hurried forward and practically leaped up onto the third step. She wasted no time climbing up to the second floor, only stopping once she reached the landing. Alena clutched the safety rails as she leaned over them to peer down at the hall entrance. She half-expected something to crawl out of it and give chase. However, she was still alone. The hollow feeling grew.

At that, Alena headed into the main bedroom. It was a large space, much like the living room, but also similarly filled to the brim. She glanced over the knick-knacks and antiques, thankful her grandfather had left a clear path on the floor to the enormous king-sized bed.

Alena slowly entered the room. The way to the windows was blocked, but luckily curtains already covered them. Alena made it to the bed and ran her hand over the old comforter. It felt unlike anything she had before. It was thick and red, with a gold pattern embossed on it. They certainly didn't make them like that anymore. She imagined it would be warm, but doubted the hard material would be comfortable.

There was also the concern of whether her grandfather had... died in this bed. The thing did look rather unlived in, though, so that theory was probably untrue. But the thought was still enough to unsettle her. She gripped the comforter and tugged it off the bed. While she was at it, she also removed the sheets and discarded them all onto the floor.

Alena climbed onto the bare mattress. Her own blanket was still packed away, and she didn't feel like going back downstairs to search for it in her boxes. Especially not now, as the sun went down. Even though she was alone without anyone around for miles, something else lingered heavy in the air. Perhaps even more than in the city. Not for the first time, she hoped she hadn't made a mistake in moving there. And it likely wouldn't be the last time either.

As Alena laid back in bed and curled around herself, it was not lost on her that it was designed for more than one person. She hated big beds like that. The hollowness creeped further down her limbs, but it stopped when her mind snapped elsewhere. Alena froze as she caught sight of the bedroom door. She had left it open, not thinking anything of it and could see out onto the landing. The sun had gone down. Alena's breath hitched. The darkness from the eerie hallway had crept out and engulfed the rest of the house.

Alena leaped up from the bed and bolted towards the door. She slammed it shut as if to keep the shadows out. However, she knew it to be a silly thought. There was nothing out there in the dark, and surely she was far too old to be scared of it. She let out a soft chuckle to chide herself. Either way, she reached down towards the doorknob to lock the room but found... nothing. Alena blinked as she looked down to where the handle should have been, but there was only an empty hole. Alena swallowed, her throat gone dry.

That was something she couldn't easily buy a replacement for and so she could only hope she'd eventually find it among the garbage. Until then, she had no other choice than to leave it be. Alena glanced around the room until her eyes landed on a footstool. It would have to suffice. She dragged it over towards the door to place it in front. That way, at least she could keep the door closed, even though her stomach churned knowing it was the only thing keeping it shut.

The floorboards creaked underfoot as Alena backed away and returned to bed. She fell onto it and despite the lack of blankets and other human bodies to share it with, made herself comfortable. However... as the world around her further darkened, she realized her mistake. She tensed and glanced back towards the door. From the empty doorknob hole, she could just barely make out the shadows that grew and danced within the foyer. And almost, just almost, she could imagine them creeping and crawling through the hole into the room with her. She had been unsuccessful in her attempts to keep it out. Alena curled into a ball as she shut her eyes tight. Her candles would be among the first things she unpacked.

The old house creaked, and Alena got little sleep that night.

Chapter 4

There was a gentle breeze the next morning as Alena carried a crate towards the car. The candles inside rattled with each step. She was extra careful as she opened the back door and set the crate on the floor of the car. With that done, she was ready to take her trip into town and went to open the driver's side door. Nerves made her brow damp which her brunette hair clung to. The exact opposite of her eyes, which felt dry and heavy. She must have only gotten a few minutes of sleep each hour before the night was up, starting at every creak and whisper of wind. Alena felt rather silly now that it was morning and everything had turned out fine. It was just because of being in a new place. That's all that it was.

'Yeah, that's all it is.'

The sudden sound of scratching met Alena's ears and made her drop the keys. They clinked as they fell into the dirt. The sound came from behind her. Came from the house. To her it sounded of knives on wood, but she was so dreadfully alone, how could that be. She was *supposed* to be alone. Alena took a deep breath and whirled around, expecting to see some assailant trying to break into her house.

"Hey!" she yelled out on impulse, but it was no human she faced. Alena balked.

On the porch was a small and sleek animal. It crouched near the crack of the door, desperately clawing at the old wood. As if it were trying to enter. At Alena's call, the animal froze and turned to look at her. The eyes were a vibrant green, familiar in the way they stared. They were the same eyes she saw from the shadows the day prior. The mysterious animal.

A second later, the animal turned tail and bolted down the old porch steps. It slipped through a crack on the lattice placed around the deck and vanished underneath. Alena watched its thin black tail lash out as it went, and could only stand there for a moment in shock. It appeared to be an animal once familiar to people, but she herself had never seen outside of old photos. They considered it to be a diseased vermin in the kingdom of Lenoria. One that was thought to have been hunted to extinction due to their demonic ways. A house cat.

Alena wondered if her eyes had been playing tricks on her from lack of sleep. The cat looked to be pure black, almost as if it was formed from the shadows that creeped around the old house.

She didn't have time to dwell on it as she hopped into the car, shutting the door and putting the key into the ignition. So far so good. She grabbed the pamphlet from the glovebox, which seemed to be an old (and possibly outdated) learning course about how to drive and the rules of the road. Alena frowned.

This was going to be yet another long day.

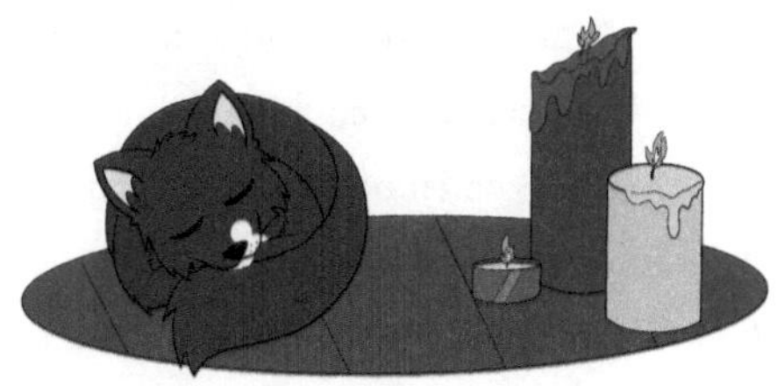

Alena nervously made her way back down the mountain road. She swerved and ran over foliage on the side of the already trodden path, the ride far more bumpier than when Lady Chambers had driven. Alena wanted to stay as far away from the cliff-side as possible. The last thing she wanted was to get back into the city by rolling the car all the way down.

So Alena went as slowly as she could to not upset her stomach too badly. As it neared midday, she finally rolled out onto the city streets. The car jostled Alena around as it bumped along the old road that was little more than torn up asphalt full of cracks. Something left over from when cars were commonplace. It was a large effort to repair the older roads, one that the government and P.O.E. gave little time. They had much more pressing issues.

Alena headed towards where her old apartment building was. Luckily most people in this part of town didn't linger about outdoors except for going to and from where they needed to go. Alena pulled up onto the side of the road and parked. She took note of the man that loitered around the entrance to the shop she frequented. He wore an old tattered jacket and had shaggy dark brunette hair, features she immediately recognized. This man and his brother were regulars to the store, so she wouldn't pay him much mind.

Alena slipped the hood of her hand-knitted sweater over her head and got out of the car. When she fetched her crate of candles from the back, the sound of the car door shutting felt far too loud to her ears. Alena flinched as the uncommon noise made the man look up. He too usually minded his own business, but now he openly stared as Alena approached the door. He looked between her and the car.

"Where'd you get that?" the man asked, which took her aback. Why was he talking to her? Deep down her stomach flipped in excitement, for no one ever talked to her. However, the good mood was quickly beaten down as Alena reminded herself she purposely wanted it that way.

"Borrowed," was all Alena got out as she threw open the shop's door and hurried in. She approached the counter where the shopkeep stood. She set the crate in front of him. The shopkeep was still a person she would have to communicate with, but one she knew a bit more.

"Didn't think I'd see you again so soon," the man chuckled as he accepted the crate, glancing at the contents.

"I wanted to see the new place first," Alena simply stated. The shopkeeper, her ex-landlord, already knew of her departure. Though the details of how she had come into possession of the land remained a mystery. Alena would only tell what needed to be known. She fiddled with the singular blonde patch of her hair, caused by a natural birthmark, as the shopkeep pulled out each of her beeswax candles. He examined them carefully before setting them aside, hesitating on one that was supposed to be shaped like a horse. Though Alena would admit it was a bit crude.

He gave her a look.

"I'm experimenting with making them different shapes," she explained. "That one turned out the best."

The others had been failures, but they were still her creations, and she loved them. The failures, she kept for herself to burn, so they would at least still get some use.

"Will it still burn brightly?" the man asked and this time Alena didn't hesitate as she nodded with enthusiasm.

"Of course!" she exclaimed. "I always pri... I always make sure my candles are the brightest around."

"Then they're good enough for me." The man shrugged as he set the horse candle to the side. Alena let out a breath of air as the word she almost said danced around her head. Alena *did* always *pride* herself in having the best candles on this side of the kingdom, but voicing it... Well that wouldn't have ended well. *Pride.*

The shopkeep was none the wiser to her near slip up as he motioned to the rest of his store. It was a small thing, but he managed to fill every space to the brim with homemade objects and foods. He said, "Since you no longer have a room with me, I'll go ahead and let you take anything you can fit into your crate."

Had Alena felt comfortable enough to express herself, would have beamed. She bowed her head in thanks as she gathered up her crate and walked off to do her shopping. That was the deal she had with the man. He would let local artisans stay in his apartment building behind the shop for free as long as they traded their wares there. The price was that he usually got about half of the product for himself, but the rest of it was allowed to be traded for other items in the shop. Items made by the other patrons that lived in the building. He usually only allowed Alena one or two items for each of her candles, depending on what it was she wanted. So this was a great opportunity she wasn't about to pass up.

"I'm still waiting on monthly rations from the P.O.E." The man made small talk as Alena browsed. "There's been a bit of a delay for things like your beeswax, so there might be a shortage for a while."

"I still have a good amount," Alena responded. She felt a bit at war with herself as she wanted to talk to the man further, but also wanted to hide to avoid the conversation going south. This involved her, though. "Why the delays?"

"Word on the street is one of the suppliers got caught," the shopkeeper said and the simple words made Alena freeze. She dared a glance at him. The man's face pinched upwards in utter disgust at the mere idea. "I hope that isn't true, I'd hate to think I ever stocked something made by one of those *demon worshipers.* Fucking vile people."

Alena's throat constricted and cut off her words. She didn't like thinking about people who worshiped the demonic. She had never seen a demon before, but the idea brought those darkened claws to mind again. Maybe they even had poisonous fangs.

The shopkeeper huffed when she didn't respond, clearly still riled. "Well, I just hope King Byron gets to the bottom of this."

And surely the Paladins of Exorcism's great leader would. Alena continued to shop as silence rose up around them once more. She was lucky the shopkeeper knew she was a quiet one already. And he didn't seem to fault her for that usually. Not like her parents had.

Alena passed up most of the crafts to head straight to the food. Pretty much all of it was pickled or salted to preserve them, the act of which was done by a kind old lady who had lived a few rooms down from Alena. They had only met a handful of times, but she was still silently thankful as she picked through the selection. Alena made sure to get a variety. Jars of fruits and veggies were a must, along with a few slabs of cured beef from one of the few sellers that didn't live in the building.

She moved on to her more guilty pleasures, so a few loaves of hand-tossed bread were quickly shoved into her crate. Not only that, but she couldn't resist snagging one of the larger bags of coffee beans. That in of itself was one of the more luxurious items in the shop, one of the so-called rations the P.O.E. would drop off. Coffee was a pricy oddity, a mutated variant of what it once used to be, preserved by dedicated botanists who devoted their lives to saving it along with some others. She seldom was ever able to afford it with just her candles. Alena even made sure to grab a bag of sugar to go with it. Her day was brighter now as she did a final once over and began to head back towards the counter. Just as she was about to pass by one of the tables, she froze.

Alena glanced over it and examined the tank full of water that sat firmly on warped wood. Inside she could see some fish from the local river flitting about. They were also used as food, but kept that way to remain fresh. Alena thought back to the cat she had seen and how thin it had looked. She knew better than to have anything to do with the damned creature, and yet... Alena couldn't get it out of her mind.

She turned away and returned to the counter to set her crate on it.

"Um, hey could I have a few of those fish?" she asked, to which the shopkeeper glanced over at the tank. His eyes narrowed as if he were unsure of the request. Alena didn't want to stretch out his generosity and so added, "They don't have to be large. I'm fine taking the little ones."

At that he seemed to relax and came around from the back of the counter. "Sure thing. Let me just grab those for you."

She thanked him again and looked up towards the wall behind the counter, just then noting a painting that hadn't been there before. It showed a field full of wild flowers beneath dark clouds that promised a storm. A single beam of light broke through the clouds and shone down on a lone person of indeterminate gender. Their long hair looked like pure gold in the light.

"Hey, if you don't have a way to keep these fresh, you should eat them today," the shopkeep said as he came back with the fish neatly wrapped up. Alena blinked out of her reverence and accepted the fish.

"That painting is new," she pointed out as she set the fish in her crate. The shopkeep went back behind the counter and began to trifle through the things she had bought. He took note of the inventory on a piece of parchment as he beamed.

"Yup, that there is a Saffron Flowers original," he said with what could only be described as pride. But of course, that wasn't allowed to be acknowledged. Instead, Alena noted the craftsmanship. She had never met Saffron Flowers, but the woman was relatively well known in the artisan community. Saffron was one of those high end types that lived closer to the main P.O.E. headquarters where King Byron resided. Alena was unable to imagine living near such a place. It unsettled her and so she focused on the art. Saffron definitely did have a way with colors and somehow managed to capture a beauty about the world that Alena, herself, had never seen.

"That probably cost you a lot," Alena said as the shopkeep finished checking her loot and recording it down.

He smiled. "She seems to be quite the fan of coffee, like you." He chuckled. "Gave her a whole barrel full!"

"That makes sense."

"Well, anyway, you're good to go now." The shopkeep folded up his parchment and set it aside. Alena gathered her crate of goodies and headed to the door. At once she remembered the man that stood outside and stopped in her tracks. Was he still out there? Would he speak to her again?

"Don't worry about that ruffian." She heard the shopkeep speak up and when she looked back at him, his disdain was clear. "Noticed him leaving a while ago."

With that she waved him off and exited the building to go back to her vehicle. Alena wasted no time in driving back the way she came. Soon enough the forest road came into view. Almost immediately a weight was lifted from her shoulders. She could breathe again. And yet the relief was short lived as the loneliness settled heavy into her bones. Once more she reminded herself that this was for the best.

Chapter 5

Alena clutched onto the package of fish and exited the backdoor with haste. She crossed the back part of the wrap-around porch, stopping just short of the stairs and staring out into the forest beyond. She couldn't see anything but plants, the slight breeze making them gently sway. Alena didn't want to think she had just imagined the cat that morning. The image of it had been so distinct, she knew it to be true.

Alena slowly crouched down and set one of the small fish onto the scuffed-up wood. She waited a minute more before she stood and retreated indoors. She sat the rest of them on the dining table beside the door and went to put the rest of her food away. Alena began placing the jars and such within the cupboards, immediately noting she still didn't have enough to fully stock them. That was fine though, she didn't need much. Alena set the bread and coffee grounds to the side, in contemplation. She would have to dig her burner out of her luggage so she would have something to prepare the latter with. She imagined how nice it would be to sit at an actual table in the mornings with a fresh cup while she worked on her candles. It sounded much more pleasant than what she had done before. Likely far better for her back as well.

Alena glanced out the window to see the fish was still untouched, and so she shrugged it off and headed back into the foyer where her few boxes were. Alena knelt down and began to pull her candle making supplies out of one, along with most of her personal candles. She would have loved to burn them all night to light up the darkened space if she had any confidence they wouldn't burn the place down.

'I'm sure it'd be fine. Probably.'

Alena stopped and glanced towards the hallway. It was also left untouched, and she was unsure why she thought it would be any different. Maybe she could take a candle and explore its depths. She bit her lip. No. She wouldn't do that.

The sound of knives on wood made her jump. Just like it had that morning. Alena wasted no time as she leaped up and rushed to the kitchen. The sound came from the backdoor. As she reached the dining table, she snatched the rest of the fish and threw open the door. Perhaps with a bit too much force.

The tiny cat yowled and practically jumped two feet into the air. Its green eyes flashed in alarm as it turned to bolt.

"Wait!" Alena called as she fell to her knees, apologetic that she had scared the thing. The cat froze before it could leap from the top step. It stared at her, back arched and fur fluffed to make it appear much larger. Alena willed her pounding heart to settle as she grabbed a hold of another fish and offered it to the feline. The cat looked from her to the offered food, its sides heaving after its fright. Very slowly the cat lifted a white-tipped paw and took a step forward. Alena held her breath.

The cat reached out with another paw and very carefully snatched away the fish. It jumped away again, this time with its prize. Alena could breathe again as the cat crouched and scarfed down the food as if it hadn't eaten in a while. Still it made sure to keep its eyes on Alena, just as she couldn't take her eyes from it. For her this momentous occasion felt as if she stumbled upon bigfoot itself.

Alena's hand twitched with the desire to reach out and touch the mystical animal, but the cat remained vigilant and tensed at the slightest movement.

"It's okay, I won't hurt you," Alena whispered to the cat, watching as its ear twitched in her direction. She thought of how the creatures had been outlawed, and were always pictured as monstrous saber toothed beasts. The tiny and frail looking thing in front of her was a far cry from that. Even as the cat gorged itself on fish, Alena couldn't help but think it was rather cute. It was mainly black, she was right, but had a couple splotches of white on its chest and face—each of its toes too, making it look like the cat had traveled through white paint.

Its whiskers and tail twitched slightly as it grumbled with each bite. Alena tilted her head to the side as she gazed into the cat's vivid green eyes. They were wild and perhaps held some truth to the lore she had been told. Alena whispered to the cat, "They say you can speak with demons."

The cat licked its chops, the fish having been fully consumed. It stood and Alena caught sight of something glinting on its neck. She leaned forward to look, when the cat glanced past her, almost as if it could see something just behind Alena within the depths of the house. A heavy weight befell her shoulders and the feeling of being watched made her spin around. The cat was forgotten.

However, there was nothing there. Alena had to remind herself she was alone. Well... not entirely alone. She turned back towards the cat just in time to see it zip into the house and right under the dining table.

"Hey!" Alena called out as she moved a chair out of the way in an attempt to get to the cat. She bent down and found the thing fearfully pressed up against the wall. Having a cat inside would be troublesome for Alena. Hell, having one anywhere near her would pose an issue. She hummed in contemplation, as she thought about how it had been in the house to begin with. Likely one of the squatters Lady Chambers had mentioned... Unless...

Alena looked at the shiny trinket that shone on the cat's neck. It wore a dark purple ribbon that nearly blended in with its coat. Attached to it was a coin. Alena leaned forward to grasp hold of it only for the cat spit and swat at her. Alena yelped and withdrew her hand quickly.

"Okay, sorry about that," Alena whispered and stood up. She grabbed another fish and placed it on the floor. Ever so gently the cat eased up, but it didn't come out from under the table. Alena left it there to shut the backdoor, not wanting to invite in anymore stray forest creatures. It still didn't come out. She supposed she would have to deal with it later. Alena fidgeted. She couldn't just have a banned animal within her house. If she was found out... She wondered when the P.O.E. agent was due to show up? She had only been at the house for a couple days, so she still had plenty of time before a month passed.

Alena walked over to a cupboard to grab a can of beans. The cat watched her every movement as Alena clutched a spoon and slowly crept out of the kitchen to leave it be. She instead went to the living room. Alena stepped over some of her grandfather's... collection, to throw herself down onto the nice couch. It was soft, perhaps much more than the bed. Had a skilled artisan, or a machine, made it? She wished to know. Alena couldn't help but wonder what the man had been like as she looked around at his discarded belongings. His life.

She cracked open the can and munched. It was no use trying to figure out a man she would never again meet. She sat there in silence until nearly half of the beans were gone. At that point she heard a soft padder against the hardwood floors. She blinked and turned around to see the cat power-walking its way from the kitchen. It slipped into the living room and rounded the corner of the couch. It immediately froze and puffed up when it noticed her sitting there. Once again they looked at each other and Alena noted how sure the cat was of the area. How comfortable.

"Did you know my grandfather?" Alena asked, though as it was a cat, she received no answer. She couldn't just let it live here anymore, but Alena had to admit, it was kind of nice having something to talk to. She could feel that hollow loneliness shrink ever so slightly. Perhaps a pet was what she needed. Something she wouldn't have to feel on edge about.

Alena sat the rest of the beans on the coffee table in front of her before she leaned back and lightly patted the cushion next to her. The cat watched every movement and she was sure it wouldn't accept the offer. Alena was proven wrong as it gracefully leaped up onto the sofa beside her. She froze to not startle the cat as it carefully made its way to her. Alena reached out her hand and the cat met her half way, tentatively sniffing her fingers. The cat licked at her, still smelling of fish. Alena wanted to gasp. Its tongue was so rough.

Feeling bold now, Alena moved her hand forward and sat it against the cat's cheek. Its chest made a rumbling noise as it leaned into the touch and rubbed against her hands. She lightly scratched the cat's head before reaching for the bit of metal tied around its neck. It truly did resemble a coin for the most part, but the bottom was elongated and had a jagged chunk taken out of it. Alena spun the coin around to see a name engraved into the metal. *Lily*.

"Oh, is that your name?" Alena asked. "Lily?"

The little cat's ears perked up and she let out a soft mew. Alena couldn't stop her smile, the feline was just so cute! She had a hard time believing the government would outlaw such a precious animal and claim it as demonic. If Lily did truly belong to her grandfather, Alena could perhaps understand why he had harbored her there.

She felt a tentative paw press onto her leg which made her go completely still. Lily watched her curiously before crawling into her lap. The cat sat down for only a moment before she curled up into a ball and fell asleep. Alena gently ran her fingers through the cat's fur. Her own eyes grew progressively more heavy.

Sleep had hit Alena hard, the exhaustion from the past few days being too much to bear. Even as she slowly came to, she felt far more asleep than awake. Alena rolled over and tried to keep her eyes shut tightly, not yet ready to return to the world of the waking. The world in which Lenoria existed. Next to her, something heavy stirred. The sounds of a deep rumbling breath met her ears and Alena woke up just a little bit more. Lily? No, that was far too loud for a tiny cat.

Alena's eyes crept open and were met with something... someone? Standing beside the couch and hulking over her. Alena let out a shriek that echoed throughout the empty house as she leaped from the couch. However as her eyes adjusted, she realized... there was nothing there. Alena was only met with the dark of night. Though perhaps not an ordinary dark. The shadows from the hallway had crept out.

The house had grown a chill during the night that made Alena wrap her arms around herself. How long had she slept for? It looked to be rather late. Alena looked around the pitch black room, each antique morphing into horrid shapes.

"Lily?" Alena called out and half wondered if she had dreamt the cat. That wasn't the case as she heard the faintest meow come from somewhere else deep within the house. Alena steeled herself and slowly made her way into the foyer, careful not to get tripped up on anything. As she entered the entranceway, Alena kept her head down to stare at her feet, she couldn't look at the hallway. Not there in the dark. She called for the cat again. She got another meow, this time further away.

Alena's blood ran cold as she finally looked up. The sounds had come from the hall.

Chapter 6

N^{o.} Alena's heart pounded painfully against her ribs as she stared into the shadows that ebbed and flowed from the hallway.

"Lily?"

Another meow, and Alena dug her nails into the palms of her hands. Okay, so the cat actually had gone there. She was sure Lily would be fine and come back whenever she finished exploring. She should just go back to bed.

The sounds of distant scratching met her ears. Alena's breath hitched. What if the cat had gotten stuck in a wall or something and needed help? Alena couldn't just leave her there.

She hurried across the foyer to snag a few candles that were still left in a box from when she was unpacking. She shoved a couple in her pocket, but held fast to the largest one she could find. Alena rustled through the box until her fingertips brushed against her flint and steel. She let out a breath as she carefully set the candle down and brought the items to it. With a spark, her candle was lit. It burned hot, and it burned bright to illuminate the darkened room.

She clutched the candle in both hands and turned to the hall. Even with the candlelight, the darkness was stifling. Alena feared her breath was too loud as she finally entered the hallway. The air around her grew heavy and somehow even staler than the rest of the house. Her legs shook as she moved forward, but her hands remained firm on the candle. She glanced around as she went, hoping to find the cat before she had to go any deeper. Lily was nowhere to be seen. Neither were the hordes of old furniture and knick-knacks that were present throughout the rest of the house. Somehow, that unsettled Alena even further.

Eventually, after what felt like an eternity, she reached the end of the hall. Alena frowned as she waved the candle to look around the area. Still no cat. *Where has Lily gone?* What even *was* this hallway for?

Alena turned and wondered if she should head back, when her breath hitched. Before her, she saw the hall hadn't simply stopped. There was another that broke off to the side and traveled the entire length of the foyer and living room. But why? Alena wanted to call out to Lily, but couldn't find her voice as her throat tightened.

In the distance, a soft mew called out.

Alena picked up the pace and nearly stumbled over her own feet. Why was it so dark? Alena looked towards the outer wall. There she saw windows that followed the length of the hallway. However, they were boarded up. If the circumstances had been different, Alena would have lamented about how much she and the old man had in common.

There was no time for that now as Alena followed the sound of the cat's frantic scratching. As she neared the end of the hall, she passed by an end table; a poor abandoned potted plant sat on top of it. It had long since shriveled up. A little further down was a lone bookcase where the sounds came from.

Alena tiptoed towards it and there she found Lily. The black cat nearly blended into the darkness as she frantically scratched at the crevice where the shelf met the wall. Alena let out a relieved sigh as she found the cat to be alright.

"Lily," Alena whispered, though still her voice sounded far too loud. The cat stopped and looked up as if she were expecting something from the other. The candlelight danced across her vibrant green eyes. Unsettled, Alena looked away from the cat's gaze to the bookshelf. It was carved from pure oak and looked incredibly heavy. Alena leaned forward to examine the equally thick and weighty books that stuffed the shelves to the brim. At first glance, most of them were about math and accounting. Alena wrinkled her nose. Bleh.

"Let's get out of here, Lily," Alena whispered to the cat as she stepped away from the books. Lily grumbled and turned back to her previous task. She whipped up a singular paw to slap it against the bookcase, her ears drawn back, determination in her tiny form. Alena didn't understand why. Was this just normal cat behavior? She leaned down to pick Lily up when the candlelight cast a strange shadow across the floor by the bookshelf. Alena paused.

Wait.

She reached down to the floor, not far off from where Lily was, and brushed her fingertips against the hardwood. Those weren't shadows. Alena further pressed her hands against the divots in the wood, evidence of something heavy being dragged across it. She looked up at the bookshelf. Something cold settled into her gut.

Lily continued to scratch.

Alena leaned over to where the bookcase met the wall. She noted it didn't fully rest up against it. Alena carefully slid her fingers behind the bookcase and gave it a light tug. It wasn't as heavy as she initially thought and easily slid across the wooden floors. It had wheels underneath she hadn't noticed before.

There was a soft clank and Alena couldn't move the bookcase any further. However, now there was enough space between it and the wall that she could fit her hands through. Well, she wasn't about to do that blindly.

Alena lifted her candle to see whatever was behind the bookcase. The light from the flame glinted off a shiny chain, much newer than the other things in the house. It connected to the back of the bookcase, and on the chain was a thick lock. What?

Alena readjusted her position to see what was attached to the other end of the chain. Her light shone into the dark crevice, but she couldn't see it... All Alena could make out was the first step of a staircase. She stepped back from the bookshelf, hands clammy against her candle.

It was a door.

Just as the realization came, Alena's candle snuffed out with a hiss and casted her into darkness. Unable to see, Alena screamed. The same feeling she had on the couch returned tenfold. Something watched her. She could feel it. Alena dropped her candle, forgoing the spares in her pocket. She nearly slammed her head into the shelf as she blindly grabbed for the furriest thing around. Lily yowled and dug her claws into Alena's arms as she brought the cat to her chest and bolted.

She ran back the way she came. Even when her hip slammed into the end table, the potted plant jostling over, she kept going. Alena's legs felt numb as she wheezed in painful breaths, her ribs constricted, her chest burning. It was almost as if the void-like space dragged her down and threatened to crush her. Blood roared in her ears and in her panic, she almost ran right into the wall at the end of the hall. Her eyes adjusted just enough that she caught herself and could scramble down the other hallway.

She could see the foyer. Only a few more strides.

Alena burst out of the dark hall and bounded up the stairs onto the landing. She didn't stop until she reached the bedroom. Once there, she slammed the door shut and whipped the stool in front of it.

She still held Lily tight to her chest despite the cat's squirms. Alena couldn't catch her breath. Her lungs were on fire. She could only stand there and stare wide-eyed at the door as she expected something to slam into it after her. She waited.

Nothing happened.

Only then did Alena ease up and finally release her death-grip on the cat. Lily huffed and scrambled out of Alena's arms, landing on the floor with a soft plop. Alena took a deep breath as the adrenaline came crashing down.

She stumbled, light-headed, as she peered through the empty knob socket on the door. Alena saw out onto the balcony that oversaw the foyer. It was dark out there, but not so much that she couldn't see. The dark of an oncoming dawn. Other than that, there was nothing. Alena whimpered as she was a husk of exhaustion. She left the door and staggered to the bed, collapsing on top.

Lily grumbled out a concerned meow as she stared daggers at Alena. Mentally, Alena apologized as she patted the bed beside her. Despite Alena's rough grab, Lily leaped up beside her, though the cat kept a foot between them.

"It's okay, we're fine," Alena whispered as she reached out to stroke Lily's soft black fur. The cat allowed it and Alena could feel the beginning of sleep take hold. She succumbed to it. Not because she wanted to, but because she had no other choice. In the back of her head she could still remember the feeling of someone... some *presence* looming around her. What was that? Alena could no longer think about it as she finally passed out and yet...

The feeling never went away.

Chapter 7

Alena, yet again, got little sleep. And so she went about her day in a daze. She staggered out of bed with a jolt of pain in her hip from a bruise the end table had given her. Still she made her way downstairs. Alena hesitated before she could cross the dark hallway. It stood there like a portal to the void. Gaping and aimless. She imagined perhaps some vile demonic creature lurking in the depths, but had to remind herself that wasn't possible. Yet she could still vaguely remember the fear she felt the night before. Even as the exact events tried to slip away from her memories. It all felt like a blur.

Lily rubbed up against her leg and purred with a rumble, breaking Alena out of her stupor. Alena, despite the way her eyes drooped, gave a small smile and looked down at the cat.

"Do you want some breakfast?"

Lily caterwauled loud enough to echo off the walls as she bounded down the rest of the stairs and into the kitchen. Alena followed and hurried past the hall. Her ears roared like they had the night before, but she could mostly ignore it this time, figuring it must have been a leftover spark of anxiety.

It was just a normal hallway. It was just a— She thought of the bookcase.

What was behind it?

Alena tried to chase the thoughts from her mind as she stopped beside one of her boxes and fetched her burner. She entered the kitchen and winced at the putrid smell of the fish she had left out. Lily was on top of the table, already scarfing down whatever was left. Alena sat the burner on the counter and lit the candle under it to heat up the water and coffee. She was still in a daze as she went back to the boxes and fetched the one filled with her candle-making supplies. Lily observed Alena as she set it on the dining table and spread out the items. The more she placed, the more Alena felt like dragging her feet. She was far too tired for this. But had to make sure she had an excellent selection.

After tying up a piece of rope on the opposite wall to hang dipped candles, Alena yawned and sat down in one of the dining chairs. Lily had now finished eating and licked her paws. Alena watched the cat for a moment as her eyelids grew heavy. They slipped shut.

The image of the hallway flashed behind her eyes.

Alena jolted awake, which made Lily jump.

"Ah, sorry," Alena murmured to the cat as she rubbed her eyes. She stood to fetch her coffee and dumped entirely too much sugar into it. She didn't care at the moment as she took a large gulp. It wasn't too hot yet and the sweetness severely overshadowed the bitter taste. Just how she liked it. Alena felt more awake. She blinked and stared down into the cup, watching the sugar particles swirl around.

'Oh, how unhealthy.'

Alena chased away the unwanted thought as she took another sip and returned to the table. For the next hour, she truly *tried* to work on her candles. Alena managed to dip enough wicks to completely fill the drying line she set up. The still wet wax dripped from the hanging candles onto the floor, but she didn't mind it. With that done, she focused more on her larger candles she made days prior. She warmed the wax just enough to try sculpting them. It was a new venture she was excited about. However, her mind drifted. Images would flash in her head and she'd flinch back to reality. She kept seeing that blasted hall, that damned bookcase.

It wasn't her problem. She didn't need to know what was in there.

Alena grimaced as she set down her tools. But it *was* her problem now, wasn't it? '*You live here now.*' Permanently. Alena laced her hands together and set her head down. She could feel a headache coming on. She didn't think the realization truly hit her yet. This wasn't just some house she was staying in for the foreseeable future. She should've been trying to make it her home.

She had agreed to take the place to live a quiet life out in the mountains. She couldn't even hear the city sounds from here. Wouldn't it have defeated the purpose if Alena kept that damned hallway constantly in the back of her mind? Would she spend every night in fear *and* loneliness rather than just the latter?

'*What are you going to do about it?*'

Alena clenched her fists and stood. Lily carefully watched her stomp into the foyer. The cat let out a loud mew just before she leaped off the table to follow. Alena gathered up as many candles as she could, along with her matches. She strolled right over to the hall, only stopping once she was in front of it. It was just as shrouded in shadow as she remembered. They twisted and danced as they beckoned her. However, it was day now and Alena wouldn't let the fears she felt during the night stop her.

She lit one candle and entered.

When she was down the first hall, she sat the candle down and lit another one. She carefully watched Lily approach her, hoping the cat wouldn't knock it over, but she appeared more curious than anything. Alena lit another candle and made her way to the end table in the second hall. Dirt and dead leaves scattered across the wood from the pot she had knocked over. The bruise on her hip throbbed in memory.

Alena brushed aside the dirt and set one of her candles on the table. The warmth of her candles settled her frazzled nerves, but not even they could completely keep her fear down as she turned towards the bookshelf.

It still stood there proudly in the shadiest part of the hall, and even with the flames nearby, it looked far too dark. Alena took a deep breath and moved forward, lighting another candle as she went. She set it at the end of the hall as she pulled open the bookshelf as far as it would go. The chain that held it in place strained with the effort. Oh yeah, the lock.

Alena hummed as she lightly tugged on it, using the light from her surrounding candles to inspect it. It was thick and heavy, the kind that could only be open with a key. She examined the keyhole, rubbed her thumb over the jagged entrance. Wait...

She turned to look down at Lily, the cat ever so loyally sitting within reach. Alena's eyes landed on the strange coin the cat wore. Could it be?

"Lily," Alena said, to which the little feline dipped her head. As if trained to do so. Alena slowly reached out and grasped the ribbon around Lily's neck, easily slipping it off. She took the coin to the lock, and with ease, it slid inside. Alena held her breath. There was no way... She turned the coin.

The lock clicked open.

Behind her, Lily perked up as she awaited Alena's next move. The latter finally allowed herself to breathe as she removed the lock. The chain loudly clattered to the ground, making her tense. Alena half-expected something to jump out at her.

When nothing happened, Alena pulled the bookshelf forward. It creaked and slowly swung open. Before she could do anything more, Lily bolted into the pitch black room that lay beyond.

"Wait!" Alena called out, but the cat didn't answer. Not wanting to lose track of Lily, Alena wasted no time to fetch the candle she set aside. With it, she walked through the doorway and onto the first step of the staircase. Was this some kind of basement? She stared down into the darkness as if she were at the foot of a cave. Alena descended.

Each step creaked and the further down she got, the harder it was to breathe. Alena was not a claustrophobic person, but at that moment, she thought the walls were far too close together. Eventually Alena reached the concrete floor, her head light from her heavy breathing. The air was stale and uncomfortably warm.

"Lily?" she called out, her words echoing around the large room as she looked around. It was a basement, made of stone, and looked to be about the same size as the living room. From what she could see, anyway. Alena wondered if it sat right under it, the thought unnerving. Despite that, she took a few steps forward. There were a few more boxes littered around. More storage. Alena huffed at it all. "You've got to be kidding me."

Well, either way, Alena felt slightly relieved. She had satiated her curiosity. It was just a basement, nothing more. Though why her grandfather would keep it so hidden away, she didn't know. And she would likely never would, just like everything else about the man. She frowned. That was just the reality of the situation. Now, Alena just had to find Lily and get out of there. Maybe later on she could bring down the rest of her grandfather's things. If she ever got around to cleaning the place up.

Alena made her way through the basement. She still couldn't find the cat, however, and wouldn't completely calm until she did. Alena looked around the surrounding boxes, wondering if she might catch sight of Lily amongst them. Unfortunately, Lily's black fur was too well camouflaged in the dark room, even with candlelight. The flickering flame made the shadows dance. Alena rubbed at her eyes as she passed by a box with writing scrawled on it. She immediately stopped and read the words.

Lily. Well, that wasn't exactly what she was looking for. Yet, Alena's curiosity got the best of her. She opened the top and out puffed a cloud of dust. She wheezed as it settled and the air cleared. Alena peered into the box. There she found a thick cushion with dark cat hair plastered onto it. She grabbed it, noting how soft it felt, before she moved it to the side. Alena was unfamiliar with cats and their needs, but she could tell the contents were definitely for her feline friend. What looked to be old cat-themed food bowls and mouse-shaped feathery toys filled the box. They must have been from the Before Times. So Lily *truly* belonged to her grandfather. Alena frowned. Why did that thought... make her sad?

No, she knew. Alena could imagine her grandfather having a close call with the P.O.E. and packing away these items. He probably wanted a better chance of hiding away his little cat. Maybe he sobbed as he did so.

'*Yeah, that was it.*'

Alena glanced around the room and her eyes landed on a large black safe with a keyhole shaped differently than the one on Lily's ribbon. Suddenly, the boxes took on a new meaning. Perhaps *all* the things in the basement would have brought on the worst of punishments by the government. Cold sweat dripped down her brow. Was she sitting on a trove of illegal items?

She didn't want to think about it and didn't want to look through them. What type of items would she find? The possibility of someone from the P.O.E. stumbling upon this stash made her feel weak. Surely, they wouldn't believe Alena had nothing to do with any of it.

She turned back to the cat box. This one wasn't that bad, but was still likely a banishable offense. Alena reached in and moved some things out of the way. That's when she saw it. A small book, the same color as Lily's ribbon. Alena slowly reached in to clasp it in her hands and bring it closer to the candlelight. When she flipped it over, she saw a singular word written across the book, the same handwriting as was on the box. Alena's eyes took in the word and the book nearly fell from her hands.

Lilith.

Wasn't that... A demon?

With shaking hands, Alena opened the book and there she saw a photograph. An actual photo like they used in the Before Times. It was hard to make out exactly what it was at first, but as she squinted, she realized it was a picture of Lily. Just a much smaller and scrawnier looking version. It must have been when the cat was just a baby. Alena flipped through the pages, each one with a slightly different picture of the cat, and soon Lily's entire life flashed before Alena's eyes. Then finally, Alena came across one last photo.

She recognized the living room and the couch Lily laid on, but the aged hand that was lovingly on top of the cat's head was unfamiliar to her. Her grandfather. In the picture, Lily's eyes shone so brightly, as if she truly loved the old man as well. Oh Lily. She must have been so lonely without him around. Alena could relate and wondered if the cat felt the same hollow sensation in her chest.

Alena shut the book and once more the name flashed in front of her. Her shoulders tensed at the sight of it. Lily. *Lilith.* Why would her grandfather name the cat after a demon? Alena felt the furthest from her relative then. She could never understand him. As Alena set the book back into the box, her hand brushed against something that felt like plastic. Curious, she pulled it out. It was square and had what she could only describe as glass eyes. She thought maybe it was the contraption that took the pictures. A camera, were they called? It even had a slot at the bottom for the photographs to come out of. Alena wondered if it still worked...

Thump.

She immediately dropped it back into the box. The sound had come from somewhere a little further into the basement. She peered into the dark, though by now her eyes had gotten used to the lowlight.

"Lily?" Alena called out.

Another thump.

Ah, maybe the cat was trying to get into something again. There certainly was a lot of stuff for her to hide in. Alena went deeper into the basement where the sound had come from, and soon reached the end of the room. There, against the wall, was a large white tarp that covered some other hidden piece of furniture. How peculiar. Her grandfather hadn't covered up anything else in the house.

The tarp gently swayed, and another thump came from within it.

Lily must have somehow gotten under it. Alena let out a tired sigh as she sat her candle down on the nearest box before she turned back around and called out for the cat. She didn't get a response that time. Alena gripped at the edges of the tarp and carefully pulled it away from whatever furniture lay underneath.

The flame from the candle danced in the sudden breeze from the tarp's movement. The tarp fell from Alena's hand.

She stood face to face with a skull.

Alena's gaze bore into the empty sockets of some carnivorous beast with thick fangs that hung on the stony wall. Gruesomely carved into the bone on its forehead was a symbol Alena never saw before, colored a darkened red. Below the skull was a table that matched the same wood as the bookshelf. In the center was an eloquently curved dagger and beside that, a copper bowl with an old piece of food inside. Scattered around them were a variety of shiny rocks and crystals, the largest one a deep black and shaped like a human skull. On the edge of the table, the statue of a gargoyle perched, a sneer on its gnarled face.

No, it couldn't be.

Alena took a step back and her eyes strained. She couldn't find it in herself to look away from the altar.

'Oh, but it is.'

Her grandfather was a demon worshiper.

From behind her, the air grew heavy and a scorching breath blew against the back of her neck.

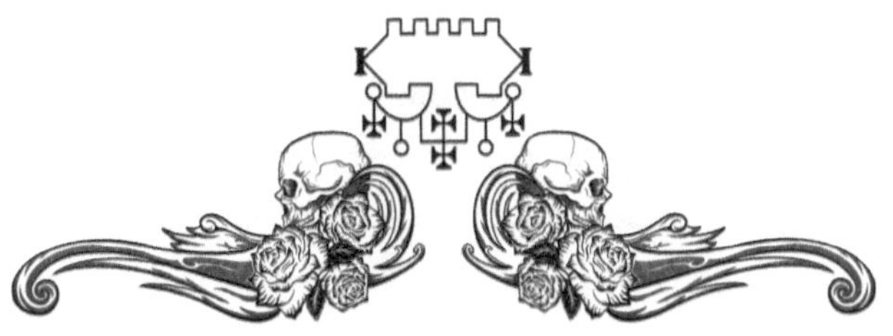

Chapter 8

The only thing Alena could hear was her own heartbeat, and the heavy breaths of whatever was in the room with her. It was so loud. She couldn't move, like the creature had her frozen to the spot. She didn't want to turn around. To see what horrid entity stood behind her.

It felt like an eternity passed. But in reality, it was only a few quick seconds.

Alena couldn't wait any longer. She couldn't let the demon get her. She spun around, and just like all the times before, there was nothing there.

No. There *was* something there. She knew it to be true by the way the darkness beyond her candlelight rippled as if an invisible foe stood there.

Alena jolted forward and snatched her candle, spilling wax onto the floor as she went. She rushed to the stairs and, by some miracle, managed to not stumble on any boxes. Alena pushed her luck further by taking two steps at a time.

She dashed out from behind the bookcase, not bothering to lock it back up. Alena followed the light of her candles down the hall. She ran past each, leaving them to burn. Alena bolted from the hallway and crossed the foyer. She threw open the front door and stumbled out onto the porch.

Her knees crashed into the deck's wood, sending splinters into her shins. Still, she didn't stop. Alena clawed her way up and bolted down the stairs onto the dirt driveway. She ran to her car, but as she pulled on the handle, found it to be locked. She didn't have the key.

Instead, she ran around the car towards the old worn-down road that led to the city. She only managed a few more strides before finally her energy depleted. Her achy knees buckled, and she went down hard onto the ground.

Pain wracked through her body, and still she pulled herself forward. Alena scrambled to the nearest tree next to the road. She pulled herself up just enough to lean her body against it, wheezing for breath. As she regained herself, her stomach twisted, and she gave a heavy, dry heave. She had... she had to get out of there. But her vision was practically black at the corners. She wasn't going anywhere.

Alena looked towards the house. It towered over her, empty and dark. A skeleton of the past that somehow still stood. She waited for the demon to burst out of the door, but nothing ever did. Had it... had it all been in her head? Was the breath on her neck just a breeze? The ripples, a trick of the light? *No.* Alena knew what she felt. The feeling of being watched. It was a feeling she had while living in the city. Every time a Paladin passed by her window. Every time a random person on the street acknowledged her.

Still, it made little sense to her. The P.O.E. drilled into everyone's heads that demons were enormous monstrous beasts with sharp claws and fangs that could fell a human in an instant. *No mercy.* Why was it invisible? Could they do that? She wished she knew more about what she was possibly dealing with. However, knowing such things could get her banished, or worse.

Alena leaned her head back against the tree. What was she to do now? The most logical option would be to report the experience to the P.O.E. but... what would they do with her?

A sob broke from Alena's throat as she leaned forward and wrapped her arms around herself. Maybe she should've never left the city. She wouldn't have to deal with being on the government's radar if she hadn't. She wouldn't have to worry about stumbling upon demonic activity. Why had her grandfather done this to her? *Who* was he?

"Mew?"

Alena blinked the water from her eyes and glanced beside her. Lily sat there, the little cat's face looking concerned. She reached out a paw and Alena flinched away. The sudden movement made Lily's ears flatten, her tail slightly puffed.

"Are you a demon, too?" Alena asked, scooting away from the cat. She had no more energy to run. Lily chirruped, not understanding why the kind human suddenly wanted nothing to do with her. It made Alena... feel bad. She sighed and deflated, reaching out a hand. Lily happily met her halfway with a purr.

If Lily was a demon, she had plenty of time to harm Alena before now. And the latter supposed she could say the same about any demon, if there truly was one in the house. Alena's chest burned. She didn't know what to think.

Lily licked her hand, and Alena frowned. Ignoring what might happen to herself if she reported this experience, the Paladins would definitely kill Lily if they found her. And the house would get condemned with whatever dark secrets her grandfather hid. It'd tarnish Alena Usher's name even if she got away with a slap on the wrist.

Who did Alena have a better chance of surviving against? Her government or a demonic entity from hell?

Alena held Lily close to her chest as she struggled to get up. Her legs still felt like jelly as she staggered back towards the house. Each step up the stairs onto the deck felt like walking on glass. She paused before the front door. It was still wide open from her harrowing run. She could see straight through the foyer to the hallway. It was back to being pitch black. The candles had gone out somehow. Maybe when she dashed by?

Alena didn't want to go any further, but hesitating any longer would delay the inevitable. She leaned forward and poked her head in, glancing in the living room's direction and then the kitchen. Again, no one was around and she was alone. The fact hung heavy on her shoulders.

"Hello?" she called out to test the waters. Only when nothing leaped out at her, she finally stepped back into the house. Her hands stroked against Lily's fur as she stood there and waited. Still nothing.

'Don't be a coward.'

Alena stooped down and released Lily onto the floor. The cat trotted further into the foyer without a care in the world. That made sense. If there was a demon there, Lily had lived with it all this time. Maybe cats *could* speak with demons.

"If that's true," Alena murmured, "could you ask it to go away?"

Lily simply blinked up at her. Alena felt ridiculous as she turned around and shut the front door. Her hands paused on the latch for only a moment before she locked it with a soft click.

As nothing continued to happen, Alena felt herself calm further. However, she knew there was one more thing she had to do before she could rest.

"Okay, let's do this." Alena shook out her limbs in preparation. She tiptoed her way back through the first hall and fetched the candle she left there. She relit it, casting away the darkness, though its warm glow did little to comfort her. Alena glanced around to see if she could sense the feeling of eyes on her. Things felt... empty. In a good way.

Pushing back her fear, she hurried back to the bookcase. Behind her Lily let out a surprised meow and quickly followed after.

Alena passed her other candle. Something had toppled it over. She didn't stop to dwell on the implication as she approached the bookshelf. She wanted to get this done fast.

She set the candle to the side and gathered up the chain and its lock. Alena turned towards the basement door and only then did she pause. She stared into its depths and the feeling finally returned. From the darkness, something glared back at her. From even deeper in the basement, she heard a thump.

Alena's grip tightened on the chain.

'Well?'

Alena swallowed her nerves and reached into the doorway to wrap the chain around the railing by the stairs. Pulling it closed, she released the lock, and it swung behind the bookcase out of sight. And that was it. She fetched her candle and hurried the way she had come. Alena could only hope she would never have to go back to the basement again. Maybe she *would* board up the hall, the P.O.E. be damned. As blasphemous as that thought was.

'Why are you running away from your problems? You're weak.'

Alena winced at the thought as she came to a stop just before she entered the foyer. She looked behind her into the hall. The bookcase didn't reach her sights, but she knew it was still there. Of course, she had to run. What else could she do?

'Stay.'

Alena left the hallway.

Chapter 9

Alena had another restless night as she tossed and turned in bed. Even with her own blankets on it, she simply kicked them off. It was far too warm. Lily had already long since vacated the area, not wanting to deal with such a squirmy human. Alena ebbed and flowed between the state of being awake and asleep. Wild and sometimes horrific images vividly presented behind her closed eyelids. Within the darkness of her mind's eye, she'd see the trees which surrounded the house, gnarled and threatening as they reached up towards the sky. Blazing flames cast eerie glows from her candles, and just past that, the faces. Oh the faces, twisted and pale things they were.

She was never one to suffer from nightmares, or whatever these pre-sleep images were. So all she could do was roll over and press her face firmly to her pillow, hoping the nothingness of sleep would take her soon, worried the pictures wouldn't stop when she did.

A numbness washed over her. She wasn't tired and yet she didn't feel fully rested, either. Alena blinked and dragged herself up into a sitting position to look around the room. There was nothing but the void surrounding her, an inky blackness she couldn't see through. She looked downwards and even the bed was gone. Alena wrapped her arms around herself. She should've been afraid, but no matter how hard she tried to feel, the emotion eluded her. She felt like she should've been cold here, but there was nothing. Alena stood on jelly-filled legs.

"Hello?" she called, only for her own voice to echo back at her. "Are you here?"

Who was she looking for? Alena had to find someone. Lily perhaps? She stepped forward and began to walk. It was like trying to wade through a marsh full of sludge. That was about the only thing she could sense, the weight of it all crashing down on her. Alena called out again as she slowed. Still no answer, but there it was. The spark of something. She could finally sense something. A small feeling as if someone stood behind her. She immediately stopped.

Alena slowly turned around. She saw only a wall of thick ink, but perhaps if she narrowed her eyes and stared long enough, she could see it form into a shape. A rather humanoid one.

There it was.

The fear.

The emotions all hit Alena at once. Her heart pounded and a heavy ache settled in her limbs. Alena turned and tried to bolt, but the murk clung to her like a vice and she only grew slower and slower.

'Why do you keep trying to run?' her inner voice asked her, but somehow it was different. Distorted and warbled. Was that even her? Alena sank further and further in the surrounding void, her legs losing more feeling by the second. At that point, she clawed at the air, her fingers slashing at nothing as she tried anything to pull herself away from the presence.

A deep rumbling growl met her ears and all at once, Alena could no longer move. She laid there helpless and vulnerable, only able to move her head enough to glance behind her. There she saw the wall of void bubble and pull apart as something breached through the murky waters. The black ink dripped away to reveal an aged animal skull, the same carnivorous creature that hung on the basement wall. The symbol on its forehead blazed a vibrant red. Alena gasped for air as the skull floated there before her, much larger than she remembered it.

"What..." she got out, her tone far away and jumbled. The skull floated closer and whispered something in a language that Alena couldn't comprehend. One word amongst them all stood out to her. *Belial.* She let out a soft wail.

"I don't understand!"

The symbol on the skull burned hotter and in an instant, its bottom jaw cracked open. A copper key tumbled out and fell somewhere deep into the darkness with a plop. She couldn't see it after that.

There was a sharp jab of heat against Alena's face. Wincing, she fully sank into the sludge and fell further and faster. She was aware enough to let out a yelp as she roughly slammed onto her backside. The ground was hard, the world around her no longer the void but still sparse of anything. There was the bite of a chill, however.

'Aleeeeeeena...' she heard the skull's voice and immediately scrambled onto her feet. She spun around, but couldn't tell which direction the voice came from.

"Please, tell me what you want from me?" Alena called out, unable to do much more. Her body grew heavy and she could only allow her arms to dangle as her knees buckled. Alena nearly cried under the weight of it all.

Suddenly there was the hiss of a flame, and the surrounding area lit up. Alena blinked and turned towards the source. Several of her candles gathered around a large black safe. She gasped. She was in the basement. The safe shook as if there was an earthquake and then the door burst open. Despite the candlelight, she couldn't see what the safe contained. It might as well have been a doorway back to the void. She wanted to take a step back, but somehow her muscles did the opposite. She moved forward.

There from the void, something else began to form and a shadowy human-like arm slipped out of the safe. In its large hand held a tiny black book, the same symbol from the skull painted on its cover in a similar red. From its depths, Alena heard another deep guttural growl.

She shrieked, lungs burning as she clutched at the sheets in her waking breath. The fabric had tangled between her legs from a desperate kicking as she fought against her fright. Alena looked around. She was back in bed. As she came down from her terror, she was left to wonder. Had it all been a dream? It seemed so vivid and real in her head, she could even remember the sensation or lack thereof.

Alena just laid there and tried not to get sick. She wasn't well.

The image of the skull flashed into her head no matter how hard she tried to *not* picture it. Alena clenched her fists. It wanted something from her, that much she was sure. She could feel it in her bones. Would it leave her alone if she didn't do anything about it? She didn't think so.

Alena gave a small whimper as she forced herself out of bed and across the bedroom. She kicked aside the footstool and walked out onto the indoor balcony, noticing Lily asleep on the first step of the stairs. Alena tiptoed over to her and gently crouched down, nudging the cat awake. Lily chirruped as she looked up at Alena with sleepy eyes.

"Lily, I'm going to need that ribbon of yours again."

Chapter 10

Alena unlocked the chain behind the bookcase, Lily at her side. This time, she carefully set the lock aside instead of letting it fall to announce her presence. Though as Alena peered down into the basement depths, she didn't doubt the creature was already aware of her. She could feel it, and so maybe it could feel her.

Perhaps she was making a mistake. It could've been a trap. It probably was a trap. She could've turned around and just left, but that wouldn't give her answers. That wouldn't stop the strange tug in her chest that told her she needed to go down into that basement.

Alena took the first step and then the second, her candle clasped firmly in her grip. Lily remained by the bookshelf, her eyes watching diligently, as if the cat was waiting for something, but only the stars above knew what.

The stone walls around Alena still felt far too close for comfort, but this time, she ignored them. She moved off the final step and looked into the darkness before her. It was stifling. She focused on her senses, those strange feelings she would get. There it was, whatever it was, distantly watching.

She slowly crept forward and passed by the many boxes. When she got to the safe, she paused to look at it. It looked just as it did in her dream, right down to the keyhole. She wondered... Alena forced herself to turn and looked at the altar. It was still uncovered, the white tarp abandoned on the floor where she had left it. She could just barely make out the animal skull on the wall, its empty eye sockets stared right back at her. Alena dragged her feet forward and approached the space. She ignored the rest of the altar items, her eyes glued to the skull. Her dream was clear in her mind. She gazed onto the symbol on its forehead.

The symbol... No. The *sigil* was vaguely skull-shaped itself. With what looked to be the battlements of a castle on top of it. They came down to two half-circle "eyes" that were adorned with medieval-styled crosses. They hung down to give it a uniformed and symmetrical look. Alena could hardly take her eyes away from the sigil, and as she stared, a singular word popped into her head.

"Belial?" she asked in a whisper and was met with a huff of hot air that blew against the side of her face. A breath. Alena went rigid. It was a trap, it was a trap, it was... She heard heavy footsteps as whatever was near her stepped away. She didn't relax.

Alena looked in the direction of the demon, but still saw nothing. She balled her fists and stepped up to the altar. She gazed back at the skull and this time made sure not to look at the sigil as she reached forward. Her hands brushed against the old bone. It was rough and littered with cracks she hadn't noticed in the dark. She caressed her fingers gently towards the bottom jaw, and could hear the demon breathe out an inquisitive sigh. With one swift tug, she cracked open the jaw.

A copper key tumbled out and landed with a soft clink on top of the altar. Alena flinched at the sound, but wasted no time as she snatched up the key and scrambled away from the table. The sooner she was done with whatever this thing wanted, the sooner she could get out of here.

She hurried to the safe, only crouching slightly to not fully let down her guard. Alena tossed a glance over her shoulder, still nothing, and thrust the key into the lock. *It fits.* Alena balked, half expecting that not to have worked, but there it was before her.

Alena grabbed the handle of the safe and, with a little muscle, pulled it open. Her palms were clammy as she peered into the darkness, but to her relief, it wasn't a portal back to her nightmare. Instead, before her was a pile of books. Why would her grandfather need to hide them away like that? She reached forward and snagged the smallest one on the very top, slipping it out with ease. *Oh.*

It was the same one from her dream. Tiny and black with the same sigil painted onto the cover. It was hot to the touch.

Alena glanced at the rest of the pile. The reasoning behind their storage suddenly made sense. She kept the black book close and shut the safe, pocketing the key with one final look towards the altar, to the skull that continued to stare at her. Heat permeated from her face, the hollow feeling in her chest gaping. She almost didn't want to step away from it.

Alena chased the nefarious feelings away. It must have been some sort of trick to keep her there. She ran back to the stairs.

At the top step, Alena found Lily waiting for her. The cat let out a meow in greeting as she hopped onto her paws, excited about something. Alena carefully stepped over her.

"I think I got what I needed," Alena whispered to Lily. "Do you know anything about this?"

She held the book up in front of the cat's face. Lily stared into the sigil before she leaned forward to bump her head against it, a loud purr sounding out. Alena sighed as she picked up the cat and took both her and the book out of the hallway. When she got back to the foyer, she saw it was daytime. The morning sun shone orange through the windows.

Alena headed into the living room to collapse onto the couch. Lily squirmed out of her grasp to instead lay beside her, watching Alena expectantly. With the book now in her lap, Alena sat up straight and glared at it. She felt as though it would come alive and bite her, but there was no use to prolong the inevitable. She had already been through the worst of things. Alena opened the book.

Immediately, a photo fell out of it. Lily pawed at the offending thing as Alena could only further stare. She slowly picked it up and gave it a look over.

It was definitely a lot older than the ones of *Lilith*, the white corners having turned yellow. Alena narrowed her eyes to get a better look. The image was of a middle-aged man. There was no denying it was her grandfather. He had a similar streak of blonde in his hair that she did. It looked as though he was in the woods, probably somewhere around the property, a huge sparkling smile on his face. In his hand, he gently held the same skull hanging up in the basement. It had no sigil on it; the old man must have just found it in the forest. So how did he get from point A to point B? Alena turned the photo over, but there was no writing on the back.

She set the picture on the coffee table and returned to the book.

To My Inheritor, the first page began. Alena balked. This book was… addressed to her? Well, perhaps not specifically her, but to whoever ended up in possession of this damned house. Her throat went dry and no matter how strongly she wanted to throw the book back into the basement, she kept reading.

To My Inheritor,

We likely do not know each other well, and for that I apologize. I am also deeply sorrowful for any pain or problems I may have caused by leaving you this house and all its contents.

Please do not hate me for it. However, it is of the utmost importance that this house does not fall into that damned government's hands. To make sure of that, I am willing for the whole world to hate me. For deep within here holds a secret, as you may have already realized upon finding this book.

Many years ago, even before the 'Before Times', one of our ancestors had fallen upon hard times. They called out to the universe for help and a passing spirit answered. This spirit was an ancient and powerful one that allowed our ancestors to rise above society. Ever since then, due to either some residual energy or perhaps a forgotten blood bond, our kin have found themselves to get involved with this being. My great-grandparents had before me, and then somewhere around my teens I had as well. Things were different back then. Those of us who devoted ourselves to the old gods were not widely accepted, but it wasn't the death sentence it is now.

That was a mistake. This society never should have happened. Our dearest lovely light bringer had made an oversight, and I do not fault him for that. But for the rest of us, the great Kings and their followers have been suffering greatly ever since. I have lost so many of my coven, so many of my friends. All due to this damned system that will kill to keep the commoners in their place.

I'm sick of it and had I been younger, I would have done something more. So again, I'm very sorry to leave you in this predicament. I wish I could have shown you the beauty of those who reside in the dark.

I wish I could have formally introduced you to King Belial.

Maybe one day things will change. For now, I leave you with the house and its "dark" secrets, and in accepting them, you have also been left to Him.

The rest of the contents in this journal will give you a starting point on your new path. However, this path is vast with many branching directions. What you might do could greatly differ from what I was able to. I only ask that you carry on the family legacy, that you do what I never managed.

With a lawless love, your relative, Rick Usher.

P.S. Please watch after my darling Lily if she is still around. And look after King Belial, as well. You'll all need each other.

Alena gently closed the book and stared ahead as she tried to process the information. It wasn't just her grandfather that worshiped the demonic, many of her family members did. Her stomach churned. Was she mad at the man? She clenched her fists. No, no, she wasn't.

She was terrified.

Alena set the book aside and brought her knees up to her chest. She rested her forehead against them, shoulders wracking with silent sobs. Alena didn't want this. She really didn't, but she was aware enough to realize it was something she couldn't fault the old man for. What would have happened if the P.O.E. had gotten their hands on the house, finding the altar downstairs along with this book? There was no question about it. Her and the rest of her family, if there were any others left, would have been rounded up. Even if they hadn't a clue about their relative's actions. It was a risk.

And yet, why did it have to be *her*? Why did she have to get left with such a burden?

'It isn't an ideal situation for me either,' her inner voice said. Alena blinked. Wait, why would she think that? She glanced over her shoulder into the foyer and for a second, she thought she saw the air ripple. Alena filed it as just another weird experience in the house and shook it off. Her eyes stung and her muscles twitched in exhaustion. Hell, if the demon didn't get her, then surely her poor health would. Alena paused. *Did* the demon want to bring her harm? If her family had such a good standing with it, then perhaps not. But what if she didn't want to worship such a being? Would it let her go?

Alena reached out to stroke the top of Lily's head; the cat's soft purring brought comfort to her. She didn't know what to do. She could further read the journal to see what else her grandfather had to say, but she was... afraid of what she might find. Alena sat there in silence for a bit, alone with the cat and her thoughts as she tried to sort through them. Her mind was sluggish, and she wished she could sleep on it, but the thought made her quiver.

The rumbling of a car outside snapped her back to attention. She blinked and wondered if someone was just passing through. Wait. She was no longer in the city. No one just "passed through" here. Alena leaped from her seat to face the window. Through the sheer curtains, she could see a silver car come up the drive.

The presence of Lily and the book burned in the back of Alena's mind as she became all too hyper-aware of both of them behind her.

The Paladins of Exorcism's emblem on the car's door sparkled in the morning sun.

Chapter 11

What was the P.O.E. doing there?! It had been nowhere near a month yet, had it? Alena wondered if she lost track of the days, but surely not to that extent. She stood there frozen, her gaze glued to the window as the vehicle pulled up and parked right behind her own.

'No escape.'

She watched as two agents got out of the car. Behind Alena, Lily let out a concerned meow, sensing her human friend was in distress. The noise snapped Alena out of it as she whirled around fast enough to make Lily jump. She took in the sight of the black cat fearfully crouched beside the equally black book with the demonic sigil on it. There was no way this didn't look guilty.

Alena rushed forward and snatched up both, fighting to hold the squirming and spitting Lily as she shoved the book under the couch. With that done, Alena mustered up what little energy she could and made large strides to cross the house into the kitchen.

"I'm so sorry," Alena yelped as she threw open the backdoor and tossed the cat out. Lily let out a shocked mew that pulled heavily at Alena's heart, but it was for the cat's own good. Alena could only hope Lily would stay out of sight as she hurried back into the foyer. Immediately she slid to a stop as her eyes landed on the dark hall. It beckoned to her. The image of the bookcase being ajar flashed through her mind. No! She hadn't locked it back up.

Behind her, there was a rapping on the door that made her skin crawl. She... She didn't have time to shut it. Alena stifled the whine that threatened to slip from her as she turned towards the door. Her chest tightened as her breathing grew more ragged. No no no no...

'Keep calm, Alena,' the voice said. It was beginning to sound less and less like her own. *'Don't let them sense your fear.'*

"Okay..." Alena whispered as she took a moment to catch her breath. She approached the door and creaked it open. Before her, on the porch, was a middle-aged man with slicked back silver hair and behind him was someone that looked to be around Alena's age, maybe slightly older. This person was perhaps on the taller side, but it was hard to tell by the way they slouched. They had a bit of an androgynous appearance with sharp cheekbones and long black hair that was pulled far too tightly into a bun. Alena looked back and forth between the two of them. Both looked like they wanted to be anywhere other than there. She forced a polite smile. "Can I help you?"

"Yes, I'm Sir Chambers and this is my intern. We're both here with the P.O.E. for your monthly evaluation," the man said, tone robotic. There was no question this was something he said often. "May we come in?"

"Of course," Alena said without hesitation. She could see the way the man's eyes kept on her. Alena stepped back as she allowed the two in, quietly watching them look about the foyer. They did it so casually, as if they were old pals invited to their friend's new house. The intern carried a clipboard and wasted no time scribbling things down with their quill. The man, Sir Chambers, caught sight of Alena's stare and waved her off.

"Just ignore them. They're taking notes," he said, which made Alena focus on him instead. She couldn't seem too shifty, she couldn't be nervous.

'You're doing a terrible job of that.'

"Ah, I just wasn't expecting you until next month," Alena said, hoping she didn't sound too guilty.

"While we usually stick with once or twice a month," the man said, "we prefer to change up the dates."

Alena nodded in understanding and didn't push it. She knew why they did that. The same reason she was so frazzled right now. To catch her off guard. The two continued to look around as they headed in the living room's direction and Alena followed not shortly behind. She could feel a sweat break across her brow as they entered the room.

"So you said your name was Chambers?" Alena asked in an attempt to make small talk, something that made her tongue feel sour. "Any relation to Lady Chambers?"

"My wife," was all the man said as he looked over the mass of boxes and antiques scattered around the room. "Haven't unpacked yet?"

"Oh, uh, this was all my grandfather's stuff." Alena shrugged. "Haven't had the chance to go through it yet."

Sir Chambers hummed as his intern walked around the couch. Alena held her breath. All they had to do to find incriminating evidence was crouch down and look underneath it. She should've hidden the book better. The intern only glanced at the sofa before paying no other mind. Instead, they paused by the coffee table. Alena's blood ran cold. The photo of her grandfather still lay on top of the old wood. The intern leaned forward—

"Well, that's enough of this room," Sir Chambers stated after he examined a singular box. He looked bored out of his mind. Alena wondered if he had ever run across any *nefarious* demon worshipers before in his time working. Well... any *real* demon worshipers anyway. By the way he held himself, she could tell it wasn't too common of an occurrence.

The intern stood at attention and hurried away from the coffee table to stand behind Sir Chambers as he moved across the foyer to examine the kitchen. Just like Lady Chambers before him, the Sir passed by the darkened hall. Alena let herself relax ever so slightly.

'*Don't!*' the voice growled, making Alena's back go ridged. '*They know what they're doing. They're trying to play you.*'

Alena glanced towards the intern just in time to see their dark eyes flick away. Oh. She looked to Sir Chambers and for the first time noticed how tense his own shoulders were. His hand remained on his belt where he had a small sheath and dagger attached.

Sir Chambers stopped at the kitchen doorway and, as he glanced around, asked, "So what made you decide to move here?" Alena gritted her teeth at the question, memories of her constant drillings flickered through her mind.

"I just wanted something different, you know?" Alena responded with a half-truth. "Get out of the bustling city."

"I can understand that." He sighed and motioned towards his intern. "You go check the upstairs."

They nodded and scampered away without so much as a glance to the hall next to them. Alena was relieved, however too brief.

"What's that?" Sir Chambers asked as he finally motioned towards the hall that had given Alena much strife. She wanted cower, but by some miracle of her own, stayed unchanged.

"Oh, it's just a couple hallways." She fidgeted her hands. "More storage, I think."

Sir Chambers hummed before he approached the hall and pulled out an antique flashlight, the kind powered by the sun. Alena felt disadvantaged by the tech the P.O.E. was allowed to have from the Before Times. She used to be thankful, so she wouldn't have to worry if her candles would sell or not. But this... she wasn't a fan of this.

She went to follow him, but was met with a singular stern hand to keep her back. Alena hesitated by the hall entrance as she watched him walk down it with his much brighter light. There was not much she *could* do but hope. Sir Chambers reached the end of the first hall and turned only slightly before he stopped in his tracks. He shone his light down the much longer hall and Alena wondered what all he would see. The end table... The bookcase... Had she left it all the way open? She couldn't remember. Sir Chambers continued to stand there and just look down the hall before Alena heard him mumble "weird" before he finally returned to her.

The intern had also left the bedroom and was heading back down the stairs.

"Get some better lighting in that hall before the next time we come back," Sir Chambers demanded. "The last agent assigned to your grandfather was clearly too lenient on how he kept his tidings."

"Oh sure, sorry it's so dark," Alena responded as the man turned to his intern. The intern finished whatever they had written and gave a small nod.

"Well, it appears we're done here," Sir Chambers said as his intern hurried back to the door without a single word. The man finally looked at Alena fully. Their eyes met as he continued, "Keep this up and don't make our jobs harder than they need to be."

It was a threat. Alena wanted to respond, but found her mouth too dry. So she nodded.

He and his intern walked out the front door without another word and Alena just stood there to watch them go. They returned to their car, but before getting in and driving off, Sir Chambers went to the trunk to pull out a bright red canister. He left it beside Alena's car before finally hopping in his driver's seat.

Alena approached the front door and waited, but the two continued to sit there in their vehicle. It all felt strange, so she waved them off and shut the door. She waited there for several long minutes until she finally heard the car start up and leave.

'Now that wasn't so bad, was it?'

Finally, Alena was able to breathe.

Chapter 12

Alena returned to the living room and stared out the window for a while, just to make sure the P.O.E. agents were truly gone. She felt an itch under her skin that she couldn't scratch. When she was finally sure they weren't coming back, Alena rushed to the coffee table to snatch up the photograph. She wasted no time to collect the book from beneath the couch and return the picture to it. The book was comfortably warm in her hands as she held it to her chest.

Alena went straight to the backdoor and opened it to let Lily back inside. The tiny cat dashed in with an offended wail, her tail fluffed up to an impressive size.

"I'm sorry, Lily," Alena sighed, her weary limbs beginning to shake. "Couldn't have them finding you."

The cat huffed, not quite understanding as she stomped away, tail held high. Alena frowned and hoped Lily wouldn't be mad at her for long. She was too tired to think over it as she decided to make some coffee on her burner. As Alena waited for it, she glanced at her abandoned candle making supplies on the dining table. She hadn't gotten any work done in so long. She yearned for the feel of wax under her fingertips, but with everything going on, how could she focus?

Alena turned the burner off and took a swig of her drink. She wrinkled up her nose at the taste. The sweetness she normally adored tasted sickening to her tongue. She poured the rest out. What now? Alena lightly clicked her nails against the book's leather cover. She should return it and lock the basement back up. That seemed logical, but after that? Well, she would just have to take one step at a time.

And so, with the book in hand, Alena returned to the dark hall. She passed by Lily, who was licking her paws on the stairs, the cat not even giving her the time of day as she went. Alena grabbed the candle she kept closest to the entrance and lit it. It illuminated her view as she walked into the shadows, the smallest pin-prick of fear stinging at the back of her head. She felt the demon's stare, as if lying in wait. Waiting for... maybe the devotion it was promised? Alena gritted her teeth. It wasn't going to get it.

'You're full of yourself, aren't you?'

"Please stop talking," Alena muttered. A sharp pain stabbed at her temple, an offended anger that wasn't her own. She began to sweat. Alena thought of apologizing, but would a demon even accept that? She kept herself tight lipped, not wanting to risk pushing her luck anymore.

She reached the bookcase and found it pushed flush up against the wall. The chain was beside it, but out of view. She breathed a sigh of relief. Sir Chambers didn't see anything. However, she would probably have to pull the boards off the windows for better lighting as per his orders. She glanced back down the hall and tried to picture the place cascaded in the light of day. Something about that thought unsettled her even more.

Alena pulled the bookcase door open, something beckoning her into the darkness. She was going to return the book and that would be the end of things. Maybe she would even go back to the city... No, she wouldn't do that.

Alena began her descent down. With each step, her muscles strained and weakened. She was far more tired than she realized. When she reached the bottom step, she staggered, but caught herself on the wall. She shook her head to keep herself alert as she pushed off the stones and headed towards where the safe was located. The further she went, the more her limbs filled with lead. She groaned as she reached the safe and gently sat her candle on top of it. Alena got down on her knees to conserve energy as she felt around her pockets for the copper key. Where had she put it?

The book felt like fire in her hands. She stopped and looked down at it. Was the sigil glowing? Alena felt her eyes droop downward. All she wanted to do was sleep. Where was that damned key? She set the book down and wondered if just leaving it there would suffice? Surely no one else would end up in that basement if Alena's luck continued.

She yawned and her eyes drooped further.

She would just have to work on finding the key after she took a nap. Or maybe after she slept for twelve hours. Both options were on the table. She went to stand, but found her limbs too heavy. Alena collapsed onto the concrete floor. She blinked, but each time found it more difficult to keep her eyes open. By the time she felt a massive buzzing energy approach her, feeling like a weighted blanket had befallen her, she was already out. The world had gone even darker.

Alena jumped up with a start. How could she have just fallen asleep in the basement like that? She wheezed for air as her body felt odd and tingly. She scraped her hand against the floor, finding not smoothed concrete, but rough stone. Oh no. She looked up to see the rocky walls of a cave. It was not as dark as the basement, the area dimly lit with a reddish hue. Alena pulled herself up to her feet. Her limbs no longer ached and felt light.

She had to be dreaming. Alena's hands flew up to lightly smack her own face. The world around her rippled, but she didn't wake up. Almost like... something was keeping her there.

At that thought, Alena heard a deep rumble followed by the hiss of air, like steam being let out of a pot. Despite everything telling her not to, Alena turned towards the sound. Further down the cave's crevice, she could see a murky black hole. Another portal to the void.

Alena let out a broken scream and bolted in the opposite direction. She stumbled and her shins scraped up against the rocks, yet that still wasn't enough to wake her from the terror. Behind her, earth-shattering steps gave chase. What would happen if it caught her? Alena's pace picked up as she ran. However, there was only ever one way to go and soon enough, she entered a dome-shaped cavern. It was only about the size of her bedroom, and was bare of anything. No place to hide.

Still, she ran until she no longer could. Alena nearly slammed into the wall on the other side of the cavern, clawing at the rock in an attempt to phase through the cracks. The steps grew closer. Alena found it hard to breathe. Her whole body quivered as she tried to wake up but was blocked from doing so. Behind her, she could feel the dark presence arrive. Alena turned to face whatever hunted her, her back pressed up against the rocky wall.

The entrance to the cavern grew so dark Alena could no longer see the tunnel she came from. Another rumble met Alena's ears just as she saw a large and clawed humanoid hand shoot out from the darkness. It gripped the cave wall beside the entrance. Another one did the same to the other side. Alena's knees knocked together, and a whimper escaped her barely parted lips. She felt far too warm.

The inky blackness in front of her parted like water as the skull that haunted her breached the surface. The only difference now is that it adorned four massive deep red horns, two that spiraled towards the sky and two that curled on the sides of its head like a ram's. The sigil blazed brightly on its forehead.

A hoof slammed forward, each step rumbling the earth in its wake. The demonic entity pulled its massive body through the tight crevice with little difficulty. Despite being in the light, it was as though the void still clung to its skin. As if the two were one.

The demon stretched out to its full height. The tips of its horns scraped against the top of the cavern and had Alena not been dreaming, she was sure her mouth would have gone dry. She felt so small. She *was* so small. Alena never thought herself to be short, but the demon still towered above her. It... *He* was practically a wall of muscle with ones that rippled over a vaguely humanoid body.

A red swirling pattern danced around the demon's dark gray body. As he took in a breath, the markings glowed brighter, as if the flames of hell burned hotly under his skin. Alena shivered. A deep red iris appeared in the otherwise empty socket of his skull, glowing in tandem with the red markings. Somehow it appeared as though the skull had smirked.

'Well, it's about time,' the demon said, his voice deep and growly. Alena could feel it deep within her core. *'This little game of yours has been trivial at best.'*

Alena's mouth gaped like a fish as the demon looked at her expectantly. Waited for her to say something. She stammered.

"Are you Belial?" she asked.

'King Belial,' he corrected, chin tilted upwards. It exposed his throat a great deal and made it clear he saw her as no threat to him. And why should he? Everything about the demon before her was massive, aside from the cloth he wore around his waist. It did little to cover the things Alena absolutely didn't want to see. Another deep rumble emitted from King Belial's chest as Alena felt a spark of agitation come from him, reaching the back of her head and all around her. There was a loud crash as a tail the size of a large tree branch slammed into the stones. Alena tensed, not having noticed it on him before. The demon still looked at her with expectations that she feared.

"W...What do you want from me?" Alena whispered as she tried her best to keep calm. It didn't work as she continued to press herself up against the wall as far as she could go.

'Shouldn't you know that already?' the demon asked her as his red markings flared. An image of the black book flooded her mind. She remembered her grandfather's letter to her. Alena grimaced. She didn't think she could trust the demonic being, let alone continue the family tradition of *worshiping* him.

Not to mention, if she was found out... that would be a death sentence. And yet... just being so close to him, she felt every nerve in her body ping as if they had jumped for joy. The hollowed feeling in her chest was no more as she felt full to the brim. Almost as if just seeing him was something she long awaited. It made her want to cry. Alena didn't know if those feelings were good or bad. She couldn't... it wasn't right. Alena curled her fingers into fists as she stared up into King Belial's eyes.

"I don't... want to..." she said, tense as she waited for the demon to lash out at her. Instead, he simply continued to stand there, as if her words were something he expected.

'Why not?' King Belial asked in such a way that was rhetorical. *'Because you allow yourself to succumb to your fears?'*

"I think it's a rational concern that I might die," she responded and even in the echoed cavern, her voice sounded small. King Belial took a step forward and as his hoof came down, Alena yelped and tried to make herself look even smaller. He only stopped once he was a foot away, still standing tall above her.

*'Alena, with me by your side, you will **never** have to fear again,'* he growled. Alena didn't know what to do, but with his eyes on her, she felt anything but lost. It uneased her. Their eyes met and soon the world grew blurry. Alena's hold on the dreamworld (or perhaps King Belial's hold on her) had finally waned as she became acutely aware of the feeling of concrete. She was still up against the rocks, but as the demon's image blurred, she could just barely make out the sight of the basement.

Her body was waking up. Alena lurched towards the feeling as finally King Belial's image vanished. However, the demon's voice still rang in her ears. *'Don't let outside forces dictate that which is your blood given right.'*

Alena snapped awake on the basement floor and sat up. She was still laying beside the safe, the black book next to her. Her candle flickered to cast a dull glow. Alena tried to gather the energy to panic, to run away, but only a cooling calm settled over her. He hadn't hurt her, though she wasn't sure if that was still on the table or not. She looked towards the altar, where she could just barely see the skull in the candlelight. It looked a lot like him. Alena frowned. She wouldn't do what he asked of her, she wouldn't do what her grandfather had hoped. She *couldn't.*

Alena collected her candle and headed back towards the stairs, leaving behind the sound of hoof steps as King Belial silently watched her leave.

Chapter 13

Even with everything going on, Alena couldn't shrug off her responsibility to help people light their homes. So, with a cup of coffee brewing on the counter, Alena sat down to get some work done. Her candle-making supplies laid scattered around the dining table along with Lily. The little cat sprawled out on the opposite end as she watched Alena cut pieces of thread from their spool. She set them aside to dip into the wax later on. This was comforting. It allowed Alena to do something with her hands.

All she could do was work and hope King Belial would listen to her pleas and accept she wanted nothing to do with him. What would the two do then? Would she simply live out her life in this house, avoiding the basement where he resided? Like some sort of weird roommate?

One of her candles flew off the table and landed on the floor with a loud clatter. Lily jumped with a surprise hiss and Alena practically did the same.

'Is that how you think this is going to go?' her inner voice asked her, warped and deep. It was clear now who the voice actually belonged to. King Belial.

"Leave me alone!" Alena yelled before she could stop herself. She felt the demon go still and so she slapped her hands over her mouth. "I, um, sorry..."

She awaited the demon to lash out at her, but instead, the air grew light as he stepped away. Alena slowly slid back down into her seat, eyes straining on where she thought King Belial might be. That was the most unsettling part about it, perhaps even more than when she had seen him in her forced dream. She couldn't exactly tell where he was until he made himself known. The only possible evidence was the way the candles on the drying line across the room gently swayed as if a breeze had gone by.

Alena slowly reached out for one of her pre-made candles and small knife to make a few divots in the sculpture she was attempting to carve. Her hands shook and ended up taking out a chunk that was far too big. She sighed and pushed her supplies to the side. She looked to where Lily perched on the edge of the table, her pupils so wide her green irises were but mere slivers. The cat stared off into a particular dark-looking corner of the kitchen, her tail and whiskers twitched.

She let out a loud mew and leaped from the table to hurry towards the corner, tail up high. Alena felt a spike of panic and adrenaline as she saw the air ripple around the cat. Lily arched her back and playfully flopped over, her purrs audible from even the other side of the room. Alena let out a sigh of relief. At least it would appear as though Lily and King Belial were on good terms. Then she frowned. A chill wracked its way through her, settling in that hollow space in her chest. Her loneliness felt like claws against her skin.

Alena shook it off and stood to step closer to where the cat was.

"Come on, Lily," she called. Alena gently picked up the cat and left the room. King Belial watched her closely as she went. As she passed the hallway by the stairs, Alena noticed it appeared less dark now that the demon wasn't lingering within its shadows. At the realization, Alena hurried into the living room.

She allowed Lily to jump from her arms onto the couch as she thought about something to keep herself distracted. There wasn't much since usually she just worked on her candles, but that was out of the picture for the time being. Maybe she should pick up a new hobby, but what? Reading? The image of the black book flashed in her head, shoved in there by an outside force. She gritted her teeth. No.

Instead, Alena looked around at the junk piled room. Maybe she could clean it up and throw things out. Distantly, there was a spark of agitated annoyance from King Belial. Alena ignored him as she tiptoed over towards the fireplace. It would be a good place to start so she could have it ready to use by the time winter rolled around. She crouched down and began to pull out the pile of papers there. She examined one. It was a newspaper, greatly yellowed with age. The date was from long before she was born, but it was an article she was still familiar with.

'President and VP murdered by The Devil!' the headline said and it was almost funny in the way it sounded like one of those trashy sensationalist articles. However, it was indeed a piece of their kingdom's history. A fact that the Paladins of Exorcism made sure all their citizens knew well. The power demons could hold.

The recliner beside the couch gently creaked and began to rock back and forth on its own. Alena tensed as she stared at the offending object. King Belial didn't make a comment on the article, but she could still feel his intense stare as if awaiting her own reaction. A little part of her wanted to ask him about it. If he knew what exactly happened, or if he had been there. All she knew, all the people were told, was that the president had hosted a ball of sorts within the White House. It was to boost morale shortly after the discovery that demons truly existed, for the country was on edge. Legends said that during the ball, Lucifer himself manifested in the building to strike down the man. The country fell to ruin not long after.

King Belial hummed as the rocking picked up in tempo. Alena abandoned the newspaper and promptly left the living room. She went back to the kitchen. Would he turn on her, kill her just like the president? She rubbed her hands together as she trotted up to her burner on the countertop. She would play this game of avoidance all day if she had to.

Alena took the cup of coffee she had left earlier off the burner and blew on it. She had let it cook for longer than normal. The liquid was dark so unlike what she usually drank. She took a sip. It was bitter but made her more alert. She thought perhaps she could get used to the taste.

'Well, it's certainly better than the garbage you drank before,' Alena's fingers tightened around the cup as the massive weight that was King Belial approached her.

In the back of her head, there was a smugness that wasn't her own as her coffee cooled a lot faster than it should've. Confused, she took a sip and found it no longer had a taste and felt light against her tongue. Almost as if the energy had been sucked out of it. There was a spark of annoyance as Alena could hear the demon chuckle besides her. She slammed the coffee down onto the counter and pushed it away. Several drops splattered onto the floor.

Alena's better judgment left as her eyes landed on the antique salt shaker left sitting out next to the sink. In one swift motion, she snatched it up, popped the top off and doused where the demon stood. A cloud of salt puffed out into the air before it pelted the tiled floors with a hiss. There was a pause and silence as Alena felt King Belial go still in front of her. Not the stillness of a demon that was successfully warded off, but the stillness of someone *shocked* by the audacity.

'Did you just...' his voice flooded her head as his energy grew thicker and more condensed, *'...throw fucking **salt** at me?'*

"I..." Alena stammered just as a massive headache slammed her skull without warning, as if his anger itself rattled her brain, "I just don't want any problems."

'Can't reap what you sow?' he asked incredulously. She felt him approach, his buzzing and wrathful energy only a foot away from her. He snarled, *'You just expect me to stand idly by while you hurl feeble minded attacks at me?'*

He... had a point. Had King Belial truly done anything to actually harm her? Aside from unnerving (and annoying) her with his presence. She took a step back from the demon, but found him to be everywhere, as if his energy were a part of the house. His anger continued to affect her body as her skin grew warm. Alena could only cower to make herself look smaller.

"I'm just gonna... lay on the floor now, " she muttered as the air around her felt far too heavy. Heart thudding, Alena slowly knelt down on her knees before laying on the floor. The tiles still felt cool to the touch as she put her hands over her head, closing her eyes tight. Maybe he would further see how little she was a threat to him, and he would take pity on her for the miniscule mistake.

How was Alena supposed to know that part of the lore was wrong? Though she supposed it wouldn't matter if it was or not, considering *she* had been the one to lash out against *him*.

Above her hovered King Belial's weighty energy, but it soon lightened up along with the demon's anger. Instead, Alena sensed his smirk. He chuckled. *'Good little human.'*

Her traitorous nerves, the ones that danced in his presence, tingled in a wave of unfamiliar pleasure. Alena's body elated at the praise from the demon that was meant to be her God. She flushed at the nefarious feelings and shoved her face further into the floor.

'You know, black candles are good for banishing,' King Belial said. *'Not that it'd have any effect on me, though.'* The image of Alena's plain off-white candles flashed through her mind. She had once considered coloring them, but it was far too expensive for what it was worth. Not to mention, certain colors could be associated with nefarious activities. So even if she had the materials, black candles would have been out of the question.

King Belial finally left her alone. She continued to lay there for a while, torn between humiliation and a desire to crawl after him like a lost puppy. Yet... Alena could feel the prickling of her mood turn sharp and bitter. There was a sour taste on her tongue and a fire in her belly. She knew now he likely wasn't going to kill her, but she didn't want to push her luck either. Alena groaned, unsure of what to do with the spite she felt in her limbs. It was aimed at him, but also at her own vile feelings. She gritted her teeth as she felt something small and furry gently press against the top of her head.

Alena looked up to see Lily. The cat mewed and purred as she lightly pawed at her. Alena sighed and finally pulled herself up off the floor, giving Lily's head a quick pat. She snagged a piece of preserved meat off the counter and offered it to the little cat who gladly accepted it. At least not everyone was against her.

Alena glanced towards the kitchen entrance where she could see straight through the foyer into the living room. It looked much darker than usual despite the large window. The reclining chair continued to rock back and forth once more. Well, if he was in there, then she was going to stay in the kitchen. Her body's feelings on the matter be damned. She returned to the dining table with her crafting supplies. Alena sat down and waited with bated breath. She could still hear the slight squeak of the chair.

Tentatively, she returned to her work, finishing her candle's sculpt. Then she began to dip her pre-cut wicks into the boiling pot of wax. All the while keeping her eyes peeled for any slight movement from the other room. Every so often she paused and waited to make sure King Belial hadn't entered the room while she wasn't paying attention. Eventually Lily joined her at the table and laid in her usual spot, casually watching the candle-making process.

Alena continued to make her candles until dusk arrived and the sky turned orange. At that point she heard the recliner's creaking stop, followed by heavy footfalls that vanished somewhere further into the house. Maybe back to the basement? Alena felt relieved as she set aside her supplies for later use and stood. She wrapped her arms around Lily and carried the cat back into the foyer, feeling safe enough to leave the kitchen.

With Lily in tow, Alena scampered up the steps before anything could reach out of the hall to grab her. That never happened, but now with King Belial's presence known, she couldn't be too sure it wouldn't. Alena entered the bath-room on the opposite side of her bedroom and set Lily onto the floor. She shut the door, thankful this one actually had a knob she could lock. She didn't doubt it would do little to keep the demon out, but it was still a comfort.

The bathroom wasn't terribly large, but she didn't see the point in having an enormous one, anyway. She lit the candle she kept in there for when the sun went down and turned on the tub's faucet. It churned and clunked until a slight trickle of water came. It would take it a moment to fully pull from wherever the source was. Alena knew it was some stream or lake around there. Maybe she should explore the forest, get to know the land she now lived on. However, Alena was no outdoorsy person.

As she sat on the side of the tub and waited for it to fill, Alena suddenly heard a loud thump from somewhere downstairs. Soon enough, the sound of heavy stomps echoed throughout the building as someone came up the stairs to the second floor.

"You've got to be kidding me," Alena snapped as the pinpricks of spite returned. She turned the faucet off as the last thing she wanted to do now was get undressed. With that, she made her way out of the bathroom just in time to see a large shadow cross the landing. Alena threw her arms up in defeat. "Leave me alone!"

'Am I simply not allowed to exist in my own home?' King Belial growled, as if *he* had the right to be offended about their unpleasant situation. Alena clenched her fists as she glared at the wall where she assumed the demon stood.

"It's *my* house," she argued.

'Is it now?' King Belial asked, and in an instant the atmosphere changed just like earlier in the kitchen. Alena froze as the demon went on, *'Tell me, exactly, **who** has lived here longer?'*

Alena's eyes went wide as she gaped, wanting to argue that she was the rightful owner of the house. Even if she had mixed feelings about the fact. However, King Belial had a point and he knew this.

'There are portals to my domain all over this place,' he went on, more matter-of-factly. *'They etch my name in the very wood you walk. They spread my energy into the air you breathe. As far as I'm concerned **you** are the guest here, **not** me.'*

She didn't respond, she couldn't. Alena felt it in the air. Could sense the energy around them that proved the demon's words to be true. The house was unearthly. Alena, defeated, like a prisoner in the house. So she dipped her head to King Belial and carefully stepped away. He allowed this without comment.

Her body felt drained, and she didn't want to keep up this losing fight. She crawled into bed and collapsed, her back to the rest of the bedroom. She expected him to leave her again. Beside her, the bed pressed down as Lily hopped up and on habit Alena reached over to pull the cat closer, except... her hand met with nothing. The air around it was thick as though she had put her hand through water. There was no cat there.

Alena yelped as she snatched her hand away. King Belial was silent as he sat beside her, as if lost in thought. By now, the sun had finally dipped below the trees and the room cascaded into darkness. Alena brought her blanket up around herself as she stared at the divot where the demon sat. Things were always different at night. In the day she had no problem with being in his presence, despite the spark of fear and annoyance he brought. But now...

She was downright terrified. Alena quaked as she reminded herself this *was* a demon. She wondered how her earlier experiences would have gone if they were to happen now. During the night.

King Belial shifted and she could see the darkness ripple slightly towards her as he reached out an invisible hand. Alena let out a small whimper as she curled into a tight ball and squeezed her eyes shut.

"J-Just leave me alone, please," she whispered under her breath. Only a second later did she feel the weight on the bed remove itself. She heard the hard thuds of his hooves as he walked across the room. The bathroom door across the way creaked open and Alena allowed herself to steal a glance. It had that look to it now, that void-like darkness. He was still nearby, lingering there.

Alena buried her face into her pillow. It was the only place she could hide.

Chapter 19

Alena couldn't do it. She had to get out of the house. The night had been full of quiet knocks and creaks as King Belial moved about. She laid in bed frozen and didn't even move when Lily finally leaped up to lie beside her.

Now in the morning, as Alena downed a cup of coffee, she dreaded the day would be a replay of the previous one. All she wanted to do was lay down, but knew the demon would use it as an opportunity to further harass her. This, perhaps, was far worse than the desolate loneliness she embodied for most of her life. That she was used to. *This* wasn't normal. Alena sighed as she set her cup in the sink and gathered several finished candles into her shopping crate. With them in tow, she bid Lily a goodbye with a quick pat before hurrying out of the door. The cool mountain air gently rustled her hair and Alena greedily gulped in the freshness. The overgrown grass caressed her ankles and threatened to wrap around them, as if they tried to get her to stay. Stay with him. It almost felt sinful.

From the house's dark windows, Alena saw the curtains shift; she was being watched. She stared back for only a moment before she packed her things and hopped into the vehicle. Alena wasted no time to zoom down the mountain.

The action still made her woozy but the relief that flooded her was so addictive that she could ignore it. For the first time, the rumbles of the engine and wild bumps from the overgrown road didn't bother her. It was elation to be putting distance between herself and the house. Yet still, Alena couldn't feel completely at ease. It was like his claws had made their way into her chest to make a home there.

Alena pulled onto the old city road and immediately the air around her grew heavy. The claws in her chest soothed and she no longer felt so utterly alone. She supposed it was because there were a few people out and about today, walking along sidewalks with their heads down. A Paladin stood by an old street sign, carefully watching them. A scruffy mutt was by his side, its leash tightly clutched in the Paladin's hold, sitting at attention. Alena tightened her grip on the steering wheel. The Paladin glanced her way and waved. Seeing her car, he must have assumed she was someone important. She pretended she didn't see him.

Alena drove up to her favorite shop and pulled her hood over her eyes. Luckily, that one man didn't linger by the door this time. Though... as she walked towards the building with her stuff in tow, she could see him and another further down the street. She hurried inside and hoped they hadn't seen her. At her entrance, the shopkeeper genuinely looked surprised and... nervous?

"Wasn't expecting you back so soon," he said, voice tight, as she set her crate onto the countertop.

"I just wanted to get out for a bit, I guess," she stammered as he collected her candles, glancing over them carefully.

"Sculpting looks to be getting better." He nodded as he put them behind the counter to stock later. "Seems like your hard work is paying off. I'll let you get eight items with these, or five if they're a bit on the pricier side. Try not to be too long. I've got plans today."

Alena dipped her head and took her crate. She didn't actually need anything, but it didn't hurt to look around. Maybe she could buy more fish for Lily, she seemed to like those. Alena passed by the food items to look around at other wares first. She never traded for anything she might not use, but today was about getting out, as unpleasant as the fact was. It felt wrong. She looked down at a table that had some rather amateurish metal workings. It was far better than anything she could do, but a far cry from smiths in the upper parts of Lenoria's city.

Her eyes scanned over a rusted knife made from old metal, much smaller than anything the P.O.E. carried. Definitely something that could only be for show and not usable. As she stared, she got the image of a stark white skull in the darkness, a glowing sigil upon it. She chased the thoughts from her mind. Alena did *not* want to think about King Belial right now.

A few feet away, the door clicked open and Alena further put her head down. She stepped away from the metal workings to go deeper into the shop. It was just her luck someone else had to get groceries the same day she came out. Alena stood at a table that had a few glass blown objects. This crafter lived in the building, but frequented the market place uptown. She grabbed a couple of jars for candles and carefully set them in her crate.

"Hey, how are you doing today?" came a soft and playful voice, yet still Alena froze. She glanced up from beneath her long bangs towards the offending voice. Beside her stood a man that appeared to be in his early twenties. His hair was shaggy and the color of sand, his freckled face beamed at her. "You're Alena right? Haven't seen you around in a while. Where've ya' been?"

How did he know her? She took a small step back. Behind him, off to the side, was the man from before. He looked tired of the situation, but kept himself close by. Ah, this must have been his brother in front of her. She had never gotten too good of a look at either of them before.

However, now, the one in front of her openly stared with an adoring light in his eyes. It made Alena all too aware of her own body, making her skin crawl as she wanted nothing more than to burrow down in her clothes, away from view. Alena held the crate close to her chest, the only barrier between them. Behind her, it felt as though the air within the shop grew hot and muggy.

"I... moved to the mountainside," she said through gritted teeth. Honest people had nothing to hide. She had nothing to hide.

"Oh, yeah?" He hummed casually, hands in his pockets. "Why's that?"

"Change of pace," Alena quipped back, short and direct. Her nerves frayed as her grip tightened on the crate-handles. She frowned. "I'm sorry, is there a problem?"

From behind the man, his brother let out a sigh and shook his head. Seemingly to himself. The other tensed and his face flushed.

"What? Oh no," he said, hands coming out of his pockets to wave them in defense. "I was just wondering about you is all."

A wall went up, her eyes narrowing in the other's direction as she dipped her head further. Her hair curtained her face.

"Why?" she asked. Alena wished her voice sounded more stern, but she got caught up on the way it whispered. "I don't know you."

"S-Sorry about that," the man responded and perhaps he was being earnest, but how could Alena trust that? He looked genuinely surprised she didn't know who he was. "I'm Archie, and this is my brother Jaxon. We live down the road."

She looked at the two of them like a chicken would a couple of foxes.

"Um," Alena stammered, "so were you wanting anything or..."

"Oh yeah, well, I was just wondering..." Archie trailed off, thrown off balance. He glanced towards Jaxon for help. The other simply crossed his arms and turned away, wanting nothing to do with whatever his brother's plot was. Alena wasn't sure if that was a good sign or not. She glanced towards the shopkeeper who was glaring daggers at the group. Alena tensed and hoped this wouldn't affect her standing with him. She sent a silent plea to the man for help.

Archie didn't notice this as he rubbed at the back of his head and continued, his face slightly flushed. "Ya' know, I've seen you here a lot by yourself. I was actually just wondering if you wanted to... hang out sometime?"

Alena blinked and took in a sharp breath. She had never 'hung out' with people and the idea was elusive. Tantalizing as a small thrill of excitement went through her. But... why would he want to hang out with her? Was it some sort of trick? From behind her, Alena heard a distant chuckle, deep and rumbly. She tensed and snapped her head around, but no one was there. She thrummed her nails against the wood of the crate in a quick tempo. There was no way.

Shaking it off, Alena looked back towards Archie, who had balked at her sudden movement. Damn it, Alena, be cool.

"Why—"

"Alena, could you come over here for a second?" the shopkeeper called and silently she let out a breath of relief and internally thanked him. Archie appeared rather down trodden as she gave him a small wave and scurried over to the counter. The two brothers regrouped as Jaxon whispered something to Archie. Alena contemplated listening in, but she wasn't sure if she wanted to know what they were saying. Something rubbed her the wrong way.

'Are you innocent or dense?' Maybe a bit of both. *'He assumes you're a pretty girl. You can figure it out.'*

I don't want to be perceived that way, Alena thought back. Half to the other voice and half to herself. Never did Alena refer to herself as a girl or woman. Nor would she use such titles as Miss or Lady. It didn't feel quite right for her and made bile rise in her throat. The energy that clung to Alena felt... understanding?

Alena shook her head as she reached the countertop, the tension leaving her muscles. She opened her mouth to thank the shopkeeper, but promptly snapped it shut. He hadn't looked at her, instead continued to stare at the two men. His brown eyes held something Alena didn't like. She withdrew her shoulders.

"You shouldn't have come today," the man whispered, his voice harsh. He finally tore his gaze away from the others to look directly in her eyes. She shied away as he gritted his teeth. "I say this because you're a loyal seller and have never given me any problems. You need to leave *now*. Go out the back door."

The hair on the back of her neck stood on end. This wasn't about getting her out of an uncomfortable situation. Something else was happening. Confused, Alena opened her mouth to speak, but the words died away on her tongue as she heard the loud rumble of a vehicle. One that wasn't her own. Without thinking, Alena whipped around to face the large window by the door. There she saw it.

On the side of the road parked a repurposed carrier truck, the kind with a large rectangular bed in the back for transporting things. It was painted silver with an emblem on the side, a raven being felled by three arrows during flight. The Paladins of Exorcism...

"Please leave," the shopkeeper said but Alena barely heard him over the roar in her ears. She saw two Paladins leap out of their truck just as Jaxon whipped his head up towards the commotion. His eyes were wide and fearful.

The shopkeeper gripped Alena's shoulder and roughly shoved her towards the back door, and only then did she manage to get her legs to move. The hand burned hot as she burst through the door out into the same alleyway below her old apartment.

The crate in her arms was the only thing to ground her to reality as she gasped for air against her burning lungs. The shopkeeper still held on tight, his grip the single bit of comfort she could latch onto. She fought to try and ask him *what* on earth was going on.

"There they are!" she heard the shopkeeper back inside the building. Alena's blood ran cold as she twisted around to find no one was in that alley with her. The burning hand that had gotten her out of the building faded from her skin. Inside she heard the shopkeeper's continued screaming, "There's those damned demon worshipers!"

Alena bolted from the alley. Her gut churned as she ran around the building to reach the street where her car was parked... The same street where the Paladins were. Alena rounded the corner and slid to a stop.

Several feet away the Paladins, decked out to the brim in tactical gear, were dragging out both of the brothers from the shop. From where she stood, she could see Archie allowed himself to be led away, eyes wide and fearful. However, Jaxon went kicking and screaming. Alena felt sick. She was going to be sick.

Jaxon shoved himself backwards and the Paladin lost their grip. The man struggled himself free and then launched himself at the one holding his brother. His fist collided with the back of the Paladin's neck and he dropped Archie when his legs crumpled. Jaxon grabbed Archie and the two of them bolted down the sidewalk in the opposite direction from where Alena was. One of the Paladins recovered and without hesitation, whipped out a bola and sent it flying in the brothers' direction.

The weapon soared through the air and struck Archie. The rope wrapped around his legs and he went down hard into the ground. Blood splattered around him as his face busted open against the concrete. Glass shattered as Alena's hold on her crate slipped and its contents scattered around her. She clutched at her ears, the world around her roaring, the sounds of her own breathing far too loud. No one paid her any mind, didn't even notice she was there.

Jaxon paused for only a moment to look back, but as the Paladins descended upon his brother, he bolted. The Paladin with the dog from across the street shouted and took off after him, the canine snarling and pulling at its leash. Jaxon likely wouldn't get far.

As he and the Paladin with the dog vanished from view, the one that tossed the bola leaped onto Archie's back. She pulled out a rope and wrapped it around his wrists, a gleeful sneer carved on to her face. The man barely squirmed and only managed a small agonized groan.

'Alena, get out of there,' King Belial's voice crackled like fire in the back of her head, though she could hardly hear him over the sound of her own blood pumping. The other Paladin returned to their large vehicle to throw open the driver's side door and slam down on the horn. The ancient truck hiccuped and wheezed, but the sound was still piercing. Villagers of the kingdom peeked out of their windows, while the bravest amongst them walked out onto the street. They knew what was to take place.

As did Alena, but still it was like her feet had grown roots in the ground. Her gaze wide and unblinking as the Paladin went to the back of the truck. He was so close to her, yet didn't notice her there. It was like a chilled sheet of shadow had been tossed over her head, keeping her from view. The shopkeeper came out of his store to watch and still paid her no mind.

"No trials for those who run," the Paladin above Archie said as she pulled the man up to standing.

Archie sputtered on the blood from his split lip, "No trials for those who stay." And so the Paladin holding onto him spat at his feet. From the truck, the other retrieved a large wooden post with a cross-shaped base at the bottom. With little effort, the well trained and muscular Paladin dragged the contraption to the middle of the street. The gathering crowd watched as he set it up on its base and Archie was pulled over.

"Should we just use gas from the car, I'm kind of in a hurry," one of the Paladins said as casually as if asking for the weather. She tied the loose end of Archie's rope to the post.

"No, King Byron was really mad about the explosion last time," the other responded. His companion rolled her eyes.

"I'll give you my own kindling if you hurry this up!" the shopkeeper called with a nervous glance towards the villagers who were his friends and neighbors. "This is a bad look for business." The Paladins looked at him as if he were a fly buzzing around their food before exchanging a glance. The larger one reached into the pack on his side and pulled out a thick bundle of sticks and other dried plantlife. He tossed it at Archie's feet and the man recoiled from it. He had a wild look as he began to thrash, but his bindings were far too tight. Archie wasn't going anywhere.

"So what *are* you doing after this?" the large Paladin asked his partner as he brought out a piece of cloth with some kind of oil smeared on it. She replied with her plans for the day as she brought a match to the cloth. Alena couldn't hear much more after that. Archie erupted into screams of horror as the Paladins tossed the ignited cloth to the kindling at his feet. Immediately, the entire bundle engulfed in vicious flames that licked at the bottoms of the man's feet. The Paladins looked at him as though he were disrupting their day.

"Honestly," the smaller one said, "you should be happy. We're sending you back to your demons."

Archie's shoes caught fire and he thrashed and kicked, his voice tearing from his throat begging for help. No one in the crowd dared approach, they only watched with hollowed eyes. There was a moment. A pause. Where Archie's eyes landed on Alena so briefly perhaps it was only an act of her imagination. Perhaps in his panic he couldn't register who stood there. Silent sobs wracked Alena's body as she dry-heaved, unable to hear anything except the screams and crackling of fire. It was growing higher now, becoming a night terror. She couldn't breathe. How long did she stand there? Dark smoke billowed into the sky, burning her throat.

'Alena, leave!' A loud voice boomed in her head and the heavy hand returned to her shoulder. She felt faint as everything else drowned out. She listened to the voice. *'Come home!'*

Alena didn't know how, but feeling returned to her legs at the command. And finally, she moved. But not only did she move. She ran.

Chapter 15

Alena didn't know when she ended up in her car. The trees of the forest blurred by as she barreled up the old mountain road. The car buckled and screeched, but still she kept her foot hard on the pedal. Her stomach flipped but her mind was miles away and could hardly consider the goings on in her own body. Soon the house came into view and Alena whipped the car into its usual spot. She slammed on the brakes and only her seat belt kept her in place as she jostled forward. Seconds later, she threw herself out of the vehicle.

She fell into the dirt and gagged on air. Alena clawed her way up and bolted towards the house. Her mind was numb as she jumped up the steps and rushed inside. She slammed the door behind her and made sure to lock it. Still, she found her grip on the knob to be deathly, her knuckles white.

Alena's knees buckled and she slid to the ground, the hardwood floors rough against her shins. Both her heart and head pounded painfully as she wheezed for air. She could hardly keep herself still as her body wracked with sickening shivers. Had her throat not felt so tight, she would have screamed. A waterfall of tears fell from her eyes despite it all. Her shaky hands flew up to her face to claw them away, but only more came. Her eyes, which had previously been so dry, burned.

"Mow?" came Lily's small meow. Alena blinked and turned to the cat beside her; Lily's green eyes were wide with concern. Alena sniffled and reached out to pull the cat onto her lap. She was warm and soft, her rumbling purrs allowing Alena's thudding heart to slow. Lily curled up into Alena's chest as she ran her hands through the cat's long fur. They sat there for a while.

On shaky legs, Alena pulled herself up with Lily still held in her arms. She paused and looked across the foyer into the dark hall. From within, she felt the burning stare from King Belial's eye sockets. She tensed, a bubbling anger in her gut that fizzled out soon after. She felt drained. All she wanted was to be left alone. She waited for him to approach, but he never did.

Alena staggered towards the living room; maybe she only imagined his eyes on her. She crossed the room to the couch and promptly collapsed onto it. Alena's head lolled back as Lily stayed faithfully on her lap. She continued to pet the cat as her eyes slid shut. Her head still ached, the combined lack of sleep and excess of stress from everything rattled her brain like a hive of bees. With what little energy she could, she rolled over to face the window. The sun was still bright overhead and she could see the yard well enough. Alena had to make sure no Paladin followed her. What would she do if they had? Run off into the forest?

Her mind wandered to Archie and Jaxon. Despite not even knowing them, it felt as though a stake had been driven into her chest. Her nose still picked up the distant scent of smoke in her memories. Even demon worshipers didn't deserve that fate. She paused as she remembered the warm hand she felt on her shoulder. Would she have found the courage to run if it weren't for that... if it weren't for *him*?

Alena's mind filled with fog. She didn't understand any of it. No matter how desperately she wanted to. She tried to live a life like everyone else. Like the shopkeeper who was in the public eye or the brothers who were often out and about.

Well, look at where it got them.

Her fears kept her indoors and made her flee to this mountain. But even as a child being raised in Lenoria she would panic and cry whenever she saw a Paladin. Why was that? They were there to protect them. Alena never felt that safety.

She knew deep down it could so easily be her tied to that post one day. Slowly beginning to burn. Whether she worshiped a demon like King Belial or not.

Alena pulled herself up and wrapped her arms around her chest. There wasn't a single vehicle coming up the mountain.

She gripped her shoulder, remembering the firm hand.

Remembered the warmth as it pulled her from the horrific Lenorian sights. Something uncertain twisted in her chest. The longing itch within her body returned, and she desperately wanted to reclaim that warm hand.

Lily sat up and puffed out her chest. The key looked like it glowed as Alena's gaze drifted over it. Her fingers tightened on her shoulder and she wondered... should she?

Damned if she did, damned if she didn't. So what truly did Alena have to lose? Her life? The last thing she wanted was to die. The last thing she wanted was to be burned at the stake.

Alena took a deep breath and stood with what little energy she could muster. She held Lily close as she headed towards the hallway in the foyer. It looked... less dark than usual. Alena's hold on the cat tightened as she walked down the long corridors. The air around her felt electric against her muscles, as if something excitedly awaited her.

She reached the bookcase and took Lily's ribbon. Setting the cat gently on the floor, she unlocked the chain. Alena pulled it open and stared down into the pitch black basement that opened up before her like a maw. The point of no return.

"You said you could make me someone who doesn't have to fear," Alena called out, her voice echoing around the empty-space. Before her, the basement grew darker.

'I can't **make** *you anything,'* came King Belial's voice from the depths. *'However, I can help.'*

Alena hesitated. Her instincts screamed at her to run away, and yet the blood that pumped in her heart sang for him, longed to envelop itself into his darkness.

"What do you want from me in return?" she asked. There was a creak on the stairs as the demon got closer, a rumble from his chest as the shadows neared.

Alena remembered her dream. The dark hand that reached out from the safe to reveal her grandfather's journal. She could almost picture it again, emerging from the void before her. However, this time it held no book. Instead, he offered his hand to her.

'All I want from you, Alena,' King Belial whispered, *'is your loyalty.'*

At that moment, there was no world around them, no death and fear. For just a second, Alena felt sound... she felt safe.

Alena reached forward into the darkness and immediately felt the warmth of the much larger hand wrap around her own. It was the same warmth she felt at the shop. The same comfort. She curled her fingers to grasp at the hand, but there was nothing physically there. Her heart thudded with the urge to follow.

Alena stepped into the basement.

Chapter 16

Alena sat in the middle of the basement, surrounded by boxes and darkness. It was quiet, aside from the heavy pounding of her heart as she wondered what would come next. Somewhere mixed in with the shadows before her, she could sense King Belial's energy. She didn't dare look at him, fearful of what she might see. Still afraid she made a mistake. King Belial huffed as her thoughts annoyed him.

'We need to have a proper conversation,' he said. His voice was stronger here. *'Come to me, in my domain.'*

The words sent a trill down Alena's spine that had her flush. She cursed her traitorous body as she shuffled, her voice small. "I'm not sure how to do that."

'It's like having a dream while being awake,' King Belial explained, his voice dragging out as though the explanation bored him. *'I can guide you through it.'*

Alena felt those large burning hands fall heavily onto her shoulders. She let out a small squeak and tensed. He was amused by that.

'Keep your back straight,' the demon said. Alena had no problem with that as she had already gone rigid. *'Shut your eyes and relax.'*

That was easier said than done. Though the thought of making herself more vulnerable pinched at her nerves. However, Alena knew she had to see this through. She clenched her eyes shut which only prompted a snarl from King Belial.

'I said relax!'

His booming voice made her tense and Alena had to take in a few breaths to calm herself.

'Now just let your mind go where it wanders,' King Belial said and by now it sounded almost tangible. Alena's mind became clear and shortly afterwards her body grew numb. She resisted the urge to twitch at the uncomfortable feeling until she felt herself floating. Alena gasped and kicked out her legs. Immediately the feeling left her and she found she was still on the basement floor. King Belial huffed out.

'Just let it take you.'

Alena crossed her legs once more and repeated the steps King Belial taught. It didn't take long for the same feeling to overcome her again. It wasn't painful in any way, but the uncertainty made her want to fidget.

An image flashed before her eyes as if they had opened, yet she knew they were shut tight. The image became clearer and she took in a sharp breath as she recognized the cave. The one where he had first approached her. He was right, this felt like a dream. And if she focused, she could still feel her body in the basement, right where she left it.

'Well, look at that, you're a natural,' came King Belial's voice, a hint of sarcasm to it. Alena blinked her dream-eyes and turned to look at the demon that stood behind her. She was met with the same enormous skull creature from before. While she should've expected it, she still screamed and leaped away. The rocks scraped up against her astral-self's spine. The edges of her vision darkened, shadows beginning to creep into the cavern. King Belial looked around at the dark corners and growled, *'Calm yourself, don't turn this into a nightmare.'*

His eyes glowed red from deep within the sockets of his skull as he stared at her. Despite the wavering of the world around them, Alena slowly pulled herself up. She hugged herself to keep calm and stable.

"S-Sorry," Alena stammered as she tried to look at him.

'If it would be easier on you, you can imagine us being somewhere else,' King Belial said. *'Somewhere that would make you more... comfortable.'*

"Where?" she asked.

'Do you need me to hold your hand for everything?' he snapped back. Alena grumbled as she turned away from him and tried to picture the world around them as *anywhere* else.

When she opened her eyes again, the two of them stood in the doorway of the living room upstairs. It was nearly an exact replica complete with every box she had memorized the location of. King Belial stepped further into the living room, his hooves heavy on the hardwood. The false sun's light shone through the window's curtains, reflecting off his skull. It was an off-white and reminded Alena of a candle. Smooth yet cracked, waxy and lovingly sculpted by the hands of whatever may have created him; perfection in all of its imperfections. King Belial's humanoid body was a wall of muscle, laid under dark gray skin that rippled with each movement. Alena's legs buckled at the sight. She could, perhaps, understand why someone would choose to worship King Belial.

It was odd to see him there physically—it didn't look right. He looked so... alien, standing next to the couch that was miniscule compared to him. Somehow, his skull face looked exasperated.

'You're not very imaginative, are you?' he asked in a tone that struck Alena's nerves like a hot iron.

"Hey!" she snapped, but piped down when his pupil slid in her direction.

'There's that fire from before.' King Belial chuckled. *'You're stupidly brave in the sunlight. But do know, I can control this land as easily if not better than you.'*

He reached his hand out to the window and the world outside turned to night. Alena shivered, which caught the demon's eye. And so, for her, King Belial made it light out once more. It was true. She felt at ease when it was bright and sunny.

'So are you just going to stand there all day?' King Belial asked. *'I've got things to do, Alena.'*

"What could you possibly have to do?" she asked, her voice quiet as she tested the waters with him. "You're always in my house."

'I can be in as many places as I want,' he growled, taking it as a challenge. *'As for your rudeness, you **do** remember I'm a **King**, right?'*

Alena carefully stepped into the room as she thought it over. She hadn't considered the word might mean more than a self-proclaimed title. That's what King Byron of Lenoria was, little more than the man that ran the Paladins of Exorcism. Though she supposed he was as close to any president or leader they currently had.

"What does that mean though?" Alena asked as she reached the end of the couch. She stayed there and made sure to keep the piece of furniture between them. "So you're actually the *King* of demons?"

'One of several,' King Belial said, a smug pridefulness to his tone. *'Our hierarchy is complex. Nothing I expect a human to understand.'*

Alena looked away from him towards the window, but it was so bright outside she couldn't see the yard. It was just white. Evidence this wasn't her normal reality.

"So what actually is this place?" Alena asked, looking at the surrounding boxes. It resembled the living room, but if she truly focused, everything rippled and shimmered.

'The astral realm,' King Belial answered. *'It's where most spirits reside and where all human dreams take place.'*

"So like..." Alena trailed off as she wracked her brain for the words, "advanced daydreaming?"

'In so few words, yes.' King Belial sighed.

Huh, that was actually kind of neat. Alena wondered what else she could do, aside from just a change of location. She imagined the space clear of any boxes and immediately they all vanished. King Belial glared at the now empty room and grumbled, but let her have her fun. A small smile slipped onto Alena's face. The room would be so much larger without the mess!

Alena imagined a new space for all her candle-making supplies. And just as she thought of them, they appeared before her. King Belial's thick tail twitched and lightly slapped against the hardwood. However, Alena could only gaze in wonder at the room.

For a final touch, Alena imagined a Saffron Flowers painting hanging above the fireplace. The same one from the shop, with the golden-haired person sitting in the wild field. Alena beamed for only a moment before her good mood fell. The picture, one of the few by Saffron she had seen in person, brought back the memories of earlier.

King Belial's eyes looked over the painting and perhaps he saw something Alena couldn't as a surprised hum erupted from his chest. The demon stepped toward the wall, the house lightly shaking as he did, to give it a closer look. He pointed to it with one clawed finger before he looked back at Alena, question-ingly.

'What's this?'

"That's a painting," Alena explained, which made the demon huff. The sound hissed out from the nasal cavity of his skull.

'I know what a painting is, Alena. I simply want to know why you've placed it.'

"Oh," she responded, and despite being in the dream-world, she flushed. "Well it was in the... shop I go to. A somewhat-famous painter made it. I really like her stuff but I can't afford the real thing."

King Belial's irises flashed in and out of existence. His own way of blinking, Alena supposed. He turned back to the painting to scan over each brushstroke. *'She better be careful with a talent like that. If she gets any better they'll accuse her of selling her soul to the devil.'*

"What?!" Alena gasped. Her fright spiked as she imagined the artist with the same fate as Archie. Alena chased the thoughts from her mind. She couldn't think about him right now. It made her stomach burn with sickness as if the memory itself was poison. Instead, Alena focused on the other thing King Belial mentioned. She bit her lip as anxiety pricked at her imagined skin. "Wait, is that what you want from me? My soul?"

'Relax, I was joking,' King Belial said. He rolled his irises around their sockets. *'No offense, sweetheart, but human souls are a dime a dozen. They're practically worthless.'*

"Okay, ow," Alena muttered as her nerves eased. Instead, they were replaced by that spiteful and biting feeling she struggled to put down. She could only act on it to settle her mood. She snapped back. "You know you're not funny, right?"

Alena stepped further behind the couch to keep it between the two of them. King Belial faced her, his thick arms crossing over his chest. He didn't seem too mad at her, but his tail twitched just like Lily's would.

'Behave yourself,' he grumbled. His skull cracked and split by the teeth as they unnaturally curled upward into a smirk. The demon chuckled. *'And if you're a good little devotee I might pull some strings to get you one of those paintings.'*

Alena blinked. "There's no way."

'I am very powerful, Alena,' he said. *'I can get you whatever you dream of.'*

King Belial's tantalizing words made her mouth water, but Alena didn't *want* to be someone who was easily swayed. But wasn't that why people worshiped demons? To get things? She wasn't sure if she even deserved to be given an opportunity like that. Alena stepped out from behind the couch and sat herself on the edge of the cushions instead. King Belial watched her carefully all the while. He looked even more massive where she sat, having to crane her neck to look up at him.

"Hey, King Belial... can I ask you something?" Her voice was so small she worried the demon might not have heard her. His slightly pointed ears twitched, however.

'That's why we're here,' he said. *'This path isn't for everyone. I pushed you here these past few days, but still I don't want you to jump straight in. Not without knowing what it may bring for you.'*

Alena nodded.

"Alright, so why?" she asked. "Why would you want to help me like this? I heard demons are all monsters made of pure evil that want to cause pain and suffering. I mean, that's what *demon* means, isn't it?"

'Daemon is what the word was in ancient times,' he spoke without hesitation, as if this was something he explained hundreds of times before. He went on, *'Back then we were seen as guardian spirits. Listen to me, Alena, I have existed before this world and I will exist far after it's gone. For millennia, demons and*

*humans have danced in a symbiotic relationship. We work beside each other. Humans give demons energy from offerings and worship. In turn, demons help unlock the power humans are owed. Just because your government has made it punishable by death, **yet again**, doesn't mean we will ever stop this dance.'*

The space between them grew silent and Alena looked down at her hands. She fiddled with her fingers as she chewed on the information. Her biggest question she wanted to ask was whether or not she could truly trust him. King Belial could so easily lie to her, but... she so desperately wanted to believe him. Alena remembered his warm hand in the shop, the safety she felt. She wanted to feel that way again. She thought back to the article in the old newspaper.

"King Belial, if all this is true," she began, slowly, unsure about bringing it up, "then what actually happened to the president in the Before Times?"

He shifted his weight, taking more time to think over that particular question.

'That is...' he began, his voice trailing off, *'not my story to tell.'*

Her voice felt small as she asked, "Were you there?"

Alena thought he would be hesitant with the answer, but King Belial's voice was quick and snappy.

'No,' he said, voice sure as anything else. *'I can promise you if I was, that situation would have turned out completely different.'*

As Alena rolled the answer around in her head, she heard King Belial's hoof step as he moved from his spot near the fireplace. Alena clenched her fingers around the couch's upholstery as his shadow fell over her. Something about the way King Belial looked down on her made her squirm. He had a slightly amused energy about him at the sight of her. Alena's heart skipped a beat in turn.

Then the enormous demon knelt down, making himself more at her level. Alena peered into the sockets on his skull. From within that void, his glowing irises peered back, and she thought maybe they looked softer than before. Less of the fires of hell and more like candlelight. It did well to sooth her frazzled nerves.

'If you truly do not wish to do this, then say it to my face.' King Belial dipped his head. *'I only want loyal followers and if that isn't you, then I'll leave you to your own devices.'*

Was he telling the truth? She scanned him up and down to remind herself how nonhuman his appearance was. Yet, still he treated her with more dignity than said people within Lenoria. Despite Alena's conviction that the basement was the point of no return, he was still giving her the option to turn back. It was... thoughtful of him, she supposed. A comforting warmth spread through her chest under the continued glow of his candle-eyes.

'So answer me, Alena,' he said, voice booming. *'Now that I've told you all of this, do you still wish to make a deal with the devil?'*

The demon before her extended his hand and this time she saw it clearly. His red markings shifted and slid down his arm, they swirled around until his sigil appeared on his palm. The mark was bright and burned so hot she felt it flush against her skin. Despite it all, a genuine smile appeared on Alena's face as she looked up into his glowing irises, her own half-lidded. She slowly reached out, her voice barely a whisper.

"Let's continue this dance, King Belial."

Chapter 17

King Belial's handshake was a blistering heat against Alena's palm. She gasped at the pain and flailed back into the waking world. With sweat on her brow, Alena realized she was back in the basement, its darkness making her disorientated. She clutched at her hand.

Alena got re-accustomed to the feeling of her body. Though her limbs had a sense of longing for that sunny living room, even if it wasn't a place in the physical. Somewhere within the basement shadows, King Belial's stare lingered. He kept his distance to let her come back to reality.

Alena looked down at her hand as the burning ebbed away and her breath got stuck within her chest. It was there. The sigil. Shining bright against the back of her hand as though the mark had transferred from his to hers. It was like a branding. Alena frantically wiped at the thing to remove it from her skin. It stayed.

'So it has been done,' King Belial stated as he finally approached. His energy felt far heavier than before, almost like she could reach out and touch him. She didn't try.

"H-Hey, what gives?" Alena's voice cracked as she glared up at the rippling shadows. "I can't go out in public like this. It'll get me killed!"

'Don't worry about it,' King Belial said, and Alena pictured him shaking his head. *'This binding mark is only visible to those touched by one as well.'*

Those words didn't give Alena any comfort as she looked at the glowing mark. She twisted her hand every which way to see it shimmer and shine. She finally lowered her hand and looked towards the shadows where the demon lurked.

"So what's next?" she asked. "What do I have to do?"

'Research,' King Belial stated. And he was a tad smug as he went on, *'Your dear late grandfather put so much effort into that little black book. Would be cruel if you didn't read it from cover to cover. Not to mention the rest of the grimoires in his stash... Weren't you thinking earlier you wanted to pick up reading?'*

Alena groaned. The thought of combing through those books gave her a headache. Full of demonic worship and esoteric knowledge. She finally stood to reclaim the abandoned book next to the safe. It was still there. Alena put her thumb on the pages to flip through them. She hesitated.

Instead, her sights landed on the altar in front of her. Tightening her hold on the book, Alena tiptoed over to it. She sat the book down on the dust that covered the old table. Though it was far too dark to make out much among the clutter, she could still see what was once a cookie in a copper bowl that served as an offering dish. It was mummified now. Alena wondered if she should tidy it up to make things down there more liveable. She glanced around at the rest of the mess around the room, unsure about the idea.

Before Alena could ask King Belial, the heavy stomp of his hoof approached her. She still tensed as the invisible wall of energy stood beside her. The heat seeped into her awaiting bones.

'All of that can wait till later,' he said, voice low, much to her surprise. *'For now, I think you should sleep.'*

"Are you going to let me?" Alena asked with a spark of bitterness. King Belial was unfazed and chuckled.

'Of course,' he rumbled, *'I've already got you where I want you.'*

Alena's breath stuttered as his words reverberated around her core. She was *almost* fearful, but the emotions from before wouldn't come. Instead, her blood turned warm, a deep electric excitement settling into her. Alena wanted to take on the world, but was quick to shelve the feeling. Lest it get her into trouble.

Alena left the book on the altar as she carefully made her way out of the basement. She locked it back up safely, but hesitated as she stepped away from the bookcase. Something in her chest clenched.

Despite everything, Alena wanted to... talk to him more. King Belial on all accounts *could* have been lying to her. If he truly wanted her soul or something else. Yet she couldn't stop the feeling of comfort that washed over her. Alena thought maybe, just maybe, she made the right decision.

She continued her way down the hall and upon turning the corner, she saw Lily. The cat stood outside the hallway, staring straight in. Her eyes flashed with understanding before she turned and bounded up the stairs. Alena followed and wondered if Lily knew more than she had let on. However, she was *far* too tired to delve into anything more and so Alena simply went into the bedroom and collapsed onto the bed. She hadn't even shut the door or put the footstool in front of it like usual.

Distantly, she felt King Belial's presence lurk around the house. Though Alena still felt unsure of him, knowing he was there settled her nerves. For the first time in a long while, she drifted away into an easy and dreamless slumber.

When Alena finally woke up, the world around her was bright. She winced as light filtered through the window curtains. Her body felt heavy and her brain groggy. She pulled herself up despite how encumbered she felt and wondered how long she had been out. It looked to be midday. Alena yawned and stretched out each limb, the strain of her muscles feeling like heaven.

Damn, she hadn't even slept that well back in the city... Definitely not.

Lily yowled as she leaped onto the bed, tail lashing. The little cat had a look of annoyance on her face as her back twitched. Soon after, she bolted off the bed and dashed out of the room. Alena watched Lily run across the landing then down the stairs. The soft padding of her paws vanished further into the house.

Alena chuckled as she figured the cat must be hungry. She rubbed the sleep from her eyes and staggered out of bed to follow her. As Alena passed the hall by the stairs, she could almost picture King Belial at the end of it, curiously observing her. He let her be though, grunting as he turned tail and vanished towards the hidden basement door.

Alena headed into the kitchen and wasted no time gathering up a few scrapes of preserved meats. She tossed it to the floor and immediately Lily pounced and started to loudly scarf it down. Alena watched the cat eat for a bit before she went and put coffee on her burner.

Then, without thinking, Alena placed a second cup of coffee next to her own. She remained there until the water boiled. Alena claimed the cups and some of her candles before heading out of the kitchen with her haul.

"Come on, Lily," she called and the cat grabbed the last bit of meat and followed with it firmly clasped in her jaws. The two of them went back to the hidden basement. Deep down in her bones lingered the threat of danger. She wondered if King Belial's energy purposefully made her feel threatened in the hallway. Or if perhaps the feeling was some leftover instinct that was part of human nature.

Either way, Alena undid the lock and as she pulled open the bookcase, Lily dashed into the dark, vanishing as her black fur blended in. Alena peered inside and saw that the basement looked the same as it always did. And yet... It felt somewhat different. More inviting.

Alena entered.

She went straight to the altar. Lily was already there, sprawled out beside it as she purred. Alena felt King Belial's gaze somewhere in the distance, watching her closely as she strode right up to the altar, as though she owned the place. Technically, she did, but to him that was debatable at best.

Alena set the coffees and candles onto the altar and left them aside as she gathered up the old half melted ones from her grandfather's time. She then turned towards the copper bowl and pried the decayed cookie out of it with a little effort. It was then she felt a sharp pain in her temple as a brief flash of King Belial's annoyance hit her senses. Finally, the demon approached her, his heavy energy invading her space far too quickly. It felt warm, as though someone had turned on a burner.

'Hey, what are you doing?' he growled and Alena could imagine his glare. *'Those are mine.'*

"O-Oh, well they're really old so I just..." Alena stammered as King Belial's possible wrath sent her heart into a flutter. Mentally, she reached out to the being in front of her and felt his anger that boiled just like the coffee. If she pushed further... If she wasn't just imagining it, then deep down she could feel a hint of worry from him. King Belial grunted and suddenly it was like he had built a wall between her and his emotions. He stepped away.

Alena smiled as she set the old offerings on one of the nearby boxes before she returned to the altar.

"Hey, don't worry, I brought you some new stuff to replace them," she explained as she set the coffee next to the copper bowl and the candles where the old ones had been.

He continued to watch, and in her head she got the image of him flicking his tail. She carefully lit the candles to give themselves more light. "If you want, I can melt down the old candles and turn them into new ones. The cookie, though, that has to go."

'I'll allow you to get away with it this time,' King Belial said as he approached, but he didn't go near her. Instead, his energy hovered around the altar. Particularly the cup of coffee.

Alena left him to it. She grabbed the black book from where she had left it the day prior. She felt slight intrigue from King Belial, but he mostly ignored her and left her to her own devices. Thankful for that, she grabbed her own cup of coffee and slid down to the floor to lean her back against the old table. With the candlelight casting a soft glow above her, she gazed at the book's cover, the same sigil engraved on it just like her hand. She brought the offending limb up to compare it to the book.

The idea of reading it sent a wave of uncertainty through her. Just holding onto it would have given the P.O.E. enough reason to bring her Archie's fate. Her fingers shook on the cover as the branches of the forbidden fruit hung over her head. She should have been terrified, but Alena only felt a thrill of excitement deep within her bones. Bones that had been sculpted for the demon beside her. She took a sip from her coffee, the bitter taste dancing along her tongue while Lily curled up into a ball and snoozed nearby. King Belial's energy warmed up the area so much the concrete floors no longer had a cold bite. Perhaps, Alena thought, this wasn't all that bad.

She cracked open the book.

Chapter 18

'Belial is an incredibly powerful and ancient infernal being. In biblical lore, he was said to have fallen right after Lucifer, though I do not believe in such stories.

He is the 68th spirit in the Ars Goetia, a group of 72 demons that were supposedly controlled by Solomon in biblical times. Whether these spirits actually could be bound is left up to speculation, for no mortal man can control a god. Crowned one of the kings of hell, Belial rules over the direction north and the element of earth. He governs over 80 legions and for his loyal practitioners, will gift them the most excellent of familiars.

Upon inviting him into your space for the first time, it is recommended to give an offering. King Belial lives up to his high ranking in the demonic courts and should be shown the utmost of respect.'

"Were you the one to write this?" Alena smirked as she looked up from the journal in front of her. It was nice to give her eyes a break, being far too strained in the dim lighting. King Belial snorted at her bold joke.

'Your grandfather had undying loyalty to me,' he said, his voice almost wistful. *'You just don't see that kind of devotion anymore.'*

And what *was* that kind of devotion, exactly? Alena tossed the word around her head, but couldn't imagine it. She could admit her current choices and relationship with King Belial were for their mutual benefit. He needed offerings, and she needed a sense of security. The memory of his warm hands on her flitted through her mind. The sharp angles of his skull and how the demon bore pure power with each movement. Yes, she had simply chosen an excellent protector. It was nothing more and nothing less.

"If I can be honest..." Alena trailed off as she tried to think of her words, "I don't really understand it."

'Keep reading,' was all King Belial said, and she got the image of him pointing one long clawed finger towards the book. She grumbled, but did as asked.

'So how did I get involved with such a magnificent spirit?', her grandfather had written. ***'It was a cold winter's day back in the Before Times around my young adulthood. There had been a blizzard and we were running out of firewood, so I volunteered to get more. I was far more fit than my grandmother whom I took care of. However, I had gotten a bit turned around in the woods and lost my way. I sought shelter in a nearby cave, but even then the cold had been violent and biting. I honestly didn't think I'd make it out alive. It was then the demonic king appeared before me. As I mentioned in my note before, our ancestor already had some sort of bond with him, and so he watches over our family line like a guardian. He said he saw promise in me which I had never really believed, even now. King Belial saved me that day. He allowed me to return to my poor grandmother and when I asked her about it, she grew excited and bestowed upon me the information that I now give you.'***

Alena mulled over the writing, but still didn't understand. Maybe she could have if she was born and raised in a different time. If she had been shown the same camaraderie of family her grandfather had. Wanting to figure it out, Alena tried to dive further.

'Ever since then, I have been a faithful follower of Belial,' the man's words continued, *'and I feel so honored to be on this path. I don't know where I would've been without him. I likely would have died in that cave, and my poor grandmother would have been left to wonder what had become of me. I never would have made my truest companions in my coven, though they are all long gone now. And I never would have been gifted my beautiful feline friend, Lilith. My little Lily.'*

Could being involved with a demon really change one's life so drastically? Alena's frown deepened. She couldn't picture herself suddenly tossing out her caution to make friends. That had never been her way. Alena looked away from the book and her sights landed on where Lily was still curled up, the cat fervently licking her back foot.

"So what's up with Lily?" Alena asked. *Lilith.* She rolled the cat's full name around in her head, and asked, "Is she some sort of demon too?"

'She's just a cat,' King Belial said, rather amused as Lily perked her ears at hearing her name. The cat purred and flopped onto her side as if being petted by an invisible force. He chuckled. *'Don't be ridiculous, Alena.'*

Alena let out a huff. "I just ask because Lilith is among the banned names you can't name your child. It's a demon's name, right?"

'The queen and mother of demons, yes.'

"So why—" Alena began, to which King Belial finished with a *'—do you ask so many questions?'*

Alena gnawed on her lip as her hot ire boiled over, but she was quick to force it down as she felt the demon look at her curiously. Was he pushing on purpose? She calmed her nerves and added, perhaps still with a bit too much bite, "I'm just trying to understand the old man. Like why would he name her *Lilith* and not like... *Little Belial?* Since he seems to be such a big fan of you and all."

He cackled, *'because nothing about me is **little**, Alena.'*

"Forget I asked!" Alena's face flushed as she set the book aside and brought her knees to her chest. It's not like she didn't *know* that. Alena had seen much more of King Belial (from a respectable distance) than she cared to admit— Modesty clearly not being something the demonic were well versed in. She grumbled as she chased the thoughts from her mind.

'Heh.' His chuckle was rough and brief. King Belial let her nerves fester as he went on with the previous topic. *'Well, if you must know. Just because he was devoted to me and me alone, doesn't mean he wasn't allowed to honor other divine demons. He loved us, for whatever reason, also a trait you do not see too often. So he named his familiar Lilith to show her respect.'*

Alena cocked her head to the side. "So that's considered a respectful thing to do?"

'Imagine it this way,' King Belial explained. *'Names have power. He named the cat Lilith and in doing so, all his love and devotion to his companion went into the name. Thus, the demon that shares the name gets that energy as well.'*

Alena supposed that made sense. The onslaught of information made her dizzy, but she couldn't deny the craving deep in her core to know more. She wanted nothing more than to sink her teeth into the knowledge. Alena glanced at the basement shadows from the corners of her eyes. She didn't dare voice this to King Belial. It would make him smug, she was sure.

Alena set her hand on the concrete and lightly scratched it. This got Lily's attention as she hopped up and trotted over.

"Hey, King Belial, where's Queen Lilith now?" Alena asked as she fondly rubbed behind the cat's ears.

'I'm...' the demon trailed off in thought. He appeared more cautious. *'Not too sure. After The Event, our courts dissolved and our kind scattered to the winds. I don't know where a lot of my former companions are. And I'm pretty sure most of them want it to stay that way.'*

"The Event?" she questioned and immediately Alena felt King Belial's heat go cold. The rippling in the air went still. For a moment, Alena feared she had said something wrong, but then the demon's energy returned to normal.

'That's simply what we call the grand ball where the president's slaying happened.' King Belial hummed. *'It's nothing for you to worry about. It's the past.'*

Something uncertain rubbed at the back of Alena's mind. Why wouldn't he just tell her more about that? What was he hiding? She bit her lip and turned to the book, wondering if her grandfather had written about it. Maybe she was prepared to scour the thing for those answers.

'I think it's time for you to take a break,' King Belial said, voice rumbling. Alena tensed, but the demon was calm and nearly tranquil. *'You'll damage your eyes.'*

"Oh, sure," Alena muttered. She didn't want to push things with him. Instead, she averted her eyes and stared down at the book. Her nails lightly scratched against the old leather, and trailed them along the pages. When she realized what she was doing, Alena pulled herself up from the floor. She took the black book with her and set it on the altar table, away from where the candles still burned.

She still felt quite energized and had nothing else to do that day. She could've worked on her candles, but... in doing so, Alena would have to think of the shop. A sickening shiver wracked her body as a picture of smoke billowing into the air invaded her mind. She wasn't ready to deal with those emotions yet. So instead, she would tidy up the darkened room around her. Alena hurried over to the nearest box and gathered it up into her arms. Luckily for her, the basement wasn't completely jam-packed with stuff and she could pile most of it in the corners.

King Belial sipped up the energy of his coffee as both he and Lily watched her. There was a hint of his mood from earlier, a deep concern as she moved things about. As Alena stacked boxes in one of the corners, she made a mental note to go through them later. Maybe there's something useful she could use.

'What's the point of this?' King Belial asked, his tone weary. *'It's fine where it is.'*

"Well, if I'm going to have to spend a lot of time here, I want it to be livable." Alena shrugged as she cleared a small section of the floor.

King Belial grunted. *'You're getting too comfortable here.'*

"Maybe...so would you want anything the next time I go into town?" she asked as she scanned the room for more candle space. Alena wondered if her grandfather had any candle-holders hidden away. This was manageable. It was a sense of normalcy to get her mind off things.

King Belial finally stepped away from his coffee to approach. Alena got the image of him standing over her, his muscles taut as he looked down at her knowingly. She shifted her footing as she looked away, unable to handle his burning gaze. There was the sound of something sliding against the floor, his tail maybe, as he put on a smirk. King Belial's energy felt like the comforting warmth of a fire in winter. It lightened up whatever dreadful mood threatened to swallow her.

'Mm, I request a hard liquor like Whisky,' he growled. *'It's been so long since **any** of my followers have given me some.'*

Alena balked at that.

"I don't think I could find that, let alone afford it..." That was usually the kind of thing only government officials and the highest elites could afford. Alena shook her head, he was going to have to settle for the coffee, and then hopefully water when that ran out. Alena further mulled over the demon's words. Something clicked. "You've mentioned your other followers, so you mean there's other *actual* demon worshipers out there? Where are they?"

King Belial's energy wall went up again, and Alena frowned. He slowly let his words out. *'That is something I won't disclose, but yes there are others, I'm able to be at multiple places at once.'*

Alena wondered if his other followers were far more willing participants. Were these other followers scared like she was, or were they just going about their normal lives? Completely fine with the hand they've been dealt. Did they feel the same strange pull in their hearts as she did?

That warm hand set itself on Alena's shoulder and the comforting safety net from before returned. It took all of Alena's willpower to not lean into the touch. Half because that would probably be an inappropriate action. The other half being she would absolutely fall to the floor with nothing tangible there.

'You should just worry about yourself right now,' King Belial said, his voice much more calm and level. Alena felt an almost painful clench in her stomach, then it growled. He chuckled. *'When's the last time you ate?'*

Now, in theory, Alena knew she should be honest with the demonic king she was devoting herself to. However, she didn't want to admit she couldn't remember the answer to his question. Before she could form any kind of answer, he spoke again.

'Alena, you need to listen to your own body,' King Belial lectured out in a deep snarl. Was this his way of expressing concern? Alena couldn't tell, but maybe he was just angry at how poor of a devotee she was. She imagined him crossing his arms over his broad chest.

'I'm not going to take care of you like Lucifer would. If you starve, that's all on you.'

Alena's curiosity perked up at the name, and she wanted to ask about him. *Lucifer.* However, she knew this was King Belial's way of telling her to move away from those thoughts. She gave a deep nod before gathering up Lily and blowing out the candles.

The basement was cast into darkness once more.

Chapter 19

What did worship truly mean?

Alena moved around the kitchen table. Her contraption for melting wax sat in front of her; she had yet to begin her work. Every time she went to start, she would just stop and stare at the bundle of herbs she would need to burn to keep the pot heated.

Instead, Alena faced the counter and grabbed a jar of dried fruits. She spooned several mouthfuls to settle her stomach and appease King Belial. Once Alena started, she had much more of an appetite and was able to fully eat her meal. Huh, Alena frowned at the bland taste. Usually she would have been fine with it, but now, she found the meal to be lacking. She wondered if it was because of King Belial or something else.

Either way, with both him demanding she eat better and ravenous little Lily, Alena would have to frequent the shop a lot more than she initially hoped. Her meal churned her stomach and Alena had to quickly discard the jar.

There was no use putting off the inevitable. If she was to keep everyone in the house well fed, she would have to continue her work. Alena sighed as she returned to her equipment and opened the lower hatch on the burning pot.

Alena carefully grasped the bundle of plants, her hands growing clammy. She set them in the bottom of the burner and brought her flint to them. They sparked alive and began to burn hot. Alena snapped the hatch shut before the dark smoke could billow out of the opening. Despite that, she still felt like it had gotten caught in her throat.

She could still see the fire in her mind. The image was crisp and clear as if she still stood there on the street. Alena hacked on the invisible smoke and shook her head to rid herself of the memory. She couldn't dwell on it. It wasn't her right to dwell on it.

Alena reached for another herb bundle to add to the fire, but only found the table's smooth wood under her touch. She frowned. That was the last of her herb supply. Alena looked towards the backdoor, where Lily lounged in the sun rays that filtered through the window. Now that she lived among the foliage, she didn't need to trade for kindling and could just step outside to get some. However, what if she didn't get the right plants? What if she accidentally grabbed something toxic?

'There you go again,' King Belial said as he entered the room, bringing with him his overbearing energy. It made the area look as though the sun had gone behind a cloud. Alena couldn't help the way her throat grew tight. She wondered if she would ever get used to his presence around her, the rumble of his voice that bounced around her skull whenever he spoke. It was surreal really.

"Is there something you want?" Alena asked and quickly hoped it hadn't come out too rude. She just wanted to be a good host, or rather, a devotee. Again, whatever that meant of her. So far she was fine with giving him offerings of coffee or whichever of her candles he desired.

'Nothing at the moment,' King Belial said and then he remained silent. Alena tried to brush off his presence as she watched the wax in her burner melt. Soon she could start the dipping process. King Belial's hefty energy pressed up against her back as he also observed. Alena sighed and took a homemade wick between her fingers before she slowly slipped it into the wax.

The demon blew hot air out of his muzzle. *'It's nice to watch how our offerings get made.'*

Alena frowned. "Do you want them?" She had just given him new candles and really needed these ones for the trade.

'That isn't what I meant,' King Belial spoke. *'Candles are a common offering — they give energy and most demons seem to like fire, anyway.'*

"Why's that?"

'A lot are fire elementals,' King Belial said and Alena pictured him shrugging. *'Though maybe for most it reminds them of home.'*

What was home to a demon? Hell? Unsettled, she wondered if it would be okay to ask about that.

"King Belial, does hell exist?" she asked. She had never been too religious until now. He chuckled.

'Not in the sense that you may think,' was what the demon left her with. *'I suppose that's what you may call the realm in which my kind live. It's a part of the astral, just as everything not physical is.'*

"What's it like?" Alena asked as she pictured the fire and brimstone from legends of old. This made Belial scoff at her lack of imagination yet again.

'It can look a bit like that, depending on where you go.' He sighed. *'Like I said, a lot of us gravitate towards tradition. Massive obsidian castles with medieval furnishings is not at all an uncommon sight to see. But there's also rolling hills and waterfalls, sometimes things that your human brain wouldn't even be able to comprehend. Like if you lived in a kaleidoscope.'*

Alena turned away and watched Lily roll over. It sounded... pleasant, almost, but Alena felt her old anxieties bubble to the surface. Those bright orange flames still burned brightly in her mind. *"We're going to send you back to your demons,"* the Paladin's words echoed.

King Belial said he didn't want her soul, but then where did that leave her? She had never really given an afterlife much thought. Why should she, when every living day was a struggle to get through?

"Is that... where I'll go when I die?" Alena asked, because she didn't quite know what to think anymore. "Is that a thing?"

'I do find your questions very refreshing, truly,' King Belial said in his more sarcastic tone. It stuck another nerve with Alena as he tended to. She bit her

tongue to refrain from saying anything she might regret, though the great king in front of her laid in wait. As if he was ready for her to give him a reason. He huffed. *'If I tell you everything, then what is the fun in learning for yourself? Death should always be the one unsolvable mystery humans must experience firsthand.'*

Alena remained quiet. Her skin prickled like needles as her heart thrummed a little faster than normal. She tried to push the feelings away, but those emotions from when she first moved there bubbled to the surface. The uncertainty. The darkness. The fear of his demonic claws tearing her open, leaving her heart bare for the crows to feast on. A deep growl echoed as those deepest thoughts and her feelings of concern reached King Belial.

'Do you regret your devotion to me?' King Belial asked, his voice surprisingly level as his energy grew ten times hot. He glared down at her from high above. *'Still think I'll drag you down to the pit when I've had my fun with you?'*

The strain of Alena's emotions tore ever so slightly. She snapped, "I'm trying! Please believe that I am. I know what my body tells me I should do, but my mind is all over the place, I..."

She thought of how it might feel to burn at the stake. The heat, too much. The smoke, suffocating. Would that happen if she was caught? That's all she wanted to know. That's all... A heavy hand fell on top of her head. The enormous thing was gentle. It chased the memories of smoke and ash from her mind to be replaced by the comforting palm she once felt on her shoulder.

'I know you are...' King Belial said, and now his tone had grown impossibly gentle. *'Do not think for a second that I don't deeply respect you for the risk you are taking for me right this second. I just...'*

He trailed off for only a second, but continued before Alena could ask what he meant. King Belial growled, *'I have to be harsh with you, Alena. I fear if I am too soft, it could get you killed. It* will *get you killed.'*

Alena's fingers curled on impulse at the words. She shivered despite the warmth he brought her as her heartbeat picked up. In her mind's eye, Alena saw him standing there, a haggard dip to his shoulders. His red markings dulled to a light flicker. King Belial slid his hand down to encase her cheek, the invisible limb tingling against that side of her face. Alena sighed with content. The emotions from the moment before all but evaporated. Only to be replaced by... something else. A foreign flutter in her gut, but she supposed it wasn't so bad. She slid her hand up to touch his, but alas, there was nothing she could grab onto.

'Mm,' King Belial's chest rumbled as an amused air rose about him. *'And truly, it would be a shame if that frantic little heart of yours was to stop.'*

Alena flushed a great deal as his words met her ears. Had he actually heard her heart beat?! She coughed. "I— um, sorry! I don't know why..."

'You're fine.' King Belial chuckled and lowered his hand away from her. It took all of Alena's willpower not to follow after him. She dug her nails into her palms to keep herself behaved. The demon's good humor still remained as he went on, *'But you are just a little too uptight. Relax a little.'*

That task from him was easier said than done, but still Alena uncurled her hands. King Belial was pleased by that and finally stepped away to give her some space, even if she could feel his energy contemplating. As if he was mulling over some sort of plot.

She took the finished candle out of the pot to pin it up on the line. Slowly she worked on several others as well, both Lily and King Belial quietly observed her. This time the staring wasn't too much. In fact, Alena found the air around them to be light and airy. It was a welcome change.

Once she had decided she had enough of the classic chime-styled candles, Alena moved onto a solid block of beeswax. She sat down in one of the chairs and examined the piece as she wondered what sculpture lay behind the excess wax. It was then that Alena picked up King Belial's interest once more.

She paused curiously as the demon stepped towards her, almost quietly. Alena awaited the comment he no doubt had on his tongue.

'I know I said I didn't want one, but...' he trailed off. Despite that, Alena sensed his intrigue at the future candle grow. He pointed at one of the discarded sculptures she had already made. A bird. He went on, *'The ones you gave me don't have fancy shapes like these.'*

Alena hesitated as she thought over her next words carefully. She wasn't quite sure if she wanted to. But this was her patron was he not? She mentally poked at his energy to see what he felt. He seemed... hopeful.

"I suppose I can," Alena responded. "What shape do you want?"

He thought for only a moment before the rippling energy moved to where Lily was sprawled on the floor. King Belial requested, *'Make it look like Lily.'*

The little cat's ears perked up as she finally stood to look up at the empty air. Alena agreed, she would love to make one like that. And so she turned back to the block of wax, now being able to see the future candle it contained. Lily. Alena smiled and began to carve.

She would carve out that cat for the rest of the day, making sure to not make a single mistake. A comfortable silence had risen just as the sun began to set. Around then, King Belial vanished to who knows where and Alena decided to stop for the night. She stretched out her back and headed to the bathroom.

Alena lit her candle and slowly shut the door behind her before turning on the faucet and waiting for the tub to fill. The mirror was fogged with age, but she could just make out her unhealthily pale skin and dark bags under her eyes. It was going to take a lot more sleep than just a night to fix that.

'And maybe some sun and fresh air.'

Alena paused and leered around. That thought wasn't her own, yet she didn't feel King Belial nearby at all. The surrounding air felt relatively empty of demonic activity, the only thing heavy being the stagnation. Alena turned the faucet off and waited, concerned about what happened the last time she tried to bathe.

But the two of them were fine now, weren't they? Carefully, under the candlelight Alena was quick to undress and slip into the water. She pulled the old curtain, despite how tattered it was, to close herself off from the rest of the room. It became even darker.

The water was chilled, but she didn't mind as it cooled her aching muscles and washed off the basement grime. There was a loud thump nearby.

"Oh, you've got to be kidding me," Alena grumbled as she put her head in her hands.

'What, do you have a problem?' King Belial asked as the air outside the curtain grew thicker. While the heat from his energy would have been a comfort in the cold water, Alena recoiled from it. Her face flushed as she wanted to snap at him, but... she didn't want to push her luck anymore. Alena bit her lip to keep herself from telling her patron to fuck all the way off. King Belial huffed.

"Why do you have to creep around like this?" she asked through gritted teeth as though to test the waters. "Bathrooms are kind of a private place, you know?"

'Well, you never told me otherwise.' King Belial snorted through the open nasal cavity on his skull. Something about his tone was... playful. Alena hesitated. Was this... a test of some kind? The demon went on, *'Some of my practitioners are absolutely delighted to spend such quality time with me.'*

"Well, not that I don't enjoy spending time with you, to an extent," Alena sighed and finally she came out with it, "but this is kind of a line you're crossing for me."

'And that's all you had to say,' he responded. The sounds of his hoof-steps faded from her ears as he stomped away.

"Hey, wait, so that's it then?" Alena spoke up. "You don't... mind?"

'You're allowed to say 'no', Alena.' King Belial's voice brought her to ease. *'I don't own you, that's not really my thing. I do, however, think you need to grow a bit of a backbone. Sticking up to me* more *is certainly one way to do that.'*

She couldn't wrap her mind around her interactions with King Belial. She assumed that to worship a demon would mean to be its servant. That's what the P.O.E. had always claimed. Alena frowned and with his words, found the courage to speak again.

"King Belial, what does it truly mean to worship you?"

'I think you're getting too hung up on the word,' he said. *'Consider this more of a partnership.'* She didn't exactly understand all that entailed.

And with that, the air inside the room grew lighter again. Alena eased up. She waited a bit, but he stuck to his word and didn't disturb her again. She finally allowed herself to lean back when her attention was brought to the faint glow coming from her hand.

Alena lazily brought her hand up to view the sigil engraved there. Curious, she dipped it in the water and gently rubbed at her skin. Nothing happened; it truly was a permanent mark and one she couldn't understand.

It also still had a slight heat to the touch. Very similar to the feeling his energy gave her. Alena couldn't help the tired smile that slid onto her face as the beginning of fondness crept over her. Despite how bizarre her life had turned out and whatever the future and her possible afterlife might bring.

Alena supposed she could eventually get used to King Belial's presence. And perhaps that was worship.

Chapter 20

Before Alena knew it, her days trickled by as she and King Belial settled into a regular routine. She would feed Lily (and herself) before she would make coffee and head into the basement. She would scour her grandfather's journal's pages, for all the knowledge she craved, until her eyes grew tired. After that, she just worked on her candles. Candles she had no clue what to do with, now that she feared the shop. King Belial would grumble at that, but say nothing.

"Patience," her grandfather had written, **"is important when working with demons."**

It made her fidget because that was something she lacked. And perhaps it struck a nerve with King Belial. He carefully watched her with those fierce eyes of his, scrutinizing every movement. Though, other than that, he seemed happy enough to just gaze at the new cat-shaped candle on his altar instead.

Throughout the days, Alena had moved most of the cluttered boxes into the corners of the basement when the studying became too much. When it threatened to crack her mind in two.

She left the safe where it was, far too heavy for her to move. Alena wondered if King Belial could. She didn't doubt it if he had a physical form, but with how things were now, he remained intangible and unable to be touched.

Alena went through her grandfather's things and found a few useful items. One being brass candle holders she could hang on the stony walls. They were much appreciated for giving her more light.

Alena just wished the space had some kind of window to let fresh air in. However, she understood why that would've been a bad idea. She knew the P.O.E. agents would eventually return to check on her.

King Belial told her not to worry about it, but it did little to settle the way it made her fret. All she could do was focus on her daily tasks to keep her mind off of things.

Alena sat at the dining table with her beeswax and wicks, carefully taking a knife over the wax. Both her food and candle-making supply waned thin so she would have to make a trip into town. It added to her building stress as a tension settled in her shoulders. It sent an ache up to her head that refused to leave. Still, she'd push through and finish her work despite only wanting to lay down in the dark. Perhaps made warm by King Belial's energy so she could take a nap. He felt amused by that idea as he hovered closely and watched her skillful hands do their job.

It didn't help her stress.

Eventually, Alena yawned as the sun began its descent on the horizon. Alena set her tools aside, then fed Lily and took a few bites of the mysterious fruit-in-a-jar before she headed off to bed. That was usually when King Belial would leave her to her own devices, which she appreciated.

The bedroom became her safe space away from it all, which allowed her to get more sleep. Alena honestly didn't remember the last time she felt so well about things. She clambered into bed after doing her nightly routine and soon afterwards, Lily leaped up and curled beside her.

Alena gently petted the cat as she laid back and watched the shadows within the room dance around. It was never as dark as those first nights, and certainly not as much as whenever King Belial was around, but it still reminded her of him greatly. Alena fidgeted as she laid there and wondered if it was normal to think so much of the demon. Did other demon worshipers do that? Or rather, *demonolaters*, as her grandfather had called them in his journal. She supposed this was simply what the feelings of worship were. It made her heart flutter with an excitement that made her excited for each day. It was... nice.

Alena rolled over and shoved her head into her pillow. She allowed sleep to take her just like she had the past several evenings.

However, this night was different.

It was around midnight when Alena snapped awake. She gasped and thrashed as she clawed herself up into a sitting position. Lily stood on the edge of the bed, facing the door with her ears perked and tail fluffed two sizes larger. Alena looked around. It was now pitch black, so she had to let her eyes adjust. Why had she woken up?

There it was again, a soft thump from somewhere else within the house, perhaps the kitchen. Was that him?

"King Belial?" Alena called out but received no answer. Goosebumps rose on her skin. Uncertainty swirled in Alena's belly. Something wasn't right.

As quietly as she could, Alena stepped out of bed. Lily snapped her head in Alena's direction and let out a distressed meow. Alena gently hushed her and gathered the tiny cat into her arms, holding her close as she made her way out of the room. She walked onto the landing and stepped up to the safety rails placed in front of the indoor balcony. Alena leaned over them to look into the kitchen. The house creaked as if someone had taken a step on the old floorboards.

A shiver wracked its way down Alena's spine in her isolation. King Belial wasn't around and the feeling grew as immense as the demon himself. Those steps sounded far too light to be him. She took a deep breath and tried to shove down her worry as she slid over to the stairs. Immediately Alena remembered her concerns over a wild animal finding its way into her house. That was the last thing she needed. Alena kept her eyesights on the kitchen archway, worried if she looked away for only a second, it might bite her.

Alena entered the kitchen and there she came face to face with a figure shrouded in shadow. Much smaller than King Belial and more humanoid. To

Alena's horror she realized there was no raccoon or squirrel. It wasn't even a demon.

It was a man.

Her shriek echoed off the house's old walls as her hold on Lily tightened. The cat yowled and retaliated by digging her claws into Alena's arms, but she hardly felt it. The shadowy man spun around in surprise and immediately lunged at her. Alena staggered back as she twisted her body around, her only thought being to protect the little cat from harm. Almost as soon as the man had stepped towards her and before he could lay a hand on her, Alena felt something large and heavy rush past her.

The man tripped and slammed into the tiled floor. Alena ran past him and hurried towards her work space. Keeping Lily held tight in one arm, she snagged her flint and steel from the dining table and prayed to Belial she could manage a spark with only one hand. Alena awkwardly stuck them against a wick and brought it to light. The dim glow illuminated the room as she grabbed the candle's base and whipped around towards her assailant. If she had to burn him to protect herself and Lily, she would.

The man staggered to his feet with a heavy groan, rubbing his elbow that struck hard against the ground. The same arm sported a crudely doctored bite mark. He turned to look at her with a glare and Alena felt the air escape from her lungs.

"Jaxon?"

For only a split second, Jaxon looked horrified, but then the expression turned into recognition.

"Alena," he stated, as if the name was foreign on his tongue. "What are you doing all the way out here?"

"It's *my* house," she snapped, her hold on Lily and the candle remained firm. "What are *you* doing here? Why did you attack me?"

The man's eyes narrowed, as if he had a right to her own house. Alena scrutinized him and for the first time, she noticed he was gaunt and covered in dirt. His eyes were dark and hollow.

From the corner of her eye, Alena witnessed an enormous shadow sneak out from behind the man. It stepped into the surrounding darkness just outside the candle's reach. She didn't dare take her eyes off Jaxon to look. She couldn't risk him getting the upper hand on her.

A dense wall of heat pulled up beside her, and a heavy hand splayed across her hip. She tensed as it nearly engulfed the whole spot. The action felt far different than when King Belial placed his hands on her shoulders. While there was still a protectiveness to it, Alena couldn't deny the action was down right possessive. The bottom of his skull brushed against her shoulder to fully encompass her in his energy. A snarl from deep within his chest met her ear.

Alena never looked away from Jaxon. He had a wild aura about him that had her on edge, even though he stared her down like *she* was the threat. Had he noticed the same Belial-related things that Alena did? She hoped not.

"Well?" she felt bold enough to ask as she shifted her weight and leaned into King Belial's comforting presence. Jaxon blinked, having forgotten she was still awaiting an answer. He looked only slightly more aware.

"Sorry, I thought this was an abandoned house," he stated, "and I thought you were a Paladin."

She spun around toward the backdoor behind her. It still stood slightly ajar from where Jaxon had gotten inside. Nothing appeared broken, so he must have picked the locks somehow.

"Don't worry," Jaxon said, voice rough and weary. "I... I got away from them. I've just been surviving in the forest."

"How?"

"By eating berries and drinking rainwater." He shrugged. It was clear it hadn't been an easy time out there by the ragged way Jaxon held himself. Alena was sure if he tried anything, she could take him in a fight.

'Still doubtful of that,' King Belial said. Well, either way, the demon was with her. Alena eased up and the weighty energy pressed tighter against her. She went ahead and shut the door so nothing else could get in and locked it up. Alena gazed out from the window into the backyard where the trees and bushes nearly blended into the night. Jaxon was truly alone as he had claimed.

Alena's gut twisted and throat went dry as she remembered the last time she had seen Jaxon. Archie's frenzied screams and the wrathful flames that consumed his body. She knew better than to bring it up. If what happened brought the feeling of claws to her heart, how did it make Jaxon feel?

Alena watched the way his shoulders drew back and how he kept one foot towards the door. He was just as terrified of this situation as she was. Alena put on a small smile, one that was just a tad bit sad. "Do you want something to eat?"

'No, send him away,' King Belial demanded. His tail slid over her torso to act as a shield between her and the man. The demon's weighty energy made her feel like she would fall before him in her devotions. At what point did her body end and his begin? Alena withheld a sigh that got lost in her throat while King Belial's energy shifted slightly. He grumbled, sensing her turmoil. *'Focus, Alena.'*

She blinked and looked at Jaxon, a hidden horror pierced her skin as she stood there. His eyes remained hollow and ghostly, but ever so faintly there was a flicker of light.

"I think I would like some food, yeah," he said.

Alena nodded and turned her body towards the dining table to finally allow Lily out of her arms. The feline gracefully sat on the edge of the table like the gargoyle on King Belial's altar, tail daintily wrapped around her paws. Lily's eyes glowed under the candlelight as she stared at Jaxon and let out a long curious meow.

He balked at the sight of the mythic beast and rubbed his eyes as if the black cat was a trick of the shadows. When he realized he wasn't seeing things and the cat was indeed there, his gaze grew even more uncertain.

"So it would seem I'm not your first fugitive to harbor," Jaxon whispered under his breath. As if the Paladins would hear him. Alena let out a nervous chuckle.

"Not by a long shot."

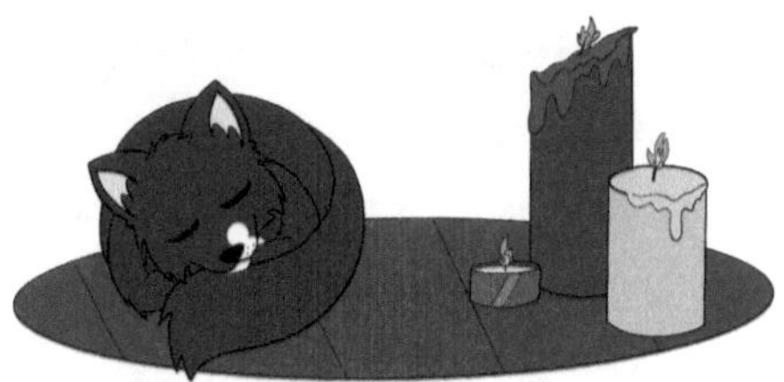

Alena and Jaxon sat in awkward silence at the dining table as he finished her final can of soup. He paid her little mind as his gaze stayed on Lily. The cat remained laying beside Alena, her tail and paws tucked underneath her as she stared back.

"So where'd you get it?" Jaxon asked, finally acknowledging Alena. She wearily wondered how much information she should let him in on. Even though he couldn't report her to the P.O.E. Alena knew she should keep her secrets close to her chest. However, he had already seen Lily and so there wasn't much she could do about that.

"She was lurking around the property," Alena said as she scratched the cat's ears. Beside her, King Belial's energy continued to emanate heat. His presence was a relief to have with Jaxon there and she thought back to their moment earlier. It made her feel warm and all she wanted was to curl up beside King Belial's altar. Bask in his energy just like the true demonolater that she had become. For now, though, Alena put her focus back onto Jaxon. She asked, "So what are you going to do after this, if you don't mind my asking?"

Jaxon's spoon froze midair, his amber eyes wide as if it were something he hadn't thought about. He lowered the spoon and ran his hands through unkempt hair.

"I don't know," he said, voice haggard and lost. Alena bit her lip. He reminded her of the first time she saw Lily. Abandoned and half starved; it struck something within her. She heard King Belial chuckle beside her.

That's what you *looked like to me too,* he said.

If Alena hadn't known any better, she would say he sounded quite fond. She cracked a smile and then quickly covered her mouth so Jaxon wouldn't notice. King Belial sent her an image just then, herself in rags, looking perhaps a little more stray-like than she actually was. If Alena hadn't wanted to keep up appearances, she would have made a sharp retort. Things felt slightly back to normal then, and Alena could breathe easy.

Still, something about the situation with Jaxon didn't feel right. Sending him off would be a death sentence. The man looked like he'd fall over at any second. Alena thought about dark smoke and violent screams.

'This is a deadly heart you carry,' King Belial whispered, his breath scorching against her ear.

"You can sleep on my couch tonight, if you want," Alena said out loud, which made Jaxon snap his gaze up.

King Belial clacked his fangs together. *'I don't want a stranger on my couch. Make him sleep outside with the doors locked.'*

Alena ignored him.

"Really?" Jaxon asked as if he didn't believe her. "But if they catch you..."

They would burn her at the stake. Just as they would if they found out about Lily or what was in the basement. Alena nodded.

"It's alright, no one comes out here that much," she said. "There are a couple P.O.E. agents that come by about once a month, but they were here not too long ago."

Jaxon was still unsure and maybe he worried she would somehow turn him in.

"You don't have to, but I thought I'd extend the offer," Alena went on as she finally looked away from him, worried she had overstepped some kind of boundary. Was it not a thing people did for one another? She glanced into the darkness where she thought King Belial might be.

"I'd... really appreciate that," Jaxon said, voice strained as if he still struggled with the choice. She smiled at him, in the hopes it would help calm his nerves.

After that, the two sat in silence as Jaxon finished the soup. When he finally had, Alena stood from the table and motioned for him to follow. Both he and Lily did as asked. Alena led Jaxon to the couch, despite King Belial's seething anger that wafted over from elsewhere.

"Sorry about the mess. It was like this when I moved in," Alena stated as Jaxon walked around the couch and collapsed onto it. He let out a tired sigh as he laid his head back and made himself comfortable for the first time in a long while. Alena shuffled her feet, not knowing what else to do. "I don't really have a spare blanket, but there might be some in one of these boxes."

"There's no need. You've helped me so much already," Jaxon said as he sat back up. He put on a smile, but it didn't last. The hollowness in his eyes went deep, like someone lost at sea in an endless ocean. She could understand that look, she thought. Alena gave a half-hearted smile as well.

"Good night, Jaxon."

"Good night, Alena, and good night, cat." Jaxon nodded to both her and Lily.

"Her name is Lil... Lily," Alena said as she stooped down and picked up the cat. Jaxon nodded and held out his hand in a silent request. Alena understood and stepped forward to allow him to pat the top of Lily's head, wishing her another good night.

With that done, Alena hurried out of the room with Lily in her arms. Her heart pounded with her thoughts fluttering through the interaction. Should she have said anything different? Alena only stopped when she reached the bottom of the stairs. She peered into the shadows of the dark hall and motioned for them to follow after her as she practically bounded up the steps. King Belial's energy encompassed her as he followed her up to the second floor. Alena noted how his hooves didn't make a sound this time.

Alena entered the bedroom, wasting no time to shut her door and press the footstool against it as tightly as she could, even though she doubted it would stop anyone that truly wanted to get in. Alena felt a sickening unease. If she had made a mistake and Jaxon wasn't someone she could trust, he could so easily hurt her during the night.

'If he was dangerous, I would have made sure he died in those woods,' King Belial snarled as he hovered above Alena. His words put her at ease, if only a little. She frowned as she turned towards where she assumed the demon stood. For once, she wished she could actually see him there. But it was for the best; it made her embarrassing reactions from earlier more manageable.

"Was this a bad choice, King Belial?" Alena asked, her brows knitted together. He grunted.

'I can't tell you the answer to that,' he said, his form engulfing the room like a shield. *'But I will say: you should send him off as soon as possible. The man cannot be good news.'*

Alena stepped away from King Belial towards the bed where she finally released Lily and collapsed onto the covers beside the cat. She shivered as she wrapped her arms around herself.

Despite it being so late, probably almost morning, she felt wide awake. Alena saw the ripples of King Belial move and head towards the door as if he were about to leave. Likely to go back to wherever he usually frequented.

"Wait!" Alena called out without thinking and tensed when she realized she had. King Belial hesitated and turned back to her. She could feel his gaze burn hotly against her skin. She was quiet then and perhaps he grew tired of waiting to hear what she had to say. He approached her, and she could feel the warmth from him grow closer.

In the dark, things always felt different and this time Alena gathered whatever courage she could muster. All she wanted was comfort from her deity. He waited beside her expectantly. Alena bit her lip and despite not being able to see him, averted her eyes. "Could you just... stay in here with me, tonight?"

She waited for a sharp retort, maybe something about her being cowardly, but it didn't come.

'I can do that,' King Belial said instead, and just like the first night they officially met, the side of the bed dipped down. Alena stared at the spot where he sat, but still couldn't get comfortable as the memories of his large demonic hands on her drifted through her mind. The warmth and safety mainly, but then there was earlier in the kitchen with Jaxon there... She tightly gripped her comforter; she couldn't just ask that. She looked up at him expectantly, like he would know what she wanted, and of course he would. But King Belial was King Belial. Alena felt his amused smirk as he stared back at her.

'You're going to have to ask with your voice.' His own impossibly deep one somehow grew an octave lower. Alena grumbled. Of course he was going to

make her request difficult. She danced about the idea of beating around the bush, but knew he wasn't one for that kind of nonsense. If she wasn't direct with what she wanted, he would ignore her. Fine then.

"Please just hold me," she stammered out and he wasted not a minute longer to give her exactly what she wanted. His massive energy invaded her space, tangible enough that she fell back into her pillow with a yelp. King Belial hovered over her and enveloped her much smaller shoulder into his massive hand. Alena's face turned a vibrant crimson, but she was so glad to have the demon there. King Belial chuckled at this as his other arm braced against her side and his tail lay flush around her. The demon, she could tell, stared at the door as if some unseen foe were there.

Alena felt like a treasure hoard laid beneath a dragon. Her body burned under his heat and all she could do was roll over and hug her pillow tightly to her chest.

"Goodnight, King Belial," she whispered as her eyes slid shut. Slowly as she got used to him there, she became comfortable once more. Even as his breath blew against her hair.

'Goodnight, Alena.'

Chapter 21

The next afternoon, Alena stirred awake and was overjoyed to discover she had indeed survived the night. Before she could sit up or do much of anything, King Belial's energy moved away from her. It wasn't as strong as it was in the night, but he was definitely still there. Her chest tightened with a fondness for the demon.

Alena still wanted to speak with him. Though perhaps with Jaxon so close downstairs, it would be too risky. Alena rolled around the idea of meeting King Belial in the astral realm. She had done it before just fine, hadn't she? Alena rolled onto her back and slid her eyes shut, allowing the sensation of floating to overtake her body.

When she opened her mind's eye, she was once again inside that dark red-hued cave chamber. With one look around the rocky walls, King Belial was nowhere to be seen. Alena wondered if she should head deeper into the caves to find him. He shouldn't have been too far. Alena called out for him, her voice echoing in the space around her. There was no response.

Before her the cavern wall rippled as she stared at the various crevices and caverns for her to choose from. Alena tried to imagine them as just a single entryway, like how she changed the astral-version of her living room. However, this time, the world did not succumb to her bidding.

She wondered if this area of King Belial's was something different from her own. Alena headed into the cavern directly before her. She tiptoed her way into the darkness and found it wasn't as bad as it looked from the outside. A few more steps and she saw a light.

It was gold and shone brightly from another crevice on the side of the cave wall. She carefully walked up to it and poked her head through.

"Hello?" she called out. She squinted as the light was far too bright and at the sound of her voice, she heard a gasp that wasn't her own. Alena's eyes adjusted just enough to see a frantic flurry of wings before the golden light dissipated. She stood there staring into a nearly empty room. The only thing within it being a lone feather that drifted down onto the ground.

Alena rubbed her eyes as she curiously stepped into the small cavern. As she got closer, she examined the object. It was large and white, tipped in a sparkling gold. It looked... soft. Alena knelt down to pick it up.

'Hey, what are you doing here?' King Belial's voice boomed from behind her, making her jump. She spun around, the feather forgotten, to see his large form bunkering down to peer into the small cavern she cowered in. There was just a hint of concern in the demon's voice. *'You shouldn't wander in this realm.'*

"Oh, s-sorry," Alena said as she went to his side without question. "I was just looking for you and I saw a strange light."

'I was in a meeting, nothing for you to worry about,' King Belial said and left it at that. His tension eased as he motioned for her to follow him. She did as asked and he let them back to the main cavern.

"So what exactly is this place?" Alena asked as she stepped into the red-hued area. The unnatural lighting was unsettling. She wondered what caused it, thinking of the strange gold glow she saw.

'It's a small part of one of my domains,' King Belial responded. *'It's the safest place for you to be when traveling my worlds. Only beings I allow can come here, but it's still a bad idea for you to be without a guide.'*

"Oh, I didn't know." She wrapped her arms around herself. The cavern suddenly looked different, more menacing. Yet it was so very much Belial she couldn't find it in herself to be completely terrified.

I should have told you before, so don't worry about it.' King Belial shrugged his mountainous shoulders. Alena was at attention as he gestured to the dark world around them. *'The astral is a wonderful place to learn the secrets of the universe. But that doesn't mean it's a safe one.'*

"I mean, I wouldn't say the physical world is safe either," Alena commented. King Belial thought it over before he agreed with a nod of his hefty skull. Alena carefully watched the way the shadows danced around the smooth ivory and cut across the sharper edges. She thought about the night before and she couldn't suppress her smile. Remembering the way he crowded over her, she whispered, "Um... speaking of which, I just want to thank you for staying with me. I'm kind of surprised you did."

'Why?' King Belial asked with a flick of his tail. He stepped forward. Alena shrank under his shadow but didn't flinch away as he slowly reached out to her. His clawed hand engulfed hers as he gently pulled it closer and flipped it around. His sigil glowed on the back of Alena's hand as he ran a claw over it. It tingled and grew warm, sending goosebumps across her skin. The demon leaned forward to get a closer look at the mark, his breath hot against her as he continued. *'I am a demon of my word, Alena,'* he said. *'You're one of my people now, and I protect my people.'*

Alena floundered as she wanted to say something, any retort, but found the words escaped her. Instead, there was a flutter in her chest. She was one of *his* people now and the thought of that brought an elation she couldn't describe. *Devotion.*

'That being said, you need to learn how to defend yourself,' King Belial growled, which broke her out of her revere. *'That man may not have been dangerous, but he still tried to lunge for you. I can only do so much without a physical form. Had he kept going after you, I may not have had enough energy to keep him away.'*

"Really?" she asked. "How does all that energy stuff even work?"

'That's what the offerings are for.' King Belial smiled at her as best he could. *Just as food gives humans strength, the energy from offerings makes us demons more powerful. It lets us have more of a claim to your world.'*

Alena made a mental note to give King Belial some extra gifts the next time she went down into the basement. Whenever that may be...

It would be far too risky with Jaxon around for the time being. Perhaps King Belial was right and she couldn't rely on him all the time. Alena remembered the fear she felt when she first saw a stranger in her house. How she had only cowered instead of doing something, *anything*, to defend herself and Lily.

"So do any of my grandfather's books have self-defense tips?" Alena asked. King Belial let out a loud cackle that made her tense.

'You can't learn to fight by reading *and not* doing,*'* the demon said as his smile turned into a wicked smirk. *'The best way to learn is through astral combat.'*

Her physical body grew cold and clammy as King Belial's tail twitched happily back and forth.

"Um, who exactly—"

'Who better to learn fighting from than me?' King Belial held his arms out to brandish himself and looked positively ecstatic by the idea. It only helped to deepen the sense of utter dread that began to creep into Alena's bones.

"You'd kill me!" she yelped as she scanned over the demon's body as if she hadn't multiple times before. Even if King Belial's massive size wouldn't be an issue, he had thick horns and sharp claws with a whipping tail. To Alena, he was designed to fight. King Belial playfully rolled his irises at her and lowered himself to her level. She shied her eyes away.

'I wouldn't go all out on you, unless you asked me to.' A wink. *'It's just friendly sparring between a human and a demon.'*

Alena forced herself to look back at King Belial and her breathing staggered. Despite him being crouched, he was still much larger than her and so much closer than usual. If she had wanted, she could have reached out and set her hand on top of the muzzle part of his skull. She resisted the urge. A grumble came from King Belial's chest as he read her thoughts. Instead, he reached out and sat his hand on top of *her* head, making Alena grow incredibly still.

'It's true that as a demon I could easily harm you, a human,' he said. King Belial's thumb began to rub circles on the side of her head. It was gentle. Soft. *'You're just starting out on this path, though. I won't go so far and push past those limits. You'd never learn that way, so we'll start with the basics.'*

Alena felt the tension leave her shoulders and she reached up to touch his hand, but he pulled away before she could. King Belial stood back up to his full height and she now had to crane her neck to look at him. He looked so unlike how she had seen him in the living room. There he looked unnatural, but here, in the darkness he seemed most at home. Most himself. Alena clasped her hands together and fidgeted.

"Um, sure, I'd be willing to try," she whispered and hoped she hadn't been too quiet in doing so. King Belial's tail slammed into the ground and made her jump, but it hadn't been in anger. The demon beamed.

'Excellent,' he said. *'You'll see, Alena. If you can last against me, you'll be able to take on anyone.'*

She wasn't sure about that, but was willing to learn, at least. King Belial shifted his stance, braced his legs, and crossed his arms over his chest.

'Stand like this,' he said.

"What? You want to start now?" Alena sputtered.

'Why not?' King Belial shrugged, and she knew it was a lost cause. Alena sighed as she mimicked his stance. It felt awkward to her, definitely not something she was used to.

"So what—" Before she finished asking her question, King Belial spun around. His tail lashed out, and Alena flew back into the rocky wall.

She gasped and clawed at her blankets as she shot straight up. Alena found she was firmly back at her body in the physical world. The attack hadn't hurt, of course, but it was enough to frighten her out of the meditation. She panted and ran her fingers through her sweat-leaded hair. As her adrenaline came down, she couldn't help but find it had been rather... exhilarating.

King Belial's energy emerged next to her as the demon hovered up and down her body, as if he wanted to double check that she was okay. When he came to the conclusion she was, he stepped away.

'From now on, I want you to meditate with me each morning on this,' King Belial said. *'We'll move onto the next phase when you're able to take a blow without losing your stance.'*

Alena's excitement still hadn't waned as she gave a small determined grin. "You just caught me off guard is all. I'll stay standing next time."

'We shall see about that.' King Belial chuckled and Alena could picture his smirk. She wanted to make a quick retort, but before she could there was a loud thump from downstairs. Alena frowned as her joyous mood vanished. Even King Belial shifted as his presence near her weakened, his voice far away as he said, *'It would seem your company has awakened.'*

Alena threw her legs over the side of the bed as King Belial left her completely. She threw on some fresh clothes from one of her still-unpacked boxes while Lily chirped at her. The cat yawned and stretched, watching as Alena hurried out of the room. No doubt she soon followed.

Alena tiptoed her way down the stairs. She crept forward into the living room and walked up to the couch. She was surprised to find Jaxon sat on the floor beside it rather than the couch itself. In the daylight, Alena could now see how much worse for wear he appeared. Not only was he half-starved, but he was covered in bruises and scratches, his clothes tattered. Jaxon stretched out his stiff limbs and rubbed at the back of his neck. The bite mark on his arm, while gnarly in the dark, had begun to scab.

"Are you... okay?" Alena asked, though she wasn't sure what to make of the situation. He blinked up at her in surprise, his gaze still so far away.

"Oh yeah, sorry," he said. "I just rolled off the couch."

She hadn't meant that, but she would take it. Alena nodded and figured making light conversation would help. "Not a sound sleeper?"

Jaxon looked pained. "I had a strange dream last night. Like a man was standing at the edge of the couch."

A cold sweat went down her brow and Jaxon noticed the way she went pale.

"Don't worry about it." His shoulders hunched. "It was just a nightmare."

Alena could only nod as she saw the way his eyes blankly looked ahead like he was lost. As Jaxon appeared to fight off tears, she realized the dream must have been about the burning. Alena didn't have siblings, so she couldn't completely understand how he felt.

"Hey, do you want some breakfast?" she asked, and she saw how Jaxon's amber eyes sparkled at the thought.

Lily let out a loud caterwaul as Alena and Jaxon entered the kitchen. The cat hopped about as she awaited to be fed. Alena wasted no time heading to the counter as Jaxon hobbled over and collapsed into one of the dining table chairs. The man looked like he barely had the strength to walk, much less leave today. Alena's stomach flipped at the thought.

She glanced across the countertop and only found emptied cans and jars, so she moved onto the cupboards only to see they were the same.

"Damn it," Alena hissed under her breath, getting a concerned glance from Jaxon. She turned towards him a little bashfully. "Sorry, I don't have much left."

The man before her looked downtrodden but didn't comment as he shrugged. Lily yowled in offense. Alena bit her lip. She would just have to... get more. She put on two cups of coffee and, from somewhere far behind her, King Belial returned. As if the possible offering had lured him into the room. Alena sighed for she wouldn't be able to give him a cup on the altar. Not this time. She could feel the demon grunt as the cups finished, and she took them over to the table.

"Maybe this could tide you over?" she asked as she set one in front of Jaxon. He clasped the warm cup as if it were a lifeline and he looked almost apologetic.

"Sorry if I've been rude." He sighed. "It's just..."

"It's okay, I understand," Alena said as she sat down across from him with her own cup. Her stomach growled as well. She ignored it and sipped on her coffee to quell the uncomfortable feeling. It was nothing she wasn't used to. The coffee, however, was tasteless and felt light on her tongue; the sigil on the back of her hand buzzed with warmth. Alena groaned. King Belial must have taken *her* coffee.

Jaxon gulped his down as if it weren't even hot. She wondered if she should fill the silence with conversation, but it felt far too unnatural so she remained silent.

Soon, Jaxon finished and set it aside with a pleased sigh. "I definitely needed that."

"I'm glad to help," Alena said as Lily ran over and desperately pawed at her leg. The cat cried in fear that she had been forgotten. The pitiful meows sank into Alena's heart and dragged it down. There was no more putting it off. Alena bent down to lovingly pet Lily, allowing the cat's soft fur to calm her before she stood. Jaxon watched as she put on a nervous smile. "I'm going to head down into the city to get some food."

For the first time that morning, Alena saw a spark of wild fear from Jaxon as he leaped up. His chair screeched against the floor tiles. The two stared at one another. Jaxon looked uncertain.

"Um, should I just stay here or...?" He wrung his hands as if they were cold.

"I'll try not to be too long, but it usually takes me all day." Alena nodded as she thought of the long drive. "But when I get back we can have a huge feast if you want."

Jaxon's eyes looked hopeful at the idea, but he remained tense.

"Be careful out there," he said, his voice genuine. "You might not be a fugitive, but..."

"I know," Alena stated as she gathered up her fresh candles to trade with. Having lost her crate, she now used a box. "Watch the house and Lily for me while I'm gone."

Alena turned and walked into the foyer. As she did, a spark of annoyance stopped her in her tracks. She looked off towards the dark hallway and felt King Belial stare back at her, offended by the words.

'I can take care of this place just fine without a human man.'

"I know you can," Alena stated, her voice soft as she grabbed her keys off the table by the door. "Take care of them, King Belial."

He huffed as she left and went out to her car. Just as before, she set her box in the backseat and hopped into the front. Alena thought of her destination in the city, the shop...

Now that she was alone, she couldn't stop the wild images that flashed through her memories. She could see the street again. Jaxon having taken out the

Paladins that held him and Archie. She remembered the two brothers making a run for it. The bola and Archie going down. His screams as the fire crawled up his body, making dark smoke rise to the sky. She wondered how long he was there for. Before he died.

Alena wheezed for air as her chest constricted and coiled like a snake. Jaxon's glassy eyes appeared in Alena's mind. She wondered if he had somehow left a part of himself with his brother.

She couldn't do it. She couldn't head back to that shop and pretend like nothing was wrong. The brothers had only been a nuisance to the shopkeeper. What would he do if he found out Alena actually was in league with a demon? She felt a sharp pain as though a stake had been driven through her heart. The dread. The foreboding. All she wanted was to be safe. All she wanted was to be happy.

Tears cascaded down Alena's face, but as they did, she felt a great warmth wrap around her. She blinked away the tears as her hand grew hotter. Her gaze landed on the sigil. It glowed brightly and sent a serene calm down her body. Alena ran her fingers across it, and the sense of safety King Belial brought to her returned.

She allowed herself to breathe before she finally began the long drive down the mountain.

Chapter 22

Despite trying her best to remain calm, Alena's hands shook around the wheel the closer to the shop she got. The shopkeeper, who she had once thought was a safe person to be around, no longer existed in her mind. However, she knew it would be far too suspicious to change her routine.

The car struggled its way onto the cracked city road, just as always. Alena's muscles ached from how tense she remained during the entire ride. She was almost there. Her heartbeat picked up as she pulled onto the street that led to the shop. The same street where the incident had taken place. Alena's breath was shallow as her chest grew heavy. She focused on each inhale, worried she would be on the verge of an attack otherwise. Sweat dripped down her brow as she pulled up beside the shop and parked. She kept her eyes on the building, far too scared to look anywhere else in case there was still evidence of what happened in the street.

The building's windows were boarded up as if abandoned. A large wooden sign was nailed to the door, big block letters painted on it. Alena leaned closer to get a better look.

'Site closed indefinitely due to suspicions of demonic activity.'

A deep and hateful laugh broke itself from Alena's throat, much to her own surprise. It was ironic, really, that the shopkeeper had reported Jaxon and Archie to get rid of what he saw as a nuisance. Only to also suffer the consequences.

'It serves him, right.' King Belial's voice met Alena's ear and she nodded in agreement. Well, at least she wouldn't have to go into the shop now, but that didn't help her. She would have to go elsewhere to get food, but... Alena worried she wouldn't be able to trade her candles easily to anyone else. She let out a sigh as King Belial's hand patted her shoulder. *'It'll be fine.'*

Taking his word for it, Alena pulled her car back out onto the road and headed deeper into the city, something she had seldom ever done, even when she still lived there. The tension never left her shoulders as she passed through the older parts of the kingdom, where the barebones of buildings from the Before Times still existed. She passed by homes and other shops she knew wouldn't accept the measly crafts she had to offer. Alena bit her lip as she slowly went along, hunkering down every time she passed by a lone person on the street. They stopped and stared, not used to vehicles.

'Turn here,' King Belial suddenly said as she came to a fork in the road where the ancient concrete turned to polished stone. Alena slowed to a crawl as her brows knitted together.

"King Belial, that leads to the newer parts of the kingdom," she claimed, palms sweaty. Alena pictured the much nicer and newer buildings in her mind to show him. Homes where only people who could afford to have them built lived. There was no way.

'Trust me,' he said, and that was that. Alena sighed and turned off onto the stoney path, heading a little ways from the parts of the city she knew. At first the land grew sparse. Most citizens of Lenoria preferred to keep their distance from the lesser parts that still stood as evidence of the old ways. Soon enough, however, Alena came upon a more suburban area with quaint little wooden cabins. Some had yards full of rich plantlife, others not so much. She wondered if that was evidence of which folks got out of their houses and which were more reclusive like her. She was curious as to what they did for a living.

Alena passed a couple of people that stood in their yard. Unlike in the old parts of the city, they barely blinked an eye at the vehicle. It did little for her comfort as King Belial lightly tugged on the steering wheel to turn the car onto a side road. A large P.O.E. truck drove past her from the other direction and Alena's breath got caught in her throat. It took all of her willpower to not push on the gas pedal to flee from the area. They had to be close to the headquarters — the Castle. As she went a few feet further, Alena glanced in her rearview to see the truck turn down the road and vanish. They hadn't been the wiser to her. And why should they?

'Keep your eyes on the road!' King Belial snarled and immediately Alena whipped her gaze up to see a man on horseback and slammed on the brakes before she could drive her car into him. The horse reared slightly and as it came back down, the man twisted himself around to glare at her. He yelled out a few profanities with a raised fist. Alena gritted her teeth and waved him off apologetically. King Belial's voice grumbled in her head, *I can't believe you. Luckily we're almost there. Turn right.'*

Alena held her tongue as she continued to do as asked; this time she didn't dare remove her eyes from the road. The path King Belial chose led her into a large grove hidden behind a few trees. They weren't like the wild trees of the mountains. Someone had planted them with purpose. A little way ahead, Alena saw the only building in the area that looked to be ancient, possibly from the Before Times. A little white chapel with chipped paint. There was a singular car parked outside of it, the only evidence it wasn't abandoned.

"Oh, are you exorcizing yourself?" Alena chuckled.

'Hush!'

When Alena neared the chapel, the trees thinned out and then she saw it. Across the street from the little building was a larger clearing where groups of people gathered around tables full of items. A marketplace. Alena balked as she pulled up to the side of the road and parked.

"King Belial, I don't belong here," Alena stammered as she tried to picture herself bartering with her little candles.

'You belong wherever you want to go,' the demon retorted before his presence waned. He still watched over her from a distance. Alena knew waiting around in the car to gain some nerve would look suspicious. She exited the vehicle and grabbed her box of candles before she took the brief walk towards the crowded marketplace. Alena's heartbeat picked up as she couldn't remember the last time she had seen so many people congregate in a singular place.

A few Paladins were standing on the outskirts, bored as they chatted amongst each other with only the occasional glance towards the crowd. Alena hunched her shoulders and went to draw her hood up to hide her face. One of the Paladins noticed and did a once over with a single brow raised. They knew she wasn't a regular.

'Keep your head held high.'

Her hands quivered on the box and she feared she'd drop it, but held strong. She didn't want to be so bold, but had to trust the demon wouldn't lead her astray. Her hood slipped off as she tilted her chin upwards and focused on her destination rather than the Paladin. Why act suspicious if you have nothing to hide? Her mother had once said that, she thought.

The Paladin shrugged and turned back to their business with the others. Alena let out a sigh of relief as she walked onto the large flat stones the marketplace sat on, which she assumed were to prevent it from growing too muddy during the rainy seasons. She shouldered past a couple of people with faux confidence. Everyone else dressed so much nicer and she stuck out too much.

'No one is even looking at you.'

Huh? She glanced around and found it to be true. Alena eased up as she went but still, she didn't want to stay there for any longer than was necessary. Alena quickly looked around for the food stalls that were her priority. She thought about the starved Little Lily and ragged Jaxon back at the house. They waited for her. They were relying on her.

Alena swallowed her anxiety and walked up to one of the tables where a crafter sold handmade jewelry. She dared not look at them, knowing not even her entire box of candles would pay for one.

"Excuse me," Alena said, her voice too small to her own ears, "Do you know of anyone who sells food around here?"

The seller blinked up at her as if surprised by the question. At the sight of Alena, they gave her a once over, taking in her means of dress. They nodded in understanding.

"Oh, of course," they said, pointing off towards the left. "Food sellers usually crowd in that far back corner."

Alena thanked the seller for their time and headed off in the direction she had been told. She passed by many tables that had wears made of the finest metals and furs. Far different than anything up for trade in her usual shop. She peered into the box at her bland white beeswax candles, some of them carved into little shapes. Their imperfections seemed blaring, chunks missing here and there where she had mistakenly taken off too much wax.

'Why do they have to look perfect if you're just going to burn them?' King Belial asked. *'Do they not do their job well? That should be their selling point.'*

She supposed he had a bit of a point. Alena always *prided* herself on how brightly her candles burned. However, that didn't matter in the grand scheme of things. She assumed these rich-types were just after whatever looked the nicest on their mantel. King Belial scoffed at the fact as if it were ridiculous. Alena sighed and continued on, knowing there wasn't much she could do to change the demon's mind.

As Alena reached the edge of the marketplace, she smelled the food long before she saw any of it. Fresh bread and recently cured hams made her mouth water as her stomach clenched in pain. The idea of having a feast that night was so tantalizing it made her want to cry. If only...

She walked up to a table decked out in a variety of baked goods to ogle at the pastries. King Belial looked as well.

"Hello there. May I help you?" the seller asked with a kind smile. Alena's palms grew clammy, but she forced herself to pry her fingers away from the box to retrieve one of her candles.

"What can I get for this?" she asked to which the seller's smile evaporated.

"Absolutely nothing," she said. "I have no need for something like *that*."

Alena flinched, and despite the fact she had foreseen this outcome, it still stung.

"Now move along, I have more serious customers to attend to," the seller went on. Alena was about to do as asked when the air behind her condensed. King Belial growled in her ear and the sound sent a wave of tingles down her spine. The demon's energy nearly coiled at the fact someone *dared* speak to one of his practitioners in such a way. The corners of Alena's vision grew dark as the demon's mood sank. The seller snapped her head up with a sharp retort on her tongue, ready to chase Alena off again. However, it soon died away as she balked at the sight of her. The seller grew tense as if she sensed something Alena didn't. She shivered, a slight fright to her eyes.

The seller practically threw a loaf of bread at Alena.

"Just take this and go," she snapped. Alena gaped in surprise as she accepted the bread and put it in her box with a small thank-you. The seller could barely look at her and waved her off. Alena took her leave and wondered how strange the interaction had turned.

'People can be so kind.' King Belial chuckled.

Alena smiled and had the undeniable urge to throw herself at the demon in thanks, but resisted. That only made her sense a smug sort of amusement roll off of him. Alena ignored it and went about her way, curious to see what else she could try to get.

Alena headed to the table of a butcher that was set up at the furthest corner of the market. He had a few cured and salted meats for sale, but to her surprise, actual live hogs as well. She tiptoed her way over and side-eyed the pigs. She had never been near one before and so wanted to keep her distance. The butcher looked pointedly at her, not at all looking impressed as Alena motioned towards the already prepared meats.

"Uh—"

"Don't waste my time unless you have something good," the man said before she could even finish. Alena bit her lip and longingly looked at the food before her. Behind her, she could feel King Belial fester once more, but this man didn't seem to have a similar reaction as the baker. His eyes narrowed in her direction.

"I don't suppose you fancy candles?" Alena asked as she forced a smile that the butcher cringed away from. King Belial grunted in Alena's head and then sent her an image. She blinked in surprise, as she saw herself clearly within her own head. There was a weird look about her, something unsettling that she didn't trust. The image waned and Alena was able to see the butcher more clearly now, able to understand the image she saw was how he perceived her... As a possible threat.

The butcher chose fight over flight. Alena stepped away as the man stood, anger rolling off him in waves. Beside her the air grew still as King Belial carefully watched over the situation.

"I said don't waste my time," the butcher growled as he looked off to the side. Would he call for the Paladins? Alena's leg muscles flexed as she prepared to make a run for it. But where would she go? She doubted she was fit enough to outrun them like Jaxon had.

Before she could do anything, something gold sparkled in the corner of Alena's eyes. It brought her attention away, as a soft voice asked, "Is there a problem here?"

Alena dared to look away from the butcher, fully expecting to come face to face with a Paladin. However, to her luck, it was not. Instead, Alena's eyes met with a much shorter and stout woman in flowy clothes. This woman had deep brown skin and dark long hair that fell around her in a halo of locs. The woman's face was covered in a splatter of freckles that gave her a youthful appearance. However, the way her eyes pinched at the corners alluded to the fact she was a bit older. She smiled brightly at Alena, making her face flush crimson.

"Oh, there's no problem," the butcher grunted and Alena noted there was a shift in his mood. He still glared at her, but didn't seem so on guard. "This riff-raff was just trying to scam me out of my finest choice cuts."

Alena wanted to defend herself, but kept her mouth shut to not further aggravate the situation. This new woman sent a curious glance Alena's way, but she could only respond with an open stare.

"Well, we can't have that now can we?" The woman said as she turned her smile towards the man. "Just add the meat to my tab, I'll get it for them."

Alena blinked. What?

The butcher let out a long and tired sigh as he stood and began to collect a few pieces of meat. He grumbled all the while. "You gotta stop doing this, bad image to keep feeding leeches."

"It's simply what my beautiful Lord has requested of me," the woman sighed dreamily. Alena side-eyed her, as an uncomfortable uncertainty settled in her belly. The butcher rolled his eyes as he handed off the choice cuts to the woman. She accepted them and turned to Alena, not even waiting for a response as she set the now-wrapped-meat into her candle-box. Alena opened her mouth to say something, anything, but her tongue felt far too dry. The woman set her hand on Alena's shoulder and lightly pushed her along. She let out a small laugh that suddenly sounded a bit nervous. "Now, now, let's leave the kind man to his business."

There wasn't much Alena could do as she allowed herself to be led away at a pace that was far too quick to not be suspicious. They made their way through the crowds and stalls, heads kept down until the two of them found a more secluded section of the marketplace. Then she finally released Alena with a relieved sigh.

"That was kind of scary," the woman said, brows pinched together in worry. "You must not be from around here, pushing your luck with that one."

"No, it's my first time," Alena finally found it in herself to respond. Though her voice sounded ragged to her own ears. Her gaze flitted between the woman and the direction they had come from. "What was that all about?"

"There's rumors around here," the woman whispered, "that he feeds people to his hogs."

"*What*?!" Alena gasped perhaps too loudly, getting several people to glare her way. King Belial stomped his hooves from somewhere in the distance. The woman in front of her promptly shushed her. Alena whimpered an apology.

"I mean, they're probably just rumors." The woman gave a nervous laugh. "But why push it? Especially with the temper he has."

Alena nodded as she relaxed at the warm aura that drifted off the woman before her. She supposed she was lucky she didn't end up as next week's choice of cut. Alena finally managed a small nervous smile. "Well, thanks for that then. And thanks for the meat, you really didn't have to."

Alena glanced down at the food currently stuffed in her box, mouth watering. Maybe, just maybe, she would be able to have that feast after all. Alena couldn't help but beam at the thought.

"It's the least I could do. I need not tell a lie about what is requested of me." The woman shrugged as if it were nothing. She reached up to fiddle at her necklace that depicted a gold plated angel. Alena wondered if that was what caused the sparkles she had seen from the corner of her eyes. Perhaps it had caught the light in such a way? The woman looked lost in thought for only a moment before her focus returned. "So what is the name of the smiling person whom I saved? And how do you identify yourself? You've got a nice nonconforming look going on."

"Oh, um, it's Alena," she stammered. "And I'm just an Alena, I suppose."

"Just Alena?" the woman asked with eyes full of humor.

"It's Alena Usher," she added on, though her last name felt strange on her tongue. The woman nodded as she took in the name and Alena's brows knitted together. So she asked, "And what is the name of my savior?"

"Oh!" The woman gasped as if the question had genuinely surprised her. A second later she bounced back and smiled a big and toothy thing.

"My name is Saffron! Saffron Flowers."

Chapter 23

What... *What*?!

"Saffron Flowers?!" Alena gasped, eyes blown wide. "Like the painter, Saffron Flowers?"

'Remember how to breathe, Alena,' King Belial stated as she wheezed. Alena calmed herself and the airflow came much smoother. Saffron still stood in front of her, a look of good humor on her face, but also maybe a tad bit of concern.

"Yup, that sure is me," the woman said with a nervous chuckle. "I guess you've heard of me?"

Alena was able to fully recover from the shock as she rubbed her shoulder. She murmured, "A lot of creatives in the area I'm from are huge fans. You're kind of a big deal for other artists."

Now it was Saffron's turn to blush as she hid her face in her hands. "Oh don't say that with such light in your eyes."

A smile broke on Alena's face as she watched Saffron's flustered floundering. Huh, it was strange meeting her face to face. It made it all the more real to Alena that Saffron Flowers was an actual person that existed. Alena almost felt dizzy as a strange sensation came over her. There she stood with another person, far away from the house and all its secrets, with King Belial still lingering nearby. It was all a bit surreal.

"Your paintings are amazing," Alena continued the conversation, though she felt just a little hollow. "Your reputation is warranted."

"Well, I appreciate that." Saffron lowered her hands as her embarrassment passed. "So where are you from? I'm not too big of a deal in this area. Most of the people here could be considered 'a big deal' in their respective fields."

Alena faltered as she pictured the decrepit buildings and ruined streets she used to call home. For the first time, she felt rather ashamed by the idea of simply mentioning it. And so she decided to omit that truth. "I live up in the mountains."

Not entirely a lie. Saffron beamed in wonder at this.

"Amazing! You're a bit far away aren't you?" she asked but then a dreamy look flashed across her eyes. "Oh I bet it's so lovely up there with the wild plants and the view of Lenoria. Can you see the stars nicely from there?"

Alena paused as she thought the words over. *Was* it beautiful up there? She didn't have the heart to tell Saffron she never went outside. Nor had she seen the stars. Alena grimaced because she didn't want to make any horrible impressions on the woman. But what could she say?

'Just be yourself,' King Belial said with a joking tone. Oh absolutely not, she couldn't do that. Saffron paused as she finally noticed the look of utter terror on Alena's face. She frowned.

"O-Oh, sorry if that was a bit much." Saffron sighed. "I just got a little excited."

"Uh, it's alright, I'm not used to..." Alena paused as she looked around at the surrounding stalls and vaguely gestured to it. "All of this."

Saffron nodded. "So what brings you here?"

Alena dragged out her answer as her old defensive wall built back up. Could she trust Saffron? She seemed so nice and Alena *wanted* to talk the painter's ear off, but she knew better than that. Alena mentally looked to King Belial for help, but the demon had grown silent. Saffron continued to look up at Alena with genuine eyes she couldn't resist.

"My previous employer is out of business for the time being," Alena explained. "I was just looking for a place to trade my crafts."

"You make things?" Saffron mused as she reached out to peer into Alena's candle box without a second thought. Alena tensed as her blush flared up.

"Y-Yeah," she stammered, her tone bashful. "But they're not good enough for around here."

"Oh, Alena, don't say that," Saffron responded with a small frown. She puffed out her chest with pride and the angel necklace glinted. "Have faith in what you do and other people will too. Passion can be contagious."

Alena's brows knitted together as she couldn't possibly imagine that were true. Either way she relented and lowered her arms to allow Saffron a gander at her wares. The other peeked inside with the same excitement as someone who had received a gift. Even as she looked at the candles, Saffron's sparkling eyes never wavered.

"These are very cute," Saffron said as she pulled out the one that was carved to look like a little bird. She twisted it around in her hands until she spotted the wick. "How do they burn?"

The question was so simple and yet it brought back King Belial's words to Alena's mind. The passion Saffron spoke of freshly bubbled within Alena's gut as she thought of the demon.

"The hottest and the brightest!" Alena exclaimed an octave too high.

"That's the spirit!" Saffron cheered as she set the bird candle back into its nest with the others. "More of that and you'll have people eating right out of your palms."

Easier said than done, but Alena was appreciative of the words as she held the box close to her chest. She glanced around and wondered if she should try again, but the previous experience was still too fresh in her mind. What if she messed up again? What if someone fed her to their hogs. She frowned and her confidence waned.

"Say... I'm not doing anything right now," Saffron said, her tone soft. She averted her eyes and pushed her locs back behind her shoulder. "Do you want help trying to sell these? I mean I understand if not, but there's a certain way you gotta handle the folks around here."

"I..." Alena wondered if she could accept such an offer. Her heart thudded against her ribs as she wanted to flee yet again. King Belial, ever present, was a few feet away, as if he also expected an answer. Alena knew what he thought, that this was a grand opportunity. A once in a lifetime chance, and he was right. Alena nodded. "I would really appreciate that, Saffron."

Saffron Flowers looked like the sunshine itself and Alena nearly wanted to shield her sight away from such a thing. Saffron causally linked arms with her, as though they were old friends and led her around the marketplace.

She pointed to each stall and happily chatted about the sellers. She'd let Alena know which ones were safe to interact with and which should be avoided. And whenever they stopped at one Alena was curious about, Saffron would patiently wait. Though most of the time, Alena's nerves gave out and she would simply move along. Only when she came upon a stall of fresh veggies and herbs, did she desperately try her hand at haggling. Alena strode up to the seller while both Saffron and King Belial watched her closely. Having an audience did little to help her worries.

"May I help you?" the seller asked as Alena strode up to them and scanned the table more closely. Off to the side they had pre-made bundles of various root-type foods. Alena pointed to it before she pulled out one of her candles.

"Can I get one of those bundles for a few of these?" she asked through gritted teeth, the seller scanned her up and down with a wrinkled nose, as though they had tasted something sour. Alena sweated. "I can give you five of them—"

"Three!" called Saffron, to which Alena flinched and quickly corrected herself, "I can give you three of them."

"I don't really—" the seller began, but in her panic Alena didn't let them finish the sentence.

"They burn really bright," she said and the basement immediately came into her mind. Her stomach fluttered as though a hundred butterflies had been released into it. Oh how she longed for its comforting darkness to embrace her.

She had been out there in the sun for far too long. Alena flushed as she held the candle close to her chest. "Just a couple of these could light a whole room."

The herb seller leaned forward as if smitten by Alena's explanation. They smiled. "Well if ya put it that way, you have yourself a deal. Feels like I usually have to burn ten candles just to light my living room."

Alena gave a genuine grin as she handed over three of her basic-shaped candles in exchange for the bundle. Once it was safely in her box with the others, Alena excitedly scurried back to Saffron. As Alena reached her, Saffron gave her a victorious pat on the back before the two continued on their way. That was how most of the interactions at the marketplace went from there on out, and soon Alena found herself with a box full of food and only a single candle left.

"Saffron, thank you so much," Alena said, at a loss for words. She had never before come into possession of so much food. It made her body feel warm. "I never would have been able to do this on my own."

"It's no problem." Saffron shrugged as if she spoke nothing but the truth. "No one should go hungry, you know?"

Alena nodded in agreement as she pulled out her final candle, the one shaped like a bird. Her brows knitted curiously together. "So what do you think I could get with this last one?"

Saffron opened and shut her mouth, unsure of the suggestion she wanted to make. It was her turn to be bashful as she averted her eyes. Saffron hummed out. "A painting?"

"A..." Alena began with only a brief moment of confusion before the realization dawned on her. A small breath escaped her lungs as a ball of excitement swirled in her belly. Even King Belial snapped his fangs together in some form of excited approval. However, Alena couldn't feel morally sound about that. She forced a frown. "Saffron no, I couldn't. Your art is worth so much more than that. I-If you want this bird, I'll just give it to you."

King Belial huffed. What did he want from her?

"I couldn't accept it for anything less..." Saffron said as she turned her usually soft eyes on Alena. A wildfire burned within them. There was also, perhaps, something else that Alena couldn't pinpoint. Some different emotion she wasn't familiar with. Saffron sighed that dreamy sigh of hers. "I genuinely want this, Alena. There's someone I love dearly who'd appreciate it."

"Um, alright." Alena gave in and handed off the bird candle to Saffron, who accepted it graciously. "B-But it has to be a small painting!"

"I can agree to those terms." And with that Saffron motioned for Alena to follow her once more. The woman led her to another stall, this one filled with and surrounded by various paintings and art projects. It was currently being watched over by someone, who looked rather bored to be there. He nodded in greeting to Saffron before he leaned back in his chair and drifted off into the world of daydreams.

Saffron motioned Alena to the table where her smaller canvases sat, before she made her way around the stall to grab a large carrier bag. Saffron began to pack up her things, which alerted Alena to the fact she would have to be quick. She scanned over each painting. She wanted to make the best choice as she knew this was likely her only opportunity to *ever* own a Saffron Flowers original. But which? Stylewise Saffron mainly did scenery, worlds so beautiful Alena knew they could have only been from the woman's imagination. Though several of the paintings, much like the one in the shop, depicted some aspect of that mysterious person. The androgynous one with golden hair. Alena had to admit the way Saffron painted them was with such love and care. The person was truly a thing of beauty.

'I don't want that dude on my walls,' King Belial grumbled as his massive energy came up behind Alena. She lightly chuckled to herself and moved onto a landscape, one that was actually familiar to the both of them. An almost perfect replica of the mountain range that stood over Lenoria, and perhaps it had also once been the kingdom. However, the painting showed an old civilization overtaken by nature in the foreground. A beaten up car surrounded by a vast array of golden wildflowers sat in the foreground. Alena felt King Belial's interest in the painting as the bottom of his skull brushed up against her shoulder. His voice sounded content. *'It's home.'*

"Home..." Alena repeated as she picked up the painting with a gentle smile. She held it for a moment, basked in its glory, before she carefully set it atop her groceries in the box.

Saffron walked back to Alena, bag now full. "Well, I'm heading out. Are you?"

With nothing left for her to get or trade, Alena nodded and the two of them walked out of the marketplace together. Saffron even went as far as to help Alena to her car. She put her box and newly beloved painting in the backseat before she turned to face the woman that had helped her so greatly. Alena felt like there were a thousand words she could say, but there wasn't the time.

"It was amazing to meet you, I..." Alena got out so she could say *something*. She smiled, a genuine one. "Your kindness to me is something I'll forever hold dear."

"I'm glad to help," Saffron said. "I just want to follow my Lord's example to assist wayward souls."

"Right..."

"Also..." Saffron began and it struck something within Alena to be on edge. Something about the woman before her had changed. She seemed more steely, serious. "If you ever return here, please find me and I'll continue to help you around."

Alena frowned, for even though the words were helpful, she could tell there was something hidden within them. She thought to speak, but Saffron beat her to the punch.

"Listen, Alena," she said, "only those with dark secrets can ever make it big in Lenoria. The butcher, everyone here, even the highest ranking members of the P.O.E." Saffron hesitated then, with a worried glance towards the guards that still lingered about. She looked at Alena with those fiery eyes of hers. "You take care to remember that and watch out for yourself."

"Why tell me all this?" Alena asked. Despite the lovely time they had with one another, she couldn't deny it felt more than a little weird. Saffron's warning solidified that. "Why help me out at all?"

"People like us." Saffron sighed. "We have to stick together."

Alena's face pinched up as she wondered what the other meant by that. Before she could ask, Saffron reached forward and brushed her hand along Alena's arm. A farewell. Saffron turned and took her leave. All the way across the street to the old chapel. Saffron climbed up its old rickety steps and only hesitated for one final look back before she disappeared inside.

King Belial's energy pressed close as he also curiously watched the woman leave. Alena sighed as she leaned into the demonic heat, seeking comfort from it.

"No I don't think we're alike at all."

Chapter 24

When Alena returned to the house, dusk began to bleed the sky into a violet hue. She parked her car and gathered her box of goodies. She set aside the painting and left it in the backseat to retrieve later that night. It felt personal to her, and she didn't want anyone else other than King Belial and perhaps Lily to see it.

She reached for the door and found it unlocked. A slight prick of concern rubbed itself against her as she entered the large and empty abode. Alena glanced into the living room, but saw no sign of either of her current roommates. Alena hurried off into the kitchen, still no sign of them, and set her box onto the countertop to deal with later.

"Lily?" she called out, and her voice echoed off the walls. "Jaxon?"

Her worry turned to fear. What if Jaxon had noticed the key around Lily's neck? What if he had... Alena was about to bolt down the dark hallway as her mind made up scenarios of Jaxon finding the altar. Only King Belial's deep growl kept Alena in place.

'There's that catastrophic thinking of yours,' King Belial said as his energy drifted off Alena towards the shadowy hall. *'You hadn't even checked the rest of the house.'*

Wait, no, that made sense. Alena allowed herself to calm and went to ask the demon if he knew their whereabouts. However, he had already gone, vanished into his basement lair. Before she could call out to him a soft meow sounded from above her. Alena snapped her gaze upwards to the indoor balcony. Lily stared back with wide green eyes. Immediately, Alena felt more than a little silly.

"You worried me," Alena said to the cat. From behind her, the doorknob jiggled. On impulse, Alena tensed and curled her hands into fists.

Jaxon entered the house and a cool rush of relief washed over Alena like fresh water.

"Jaxon, are you okay?" Alena asked and only then did he notice her there. He looked up, his eyes dark.

"O-Oh you're home already." He ignored her question. Something about it unsettled Alena as the man looked worse for wear than when she had left.

"I was just looking for you," Alena explained. "Where'd you go off to?"

"I was..." Jaxon rubbed at his eyes and the tension eased out of his shoulders. He put on a smile. "I was just taking a walk to clear my mind. And also, checking out the local flora."

"Oh..." Alena murmured, before she shook it off. If Jaxon wanted to work through his thoughts, she wouldn't push him. She smiled and motioned towards the kitchen. "Well, I got a lot of food so you don't have to worry about that right now."

The man lightened up as though she had shown him the stars for the first time. It was a look that made her chuckle, but she knew the truth behind it and led the way into the kitchen. Lily meowed loudly as she frantically jumped and clawed at Alena's shins.

"Alright, hold on," Alena said to the little cat as she reached into the box and ripped off a large chunk of meat. The butcher had not a clue his fine cuts were to be used for a feline, and would probably be horrified by the fact. It made Alena's smile grow a bit more as Lily snatched the meat with a deep growl. She scurried away with her prize to enjoy it elsewhere. Alena watched her go with love before she pulled the rest of the food out of the box. Jaxon stood by and watched her quietly. His eyes were still someplace else, but he made an attempt to focus on her.

Once her groceries were laid out Alena stared at them as if each was a musical instrument she was ordered to play. Instruments she didn't know how to. Her brows knitted together in concentration as she fiddled with her hands. Jaxon sighed and appeared a little more put together as he couldn't watch the display a moment longer.

"Have you ever cooked an *actual* meal, Alena?" he asked, which made a blush invade her cheeks.

"No... not really," Alena admitted, but she still refused to look at him and instead glared down at the meat and vegetables. "But how hard could it be?"

Jaxon shook his head and stepped up to the counter as he waved her off. "Allow me."

"What? No, Jaxon, you need to rest more," Alena said, a jolt of worry as she glanced over the man.

"I'm fine," Jaxon forced out. "I chugged so much water from your sink while you were gone. I feel like a real person again." He laughed, but she still nervously rubbed her hands together. He gave a playful glare and once more shooed her away; she sighed in defeat.

Alena retreated to the dining table and sat there as he worked on their meal. His hands moved smoothly with purpose, a knowledge of what to do within his muscle memory. It might as well have been magic to Alena, witchcraft even.

Alena lightly kicked her legs under the table as she watched. She wondered if this was a good time to throw in some small talk, but it still wasn't something she liked. Alena tapped her fingers against the old wood of the table as she thought of an appropriate topic. She thought of Jaxon's day out. "So how do you know what's safe to eat out there and what's not?"

"My dad." He shrugged as he set the meat on the burner's plate and began to chop carrots. "He really shoved all the survivalist crap down our throats growing up. Hated it at the time, but I guess I'm thankful now."

"Did he also teach you how to cook?"

"Yeah." Jaxon smiled, a sorrowful thing. "It was just the three of us for a while..."

Alena was unsure of the most appropriate response. Ask more about his family life? In a flash Alena heard the echoed screams from her memories, and could still smell the putrid dark smoke. She wanted to further avoid the topic. Instead, she said, "I never learned how to cook. I just kind of throw stuff on my burner and hope it works."

"That's no way to live," Jaxon responded like the thought made him sad. But perhaps, it had been the thought of his father and brother that made his tone so desolate. She watched Jaxon rustle through the cupboard for a couple of old plates before he placed their meals onto them.

"It's easy," Alena said, but the conversation was over. "That's all that matters."

Jaxon hummed in thought as he brought her a plate. She even felt King Belial give her a slight look from wherever he was. Alena shut her mouth and instead stared down at the food while Jaxon took his seat. It made her mouth water as she gazed upon the meat that lay next to mixed vegetables. She took a bite and was shocked by the freshness. Was that how food was supposed to be? She thought of Saffron and wondered if the woman ate this kind of stuff often. Alena wasn't much of a jealous person and instead felt a hint of longing within her chest. How the two lived in such different worlds. And yet still she was so kind to her.

"It's getting late," Jaxon pointed out when the silence had gone on for a while. He tossed a concerned glance out the window towards the darkened sky. Jaxon looked unsure about something, his shoulders tense as he stared into Alena's eyes. It made her fidget and want to look away but she stayed firm and waited for his words. He sighed, like his mental walls crumbled slightly. "If you don't mind, I think I'll stay another night. I can be gone first thing in the morning."

A shot of panic flooded through Alena's core. Sure, Jaxon looked a hair healthier, but would he last out there? Even with his knowledge of nature? She tried to search for the words. Was it... guilt? The day of dark smoke loomed over the two of them. She wished she could do something. Make it better.

Alena once more thought of Saffron's kindness and desperately wanted to extend that same hand. She thought of the Paladins, her old anxieties bubbling to the surface. Alena was already in so deep. What was one more thing? King Belial began to stir, his energy grew stronger as he approached.

"Jaxon, if you want, you can stay as long as you'd like," she finally said.

His lips parted in surprise as if those were the last words he expected. King Belial's hefty energy engulfed Alena and briefly scattered her thoughts. His hands were heavy on her shoulders as he glared Jaxon down. She tried not to focus so much on how the enormous demon hovered over her.

'Can you truly trust this man, Alena?' King Belial asked. It wasn't a demand to send him off, yet it still felt like the warning of one. Alena didn't respond. She knew it was a leap of faith, but her conscience couldn't send him off to die in the woods.

"What about the P.O.E.?" Jaxon questioned, his tone pained and gaze glassy. Having heard it being voiced, Alena allowed a deep grimace to mar her face. It was a dangerous line they toed.

"We'll have to keep an eye out." Alena sighed. "If we catch them driving up the road it'll give you enough time to run out the back door. Maybe hide in the forest for a bit. You could watch after Lily." Jaxon carefully listened and so she added a quick, "If you want to."

"Why would you go through the trouble for me?" he asked, his amber gaze fierce underneath shaggy brunette bangs. Alena was unsure if she could answer that, knowing the man likely wouldn't take pity for an answer. Just like how she didn't want to speculate Saffron only taking pity on her as well. Saffron... Alena smiled.

"People like us have to stick together," she said, but Jaxon didn't look convinced.

"Do we even have anything in common?" he asked as Lily walked back around the corner from the foyer. The two of them looked in the cat's direction as she gazed at them and licked her lips. Alena chuckled.

"We're both hiding," she answered and that was enough for Jaxon.

"Alright, I'll stay, but I'm not gonna mooch," he said and suddenly there was a newfound fire in his gaze. "Do you know about the plants around here, Alena?"

She felt her face grow hot as the answer felt almost sinful. "N-No, I actually haven't been out there yet."

"I can teach you then," Jaxon said, free of judgment. "There's a lot of resources out there for food that can ease your burden of going into the city."

Well, that certainly was better than what she had been doing up until then. However, Alena was unsure if she liked the thought of going out and just eating the things she found. With that, the conversation settled into casual talk well into the evening after their meals had been finished. Jaxon offered to teach Alena how to cook the things they would find in the woods too. However, she decided to focus on one thing at a time. Unbeknownst to Jaxon, Alena still had to do morning sparring sessions with King Belial as well.

By the time the two parted ways and went to their separate sleeping quarters, Alena felt a warmth unfamiliar to her. It wasn't like the raw primal blistering heat of safety King Belial made her feel. Perhaps it was from the natural sort of bond humans could find with one another? Either way, what Alena *was* positive of was her exhaustion from speaking to people that day. She wanted nothing more than to be alone in her bedroom for a while. Well, perhaps not truly alone. Was she ever such, these days? However, as she sat on her bed, with Lily comfortably in her lap, she waited for time to pass.

King Belial didn't go to her that night, and she knew deep down she'd be the one to approach him. Alena waited for the perfect hour, of which she knew Jaxon would be asleep. And so she stole away Lily's ribbon and key, and crept down into the foyer. Alena hesitated by the stairs as she listened for the soothed breathing of the man as he slept. When she heard no other sound, she tiptoed her way out of the front door. She left it cracked and dashed out into the yard towards her car. Once there, she snatched the painting and gazed at it for a moment, though it was much too dark.

With Saffron on her mind, Alena looked upwards.

Her breath was stolen away as the galaxy was laid out above her. The night sky was a wondrous void filled with billions of tiny sparkling stars. She held the painting to her chest and for the first time wished she could spend this moment with another. On one hand, she would have loved to see Saffron's reaction to it, knowing the woman would adore the sight. However, on the other hand, Alena wondered if King Belial had ever gazed upon the night sky like this. Though she didn't doubt there was a single sight he hadn't seen in his long existence. What exactly did that mean though? Did the stars look the same to him in whatever realm he resided?

Alena took one last breath of cool night air before she retreated back to the house. Once she figured it was safe again, Alena scurried off into the darkness of the hallway. Using her memories she made it all the way to the bookcase without so much as a misstep. She unlocked the chain and carefully set it to the side as quietly as she could.

Though it had only been a couple days since she had been down there, to Alena... to the way her heart sang, it felt like so much longer. Alena bounded down the stairs and deep into the basement. Her eyes adjusted enough to see vague shapes.

"King Belial?" she called out and immediately his energy enveloped her. She sighed as it felt like she could reach out to touch it, but Alena resisted the urge. Instead she walked up to the altar and carefully leaned the painting up against the wall behind it, as far as it would be from the candles she often burned for him. Alena could sense the smugness from the demon, but she hoped at the very least that he was happy as well.

'Look at you,' he said, his deep and gravelly voice booming in her head. He was amused. *'Proud to have gotten yourself both a boyfriend **and** a girlfriend?'*

"S-Shut up," Alena sputtered, because of course he would say something like that. But still, she thought of her day. She sighed. "It's not like that, but still today has been so weird."

King Belial's energy pressed even closer from behind, somehow even heavier this time. His enormous hand clutched her shoulder so strongly she could physically feel his claws poke at her skin. King Belial tugged Alena closer to where she assumed his actual body stood. His other hand, claws and all, gripped her chin and pulled her face forward as though to look at him. Alena's heart hammered heavily against her ribs. A thrill of excitement stirred in her belly. She still couldn't see him clearly, but if she tricked her mind, could imagine a shadowy shape in the dark.

'See?' King Belial's voice rumbled. *'I said if you were a good little devotee, I'd get you one of those paintings. I keep my vows, Alena.'*

"You..." Alena began but it felt as though the breath had been stolen away from her lungs. The demon felt pleased by this, proud even. Had he truly done that? And for her? Alena's fingers curled as they wanted to grasp the hand she couldn't touch. It astounded her really, the absolute magnitude and power of the being before her. The ability to cheat reality. Her legs quivered in their want to fall into worship, but she stayed in place. Alena whispered, *"King Belial—"*

But suddenly it wasn't so dark as the light from a candle began to flicker. The basement stairs creaked and trembled. The demon stepped away from Alena and emitted a deep growl that made her head spin, made worse she snapped around.

"Alena, you down here?" Jaxon's voice met her ears. She wheezed as her chest tightened and all she could do was settle her sights on the skull on the wall and King Belial's sigil carved there proudly and oh so visible even with what little light there was.

No no no no!

Alena whipped around to face Jaxon, an excuse on her lips, but the sight of all that was this basement was evidence enough against her. Alena remembered the first time she gazed upon the demon's altar. Jaxon's face contorted with a mixture of shock and horror. Alena knew there was nothing she could do.

The two of them stood there and stared with wide eyes at one another, with only the sound of the candle flame between them.

Chapter 25

The silence was deafening. The only thing Alena could focus on was the roar of blood in her ears. Jaxon stood before her, tense with one leg behind him pointed towards the stairs. Alena was equally at a standstill. She couldn't breathe, or rather, she dreaded if she uttered a noise it would break the fragile thread between them. They couldn't stay like this though, an eternity of unspoken words and unbridled *fear*. Alena tried to focus on King Belial's energy, but was far too frazzled to feel anything other than the humid and stale basement air.

"Jaxon—" Alena began, but at the sound of her voice he broke out of the frozen stupor he was stuck in.

"You're a demon worshiper?!" the man snarled and it was a shadow of his old self. The one that fought himself free from the Paladins. Alena flinched at the question. She wanted to respond, but her chest clenched painfully, like claws against her heart.

'Breathe easy, my dear,' King Belial said close to her ear, but his words were of little comfort this time. Alena's memory clung to the day prior, where things felt

as though they were brighter. She supposed this was the punishment for trying to open up. King Belial grunted, displeased at the thoughts.

Jaxon waited only a moment longer for her response, but when it never came, he bolted back towards the stairs. A rush of desperation flooded through Alena. She ran after him as King Belial called out, *'Don't fret, the fugitive isn't able to rat you out!'*

That wasn't what Alena feared most at that moment. All she could think was that she had to reach Jaxon. Alena's throat was tight as she wanted nothing more than to explain everything to him. To beg him to not see anything wrong with what she did. To beg herself to stop seeing what she did as something dirty. It was in her right; it was in her blood given right.

Alena chased Jaxon up the stairs and out of the bookcase. Even with the candle he clutched, the cluttered hall tripped him up, and the man stumbled. She gained on him, but still he turned the corner and cleared the distance to the foyer. Alena wheezed; she wasn't going to catch him.

However, just as Jaxon crossed in front of the stairs, something small and black shot out and crossed his path. Lily let out an enraged scream as Jaxon tripped over her and slammed into the hard floor. The cat fearfully dashed into the kitchen as the candle flew up and clattered a few feet away. The flame snuffed out and enshrouded the ancient house into darkness.

Alena leaped out of the hallway and landed right on top of Jaxon. He twisted around and tried to grab at her.

"What are you going to do?" Jaxon spat in her face. "Sacrifice my soul to the devil?"

A white hot *wrath* boiled under Alena's skin. On impulse, she dug her cracked and blunt nails into Jaxon's arms. She hissed, "We don't *do* that here!"

The man growled, grappled her, and got the upper-hand. The air escaped her lungs as her back hit the floor and the two of them rolled. She still held onto him and refused to let go. Her muscles, though weary, had far more energy than the weakened Jaxon. He thrashed about desperately as he tried to dislodge her so he could flee. Jaxon's face looked pained as his fingers dug into Alena's shoulders and tried to shake her.

"You damned devil worshipers killed my brother!" he shouted and only then did her grip loosen as she looked at his face. His waxy eyes had grown damp. Alena frowned and found a few of her own rogue tears to escape as a sharp pain sank into her gut.

"We had nothing to do with that. The Paladins did!" she wailed and at that Jaxon finally froze. His grip became flimsy so Alena finally released him. She collapsed onto the floor, panting, as Jaxon lost all strength and fell back onto his rump. His voice broke as he buried his head in his hands. Alena caught her breath as she watched his shoulders wrack with silent sobs.

"Neither of you were actually in leagues with demons, right?" Alena asked, a grimace plastering her features. A raspy sigh escaped Jaxon as he calmed himself.

"No, we've never even met a demon worshiper." His fingers parted so he could glance between them. At her. He whispered, "Until now."

"I'm sorry you found out this way," Alena chose her words carefully. She wouldn't apologize for the actual act. There was nothing she should apologize for in that regard. Despite how deeply the claws in her heart told her so. The whispers of society beat her down into the ground, and the fright covered her body like dirt. A grave of expectations. Alena wanted to defend herself, to explain the feelings of devotion. The way her heart soared and how safe she felt being around King Belial. Would that only make her look more guilty? Guilty of the wrongs he assumed her to commit. She sat up from the floor and hugged herself, wanting to hide her face. She mumbled, despite how fake it might have sounded to him, "I'm not a bad person, I don't think... I try not to be a bad person."

Jaxon fully lowered his hands and stared at her with those fierce amber eyes of his. She flushed and fidgeted under his gaze, worried he might launch another attack at her. Still on edge, Jaxon whispered, "I'm sorry for how I reacted." His voice was grave with exhaustion.

"I'm just a person, like you," Alena said. "I just so happen to have a demon that looks after me."

"What's that like?" Jaxon asked before he could realize what he had said. He shook his head, as though perhaps he feared the answer. Instead, he sighed. "Why would someone do that? Demons are evil."

"It would take all night to explain," Alena lamented, "but if you still wish to stay with me, I promise I'll tell you about it. I *want* you to know."

Jaxon opened his mouth to speak but promptly closed it. His face deep in thought as he contemplated his options. She knew very well it was a lot to take in.

From somewhere in the depths of the dark hall, a loud knock was heard. Jaxon's breath skipped as he leaped up and spun towards the offending sound. His shoulders were impossibly taut as he readied for another fight. Alena looked off towards the sound and within the shadows she could see ripples. They moved away from the archway and further into the hall. *Oh yeah.* She nodded and stood.

"Would you like to meet him?" Alena offered and when Jaxon looked at her with uncertainty, she felt her face heat up. As she looked away, her heart fluttering, she whispered, "My demon king?"

Jaxon scanned her over to read into something that wasn't there. He slowly asked, "How do I know you aren't just going to kill me?" It was a genuine question and one that reminded Alena of when she first came to this house. It felt like so long ago. She looked back at him, serious now.

"You've been asleep on my couch for the past two nights," she responded. "If I wanted to do that, I would have already."

Jaxon let out a ragged sigh and nodded. He grumbled, "I do want to meet him."

And with that, Alena offered her hand, but he didn't take it. She dropped her arm and instead walked off into the suffocating shadows of the darkened hall. Jaxon hesitated as he looked up at the grand archway that opened before him. Did he notice the hall there before that night? Alena couldn't say for certain.

She showed him trust as she turned her back towards him and led him back to the bookshelf. They descended down the stairs together and upon entering the basement, went straight for the altar. Alena grabbed her extra flint and steel she kept there and lit King Belial's personal candles to give them light. She looked up at the large animal skull that still hung on the wall proudly, examining the intricately carved sigil in the bone. The mere sight of it made Alena feel warm; her fingertips buzzed at the power the demon held.

Jaxon shuffled nervously as he glanced around, having second doubts about it all. Alena watched him as he looked disdainfully at the rest of the dust covered basement, wheezing at the musty air. Jaxon's voice was light, albeit forced, as he asked, "So do you want help cleaning this place up sometime?"

She couldn't help the awkward chuckle that escaped her. "I'm mostly done in here, but I'd love to get the living room in a more livable condition."

He nodded, eyes still averted. The two stood there, for only a moment, until there was another knock. This time it came from the actual altar. Alena smiled, endeared, as she faced Jaxon and motioned towards the space beside her. He approached with caution, his eyes never leaving the threatening skull above him.

"Jaxon, this is King Belial," Alena said, voice only slightly above a whisper. He nodded at first, but then perhaps thought better of it as he faced the skull.

"Um, nice to meet you," he said and she wondered if perhaps he felt silly to address the skull as if it were an actual living being. But to Alena, she could feel King Belial's hefty energy permeate from it at all times. Staring too long, for herself, would often make her a tad dizzy. The energy grew and she could see a shadowy shape move from the skull to linger just above Jaxon. He made no sign he witnessed the same thing as well, but Alena noted the way his muscles tensed. Jaxon had definitely sensed *something*. King Belial hulked over the much smaller human man, his energy curious as he examined him over.

'He keeps himself secured behind a wall so I can only sense fear,' the demon declared. *'Remember to remain vigilant, but for now I shall allow him to continue sleeping on our couch.'*

Alena let out a laugh and Jaxon's gaze snapped to her. He hadn't a clue what was going on. She raised a brow, curious. "Can't you hear him?"

He shook his head and Alena felt all the more flustered. Oh. She cleared her throat and lifted up her arm to show him the sigil branded on the back of her hand.

"Can you see this?" she asked, but his confusion only deepened.

"Your hand?" Jaxon asked after a beat.

"Ah, nevermind." She sighed. At least that proved he truly wasn't another demonolater. Alena lowered her hand as Jaxon watched every movement. King Belial finally stepped away from him and Jaxon's shoulders became more relaxed. He could breathe easily now.

"So, if you don't mind," Jaxon said, "I'm going to go back to bed. This was... a lot."

"Yeah, I think I might need some sleep too," Alena admitted. Jaxon nodded a goodbye as he turned and headed back out of the basement. And she couldn't blame him.

Alena decided she would follow and go back to her own bed, but she hesitated. She looked at the altar. The way the candlelight danced across King Belial's skull and she felt content. Happy even, that the interaction with Jaxon had gone as well as it could. Alena blew out the candles, casting herself into darkness.

Chapter 26

'Don't forget who you're truly devoted to,' King Belial said first thing the next morning. He stomped his way around Alena in their usual cavern meeting spot. She rolled her eyes at his playful tone. There was an amused tug at the corner of his toothy maw.

Alena couldn't help but find the look rather endearing. "Of course, you're the only one for me," she said in the hope her own tone mirrored his.

The demon's irises burned brightly from the depths of his skull. *Is that so?* The tip of his thick tail twitched with interest and Alena's face grew warm. King Belial's eyes flickered over her and he appeared to be waiting for... something. Another question from her maybe? After a few silent seconds, the demon let out a tired sigh.

'Would you like to continue your training?' King Belial asked, but now Alena didn't feel like it. What was that about? However, she decided to continue on with the sparring session.

Alena got down into her usual stance and braced herself while King Belial lifted his arms over his head to stretch out each muscle. A deep gravelly growl emitted from his chest and Alena couldn't help but to openly stare. That was fine right? That was worship, Alena thought. King Belial smirked and with a snarl, launched himself at her. *'Don't get distracted!'*

Alena forgot he wanted her to block and leaped away with a yelp. She stumbled and fell. King Belial slid to a rough halt and his hooves loudly scraped against the stony ground. Alena, not yet being completely acclimated to the astral realm, didn't feel the fall, yet she still groaned in habit. Her body, in the physical world, twitched.

'*Alena*—' King Belial started, but she wasn't in the mood nor the right mindset to handle his lecture. Alena gritted her teeth as she pulled herself up and lunged for him. She slammed into his stomach and wrapped her arms around his middle. Her side ached as if she had leaped onto the mountain itself. The demon expelled air as she had taken him by surprise, but otherwise, he didn't budge. Alena grunted and growled as she dug her heels into the rocks and tried to topple King Belial over. He slapped his tail against the ground in response, unbothered.

The demon didn't let her struggle too much longer as he gripped the tops of her shoulders and pulled her off. King Belial twisted around and rolled them both onto the ground. Had she been in her actual body, Alena knew it would've knocked the air from her lungs. She tensed as he crouched over her, his clawed hands on each side of her face. King Belial's crimson irises glowed brightly in the shadowy cavern and faintly reflected off her own.

'Never grapple with an enemy much larger than yourself,' he said, lowering himself further to sit on her. In the physical world, a foreign weight pressed down on her stomach. The muzzle on King Belial's skull quivered. *'Unless you work on your muscles or battle tactics, of course. If not, you'll keep making this mistake.'*

Alena gritted her teeth as she remembered her fight with Jaxon the night prior. If he had been someone who had wanted to hurt her, the outcome could have been much different. Still, she knew there wasn't much she could currently do. Alena felt weak and hopeless. She frowned and nodded in agreement with King Belial, but could hardly stomach to stare at his face. Instead she concentrated on the way the red striped pattern on his chest rippled and shined with each rise and fall of breath.

King Belial leaned back and Alena's gaze flickered towards his face on impulse. She carefully watched how the glowing markings made a faint light dance across his skull.

"Can you get off me now?" Alena flushed. The demon above her cackled.

'Maybe if I feel like it,' he hummed. Alena spat like a cat and kicked out her legs, lightly clawing at King Belial's thighs as if that would get him to budge. His smirk only deepened.

"You're so mean." She sighed, giving up as she flopped back down.

'I never would have imagined a king of hell to be that way.'

Finally King Belial decided Alena had enough and lifted himself off of her. She practically shot back up from the ground and stumbled into the demon before her. He grunted, annoyed, but instead of moving away he sat a gentle hand on her head. She froze and craned her neck to get a better look at him, eyes incredibly round. King Belial was still slightly crouched and not standing at his full height. He was so close.

Alena cleared her throat and finally stepped away from him. It felt colder. He straightened up, the tips of his horns brushing against the cavern's ceiling. King Belial looked contemplative as if he wanted to say something again.

'Alena, these feelings of devotion—'

"Hey Alena, are you awake?"

Her eyes snapped open at the sound of Jaxon's voice, the image of the cavern melting away from her mind. Alena groaned as she pulled herself up, her back stiff, the only evidence of her rough brawl. She looked past where Lily was still curled up on the foot of the bed to where Jaxon hovered near the door. She blinked down at the footstool that now lay off to the side, having done absolutely nothing to keep the door firmly in place.

"Yeah, I was just laying here," Alena responded. She was about to be honest about what she was actually doing, but the sight of Jaxon stopped her. Dark circles surrounded his eyes, indicative that he had struggled to sleep that night.

All of this would have been too much for him. Alena looked off to the side in search of the demon she had previously shared her space with.

King Belial stepped away from the two of them, his energy rippling with annoyance. Alena supposed she could understand that. She wondered what King Belial had been about to say. However, as she waited for him to finish, whatever it was left the demon's nerve. And so his energy became dull until it wasn't there at all.

"Um, well, I made breakfast, if you want any," Jaxon mumbled before he turned and left, to which Alena was flooded with relief. Things may have been awkward now, but that sounded like a saving grace. She leaped out of bed and hurried from the room and down the stairs. As Alena entered the kitchen, she found Jaxon already at the dining table, quietly eating. She went and joined him at her usual spot, but her belly felt far too queasy to partake in what he made.

She stared down at the light leftovers from the night prior and frowned. The air between them was fragile, like something could shatter at any moment. Alena wondered if she had tarnished any trust garnered between them, and yet... what had she truly done that was so wrong? Hide away her connection with King Belial? Was she just supposed to be honest about it with everyone and risk her life? No, she would never apologize for that. She thought of the demon and despite how he could be, felt endeared by him. She looked up and saw Jaxon openly stare, a tight strain to his eyes that held all the concern and fear he didn't voice.

Even after their talk last night, it was still awkward.

"I wasn't doing anything weird in the basement," Alena said to break the silence. Jaxon tensed, not having expected her to speak. She gave a sad smile. "King Belial got me a painting from an artist I really like, so I was hanging it up down there."

The man looked curious, painfully so. After a minute more, he dragged out his words, "How did he do that?"

"I'm not sure," Alena hummed as the air between them grew more warm. "It's kind of like he set things up. A bunch of coincidences happened which resulted in me getting it."

"Interesting," Jaxon said and he truly did look intrigued. But also, his concern never waivered. He said, perhaps far too quietly, "From what I heard on the streets, demons can possess people. Sometimes they might even make themselves look like humans. Is that... true?"

Alena blinked. "I'm not sure... I've never even seen him take a physical form. In my experience demons, at least King Belial, are made of energy. It's hard to explain."

Jaxon's brows knitted together as he took in her words and Alena wanted to kick herself. It all did sound confusing and no number of books would help with that. She thought back to her grandfather's journal. Despite all of his experience, he also didn't fully understand what went on with the demonic divine.

"Again I ask," Jaxon spoke up, "why would you devote yourself to something like that?"

Alena didn't have the answer. She only had strange and vague feelings that she couldn't explain. She remembered how King Belial looked in her living room when she agreed to be his devotee. The way the sunlight molded against his musculature, tinting his skull a light orange. Even then he had looked the utmost of demonic, something that would have chased most people off. Nearly chased her off, in fact. Yet she couldn't deny the way being around him made her feel. The way his presence made her blood sing for the one it was long ago promised to. Alena's imagination went back to that morning, the way he crouched above her. Even in the dark, he exuberated an attractive allure she couldn't deny. That was divinity.

"I really don't know the answer to that," Alena finally responded to Jaxon after what felt like an eternity. She avoided mentioning her grandfather. Following a demon just because a family member did, didn't feel like a suitable answer. Alena was desperate for her reasoning to be deeper than that. "But maybe I think there's something beautiful about the dark."

He didn't appear too convinced, for how could something like darkness be beautiful? Well, Alena wasn't sure either, but it was something she could *feel* inside of her gut. The two continued to eat their breakfast in silence. Despite not being all too hungry, Alena forced the leftovers down just to make sure she had some sort of sustenance to keep her going throughout the day.

It was when she was nearly finished that she heard a loud and frightened caterwaul come from the other room. Her blood ran cold as she recognized Lily's cry. Before Jaxon could say anything, Alena leaped up and bolted towards the living room.

"Lily, what's the matter?!" Alena shouted as she ran into the other room. She slid to a stop and balked. Her tired eyes made the room look as though it were an illusion. The piles of boxes were mostly gone. Lily was hunched down low to the ground as she kept close to the couch and crept around the room. Her tail was puffed up two sizes and her pupils were incredibly round. Lily stared into the sparse living room as though the area itself was a snake about to strike.

"What—" Alena blinked as she looked around. It vaguely resembled the version she recreated in the astral.

"Oh, yeah." Jaxon shrugged as he walked up beside her. "I couldn't sleep last night so I thought I'd go ahead and start cleaning the place up."

"What did you do with the junk?" Alena asked numbly, unable to take her eyes off the strange sight before her.

"It's out in the yard." He tossed his thumb in the direction of the door. "Figured you could dispose of it next time you go into town."

Something sharp stabbed at her chest, but it was the last thing on her mind. He had done all that without even consulting her. She wanted to mention that, but she *had* said that the two of them could clean up the living room. Something felt off about the situation, still, as though she should have gone through the items herself. What if there had been something incriminating within them?

Alena took a few steps into the room. Dark outlines of dust showed where the boxes and other old broken items had once been. The room looked so much larger, but unlike in the astral. Something about the openness felt dangerous, like she was far too exposed. The unsettled dust floated about the room and aggravated her lungs. Lily let out yet another distraught cry that made Alena flinch. She could hardly pay attention to the man beside her as she watched the little black cat quiver. Had the living room really scared her? It was far too much for Lily to handle. The cat bolted out of the room and around the staircase into the dark hall. Alena could still hear her echoed cries as the patter of her paws grew faint.

'HE WHAT?!' The roar rattled around the inside of Alena's head and nearly made her double over in pain. She winced and clutched at the sides of her head. Around her the house shook with the ferocity of an earthquake that threatened to upheave the building from its foundations.

Jaxon nearly stumbled, a panicked look in his eye. "What is that?!"

Alena floundered, but couldn't muster up the words as a thunderous boom came from the basement beneath her feet. The raucous sounds moved quickly up the stairs and down the hallway, reminiscent of a rockslide tumbling down a mountain. Alena looked towards the foyer, where she saw the room darken despite it still being morning. A large black shadow shot out of the hall before it encompassed the house around them.

Jaxon looked like he was about to be sick as the massive wave that was King Belial's form rushed past the man. Even Alena felt the need to jump out of the demon's way. His energy was a burning rage and hatred that made the house appear to ripple and bend. Alena took a step back to give King Belial space as he frantically moved about the now empty living room.

'What've you done?!' the demon howled out with a vicious lash of his tail, the heavy limb cracked against the hardwood. *'You dare do this as a guest in my house?'*

His words struck that old nerve inside Alena. It bit at her until she spouted venom. "It's my house!"

'I'm not talking to you,' King Belial said. There was a sort of desperation in his voice that pleaded with her to stay out of it. Alena knew she couldn't do that, not as the demon approached Jaxon, a massive threatening aura. Jaxon could also feel this and bolted towards the front door. King Belial moved to give chase, but Alena leaped in front of him to put herself between the two. Even though she knew King Belial could easily go through her to get to him. Despite this, King Belial came to a stop in front of his devotee.

"Y-You're out of line," Alena stammered in a desperate attempt to make the demon see reason. "He was just trying to be nice."

'ME?!' King Belial cried out, scandalized. *'He's the one that touched these things without asking.'*

"King Belial," Alena said as softly as she could; she could feel the demon's distress at the situation. The emotion was one that felt unfamiliar from him, but it was definitely there under the piles of rage. She wanted to try to calm him, but as her own anxiety spiked, she foolishly whispered, "It's just garbage."

King Belial's mood became blistering hot as if someone had turned up a dial. And yet he still tried to keep a level voice with her. Gently, King Belial stated, *'Those things were your grandfather's. You wouldn't want to keep them for sentimental value?'*

Alena groaned, feeling exasperated as the draining energy continued to bite at her. Out of exhaustion, she yelled, "I didn't even know him!"

'But I did!' King Belial shouted back. His voice caused the house to shake and rumble once more. Alena froze as she felt like a block of ice had formed in her gut. Oh... She hadn't considered... That was the final straw that snapped the fragile air that hung over their heads. Alena felt it as King Belial's form rippled painfully. The demon growled, much more lowly, *'Just leave.'*

"King—"

'NOW!' Another housequake and Alena tore herself away from King Belial to rush out the front door after Jaxon. She stumbled in her haste, like a part of her had been ripped from her chest and left behind. Still, she ran and leaped from the porch steps into the yard. The windows shuddered and the old wood moaned as the movement was almost far too much for it to handle. Alena panted as she doubled over and desperately clutched at the fabric of her pants. The desire to run back inside to him gnawed on her body. The boxes that had caused this mess laid strewn about.

Alena, despite it all, whipped around to face the house. Only for the front door to slam before her.

Chapter 27

King Belial's wrathful ire burned in Alena's chest. She could only sit down in the dirt several feet away from the house and hold herself. It still quivered now and again, and she thought perhaps, he had begun to simmer down. Jaxon sat a mere inches away from her, eyes haunted like he had just returned from war.

"I'm not going to lie," Jaxon said after a few moments. "I really thought you were just out of your mind, and there was no actual demon."

A sour laugh escaped at his words. "Y-Yeah, that's a fair assessment, I guess."

"So what now?" Jaxon asked as he rubbed the back of his head. "Looks like we're both without a place to live now."

"I think I'll just give him time to cool down," Alena stated as she finally looked up and glued her eyes to the house... her home. She yearned to go to it, just like how she felt when Lady Chambers offered her the house. That strange tug that made her want to venture into places unknown. She sighed. "I didn't consider his feelings in this situation."

"Feelings?" Jaxon uttered under his breath, as though the concept were a ridiculous one. Alena wasn't sure why, but it reignited the flame of her anger. She shook it off and finally pulled herself up.

"So since we're probably going to be out here for a while, do you want to teach me about plants like you said?" Alena asked hopefully. She didn't feel like it, but anything to get her mind off the situation would be good.

"I... guess we can," Jaxon murmured, brows furrowed. He wearily glanced towards the trees closer to the house. He stood and began to walk in the opposite direction, to which Alena hurried after. Despite the cool fresh air and sunny light, she could tell the both of them felt more than a little on edge. It was so open out here, even with all the trees and plants. Nature definitely wasn't something Alena was used to. She curiously examined each plant they passed as the ground sloped upwards. The muscles in her legs screamed.

Jaxon, on the other hand, had no problem as he pulled himself upward over roots and large rocks. It was no wonder he could survive out there with nothing but the clothes on his back. She watched him carefully as he looked back and forth in the search of... something. She didn't have to wait long to find out as the two of them came upon a large outcropping of rocks. A single tree grew against them, still somehow hanging on with roots exposed to the elements.

"Ah, there we go," Jaxon said as he motioned for Alena to come closer. She wheezed for breath but managed to leap over a ridge and get to him. "You see this?"

He pointed to a fungus that held firm onto the tree, shelf-like and bright orange in color. Alena wrinkled up her nose, but nodded nonetheless.

"They call this the chicken of the woods," Jaxon explained as he reached out and broke off a few columns of the mushrooms. "Normally I would advise against a newbie forager collecting mushrooms, but there are no toxic imitations of this one, so it's relatively safe."

Alena didn't like the idea of eating mushrooms straight off a tree, but she supposed she'd just have to get used to it. Curiously, she remembered the state Jaxon had been in the night he came to her. Alena asked, "Did you eat this when you were out here?"

He paled as he pocketed the mushrooms into his large coat. "No, you really have to cook any mushrooms before you eat them. I didn't have the time for that, and I didn't want to risk the P.O.E. seeing the smoke."

The two continued on their way. Alena couldn't imagine what it would've been like having to survive out here. She looked up at the tree branches overhead. They were sparse in leaves, but provided enough cover from the sunlight. At night, she could hardly stand to look out of the window. They looked so strange in the dark, like tall and spindly people with sharp claws that reached towards the sky overhead. The stars were beautiful, the trees not so much, and yet...

Alena moved about the mountainside. Her steps brushed over hard ground and she clambered over felled trees. She couldn't help but be in awe at the forces of nature, couldn't help but be reminded of the demon she just fled from. Her grandfather's journal said King Belial was of the earth, and while she had first questioned it, now she had no doubt about it. Everything on the mountain felt as though it led back to him. This only served to make her footfalls feel heavier as time went on.

The day slowly trickled away as Jaxon and Alena continued their walk around the woods. He made sure to never take them too far from the house as they made frequent stops. Jaxon showed her many plants that grew around her home, perhaps more than she had anticipated. Some were toxic and would likely kill her within the day, and others were completely fine to eat. Jaxon pocketed those ones so Alena could study them and memorize which ones they were.

It was a bit past midday when the both of them, especially Jaxon, began to grow tired. Alena's stomach rumbled painfully and Jaxon gave her a worried look.

"Here, eat a few of these to keep up strength," he said as he handed off a handful of berries. She quietly thanked him, popped them into her mouth, and relished in the bitter flavor. A deep scowl appeared on Jaxon's features as he looked towards the sky. They still had plenty of daylight left, but using up so much energy wore both of them down. He asked, "Do you think we'll have to sleep out here?"

Alena was unsure how to answer, so instead slid her eyes shut and tried to focus on her connection with King Belial. He was distant, painfully so, but she no longer felt the seething rage he initially exuberated. The demon's bite of annoyance still held out, but the tug between them was back, as though he were awaiting her return. She let out a tired sigh as her eyes fluttered open to look at Jaxon. "I think we can head back to the house now."

"A-Are you sure?" Jaxon was quick to ask. Alena nodded, sure of herself. Jaxon saw this and despite his own hesitations led her all the way back to the house. It looked just the same as when they left it. Alena stepped up to the porch and held a hand up. A motion for Jaxon to stay where he was.

"Let me try to talk to him first," she said.

"What? No way. What if he attacks you?" Jaxon gritted his teeth, but it only made Alena blink in surprise.

"He wouldn't do that," she responded and didn't like the incredulous look the other gave her. Alena ignored him and turned back to the house. She carefully made her way up the creaking porch steps. Alena tossed open the front door with ease. It swung and clattered like old bones as the hollow house opened up before her. Across from the door, the dark hall appeared even more shadowed. Uninviting.

Alena entered and tiptoed up to the archway and looked up. Lily sat above it on the landing, her stare full of judgment.

"Is King Belial in the basement?" Alena asked, but the cat only lowered her head to allow the ribbon to slip off. The key clattered to the ground and Alena thanked Lily before she snatched it up and continued on her way. Alena made her way to the hidden bookcase, just as she had memorized all the times before. Only this time, her hands hovered above the lock, worried she had perhaps misunderstood the feeling between them. She bit her lip and undid the lock, anyway. It clanked loudly on the floor, announcing her presence.

"King Belial, I'm back," she called as she stared down into the depths. She received no answer, but could feel his distant stare if she focused enough. He did nothing else, no wrathful snarl and certainly no shaking the house. Alena carefully made her way down into the basement and crossed the long dark room to where the altar stood. In the pitch blackness, she could just barely make out the off-white skull that hung above the old table. Alena reached out to caress her fingers across the old bone.

'Are you going to throw that out as well?' King Belial finally spoke, his energy brushed up against her side. She shivered at the slightest bit of warmth he still gave her.

"Don't be like that," Alena whispered back to him, but she shook her head. No, he had every right to be upset. Alena should have considered his feelings on the matter before she asked Jaxon to do that. She just never assumed... Alena turned away from the altar and sat down cross-legged on the floor, her back to the table. She slid her eyes shut and allowed the floating feeling to take her away.

When she opened her mind's eyes, she was surprised to find her astral form stood in the dark hallway. She turned around and looked straight into the foyer. There she heard heavy stomps as King Belial stepped into view, as though he had been in the kitchen. He stopped and turned his skull to stare at her, his breaths heavy like growls. On impulse, despite her desire to stay calm, her breath hitched. Alena had just seen him that morning, but it felt as though they had been apart for an eon.

Alena took a step forward and as she did so, King Belial looked away and continued to walk out of view. His tail slipped around the corner. She hurried on into the foyer and caught sight of him in the living room just as before. Except this time it was dark, only the moonlight from the windows cast any reasonable glow. King Belial made the couch look miniscule as he leaned over it to look at something on the other side. When he didn't so much as acknowledge Alena's presence, she walked around the couch and froze.

There was a man laid on it, one that was unfamiliar to her. He was wrinkled with age, incredibly so, and had faint silver hair. Just a singular section of it was lighter in color, just like hers. He was bundled warmly in old tattered blankets, and on his lap Lily curled up fast asleep. Alena's heart skipped a beat. Her grandfather, Rick Usher. The world shuddered, but she held onto it tight. She couldn't allow herself to be booted out of the astral, she knew this was something she was meant to see.

Her grandfather's eyes blinked open, clouded and milky, his voice shaky as he called out, "Belial is that you?"

Yes, I'm here old friend, King Belial responded as his eyes flashed to attention. His usually booming voice was low and much softer than Alena had ever heard it before. Something within her chest twisted at the sound of it.

"Ah, good," the old man wheezed. "I thought... thought you had already gone."

You should know well by now, you can't get rid of me that easily. King Belial chuckled. However, his humor wavered as he leaned closer to the bedridden man. The demon whispered, *And I'm not the one we should be worrying about.*

"Any day now, I fear..."

A sorrowful part of human existence.

"May I be frank?" Alena's grandfather asked him.

You've never not been.

"I think I'm a bit..." the old man whispered after a pregnant pause, "scared of dying."

King Belial's massive shoulders drew back as he tensed, but never let it show on his skull. *I have seen many humans die. It's nothing short of natural for your kind.*

"Does it ever get any easier?"

Human souls are born and die many times throughout their existence. King Belial nodded as if it were the most obvious thing in the world. *Your soul will know what to do when it leaves your body.*

"No, not me, for you," the old man wheezed and hacked. When he settled, King Belial hummed curiously and tilted his head to the side. He didn't quite understand what the human was trying to get at. Rick Usher chuckled, sensing the demon's confusion. He went on, "Seeing your people die, does it ever get any easier?"

At this King Belial was taken off guard as the lights of his irises flickered. He looked as though he didn't want to answer the question. However, Rick waited patiently, as if he had all the time in the world. Time they both knew was running out. King Belial let out a deep sigh that echoed the sorrows of deep lone caverns. His voice was quiet. *'While human souls live on, the person they once were does indeed die. I can remember every person I've crossed paths with. Millions of them, and no, it never gets easier. You could reincarnate tomorrow, but you wouldn't know who I am. Wouldn't remember all the times we shared. Perhaps your soul will and you'll feel a longing to reach out to me. But it is just as likely you simply continue on without so much as a thought in my direction.'*

"And if I don't want to reincarnate?" Rick sighed, rebellious.

'Then perhaps a succulent afterlife will await you full of beautiful women or men,' King Belial cackled as if there wasn't anything to worry about. He settled back down and gave a solemn nod. *'Or perhaps your old coven awaits you to play poker. I can't say for sure. You never gave me permission to look after your soul once you left.'* It was something of a tense topic for the both of them, Alena could somehow tell. Perhaps from the way King Belial's mind melded with her own.

"That sounds more delightful," the old man waivered, focusing on what the demon said previously. "I've missed my friends through the years, I wish... things could have turned out differently."

King Belial froze for only a moment, but as Rick's breathing became more ragged, he knew the two of them were running out of time. The demon would be open, if just for this once, *'I've wished for that as well.'*

The old man weakly reached out to King Belial with an outstretched hand and the demon met him halfway. He lightly grasped the other. Rick Usher's hand looked so small and frail in the massive demon's. Yet King Belial was gentle as though the old man was the most precious of gemstones. Alena's grandfather let out a small content sigh as he allowed the demon to cusp his hand.

"If I could have, I would have left you this house and everything in it," Rick rasped. His other hand slowly reached out to Lily, who still snoozed quietly. "Especially my precious little girl, I'm so scared of what will become of them both when I'm gone."

'Oh Rick,' King Belial grumbled and to Alena, she was shocked to see the look of agony that graced the demon's features. His eyes burned like fire as he looked upon the dying old man. *'If you Will it to me, I will do all in my power to find the most worthy of your bloodline to gift it to.'*

"Please do," Rick whispered as he gathered the rest of his strength to lift his arm further. King Belial noticed this and carefully leaned down. He allowed the man to splay out his hand on top of his skull. Rick let out a sigh as the action brought him great comfort. Alena noticed on the back of her grandfather's hand was King Belial's sigil just like hers. Rick slid his eyes shut. "That is both my last offering and last request of you."

Rick Usher let out one final sigh and grew limp. His hand fell from King Belial's skull. The demon stood up straight in surprise, somehow not having foreseen his follower's death coming so soon. He stood there and looked at his body for a moment and from it drifted up a bright blue wisp. It nearly resembled a bird as it fluttered upwards.

'This wasn't my plan for you,' King Belial whispered as he watched the ghostly bird vanish into the ceiling. He snarled, *'I should have been able to give you the life you deserve!'*

Alena could feel it. The demon's sorrow tore through her chest and nearly knocked her over. She staggered forward to go to him, but the image before her melted away. She blinked, and once again found herself in their usual meeting spot within the cave. Behind her, a deep darkness permeated.

'I knew him, I knew him,' King Belial repeated as his muscles quaked and tail quivered. His skull snapped upwards as though he had just noticed she was there. Alena tensed but remained where she stood as King Belial stomped his way over to her. The eye sockets of his skull narrowed and darkened as he glared. *'You may see me as a being that is incapable of feeling, but* know *that we care. We care for each and every one of our followers and it always hurts when you're gone.'*

Alena's words were lost on her tongue. What could she even say to a being so vastly different from her? Her heart pounded and she had to grit her teeth to keep from breaking down then and there. She reached out towards his skull, just as she had seen her grandfather do in the memory, "King Belial—"

'Don't!' the demon snapped as he grabbed her wrist. She tensed, but found his touch to be gentle. King Belial repeated, *'Don't... you haven't earned that right yet.'*

Alena's whole body recoiled; his words felt like a sword to her flesh. If that's how he felt, though... She would respect that. Alena frowned and tried to pull her hand away, but King Belial noticed the hurt that showed clearly in her eyes. He sighed and instead gently brought her hand to his chest. Alena immediately grew warm, even though his red markings had turned dull without shine. The sigil on her hand burned with a fierce intensity, as if it had been a candle lit for the first time.

Alena's fingers curled to grasp at his skin, but of course, she could only feel a vague tingle in her physical body back in the basement. It made her want to kick and shout. Instead, Alena reveled in her connection with him and leaned fully into King Belial's chest. She rested her forehead against him. The demon let out a breath of air as he allowed it and brought up his other hand to cup her head. That old safe feeling from the first time he grabbed her shoulder melted back into her body. Emboldened by it, Alena snuggled up against King Belial even further. She couldn't even recall the last time a human had touched her, let alone in the way she now stood with the demon.

'Alena,' King Belial grunted as she got a little too ahead of herself and slowly wrapped her arms around him for a hug. Or rather the best she could attempt one as she struggled with the sheer size of him.

"I-I'm sorry!" Alena yelped as she realized what she had been doing. She pulled herself out of his arms and covered her face with her own to calm her rapidly beating heart. Had she allowed her feelings of demonic devotion to get a little too out of hand? They were a bit too strong for her. King Belial huffed and looked as though he wanted to say something, but only shook his head and decided against it. Decided to leave her to feel her shame in peace. Instead, King Belial walked around her and the scene around them began to morph.

'You still have a lot to learn, Alena.' He sighed and maybe she caught just a hint of disappointment in his tone. Alena pulled her arms away to see they now stood within the basement. Unsettled, she could see her own body where it still sat up against the altar table. Alena forced her gaze away. King Belial walked over to his altar and examined Saffron's painting there. His eyes glowed brightly as his voice returned to being as strong as ever. 'I think it's time you do.'

Alena stared. "What do you want to teach me?"

'About what really happened during the Event.'

Chapter 28

Alena grumbled as she leaned further into the couch, her eyes glued to the painting clasped in her hands. "What do you want me to do about this?" she had asked King Belial.

'The truth is hidden within, simple,' the demon responded, an amused air about him. *Of course,* he couldn't just be frank with her and tell her himself. Now, as the next day trickled by, she found herself far too hyper-focused on the task at hand.

Lily sprawled across the coffee table and flicked her gaze between Alena on the couch and Jaxon, who sat amongst the boxes on the floor. The living room was full of junk once more, as King Belial refused to let Jaxon back in until he carried it all inside.

"While I understand you want to keep all my grandfather's things," Alena had said to King Belial. "We really can't live with it all cluttered like that."

King Belial begrudgingly agreed to let the two humans go through the belongings and throw out what was too far gone. Just as long as it was under his watchful eye. Which was still easier said than done.

"What about this... this *thing*?" Jaxon asked as he pulled out a black rectangular object with various buttons on it.

'Oh look, Lily, there's *the remote.'* King Belial chuckled, which made the cat's ear twitch. The cat looked over at Jaxon as though she understood the demon's words. King Belial reminisced, *'Rick lost that thing about twenty years before the Event. The TV was always on the same channel after that...'*

"King Belial says you can toss it," Alena said without looking up. The demon growled in response.

'I did not!'

She blinked and her eyes stung from lack of sleep. That was how cleaning the house had been. It made Alena realize how seriously demons took people to their words. Her grandfather had left the house and *everything* inside it to King Belial. And by the infernal gods, that meant he *did* own everything. Even the trash. Alena rubbed her eyes. "We already threw out the TV. It doesn't even work anymore."

'I guess I'll allow it,' King Belial responded with the mood of somebody who was being forced against their will. Alena gave a sad smile and pried her fingers off the canvas to reach out to where King Belial's energy lingered. He rumbled and the thick air moved closer, only for Alena to snatch her hand back, face flushed. Ever since the previous night, it felt like he had cracked open her shell, leaving her wide open and vulnerable. King Belial appeared more than content to let her sort whatever that was on her own. But Alena didn't know the first place to start. And so she just focused on the goose chase he sent her on instead.

Every time Alena gazed into the painting and saw the beautiful mountain she called home, she felt a strong pull in her heart. She wished things could be easier. She wished she could see what King Belial did, but it was the same old scenery. The remnants of old crivilization taken over by nature. The car sat off to the side, overgrown with weeds and a cluster of white and yellow wildflowers. One was darker than the others.

"It sure would be nice if you could help me out here," Jaxon grumbled.

"Sorry, I'm still trying to figure this out." Alena sighed as she leaned forward and sat the painting on the coffee table with Lily. Jaxon simply turned back to what he was doing, having been used to Alena's strange ways by now. Perhaps she had been a bit too focused lately. She stretched out her limbs and stood to go help him, but hesitated to glance back down at the painting. King Belial only felt amused by her struggle, not even giving her the smallest of hints. Maybe he was just messing with her and there was nothing in the painting that held dark secrets.

"Dark secrets..." Alena whispered out loud as the thought passed through her mind.

'Wouldn't that be something?' King Belial said with the flick of his tail. He felt closer to her now, his energy intrigued. Was she on to something? Saffron Flowers had mentioned dark secrets too. Alena tapped her fingers against the sides of her legs. Saffron Flowers.

Flowers! Alena snatched up the painting and glowered at the flowers. She examined them every which way and flipped the painting upside down. Alena squinted her eyes to examine the tiny details. Oh, the darker flower wasn't even a flower at all. It was so small she hadn't noticed. Amidst the cluster lay a singular feather. White and tipped in a goldish-yellow. It reminded Alena of the one she had seen in the astral caves. She nearly forgot about the experience. Now this just left her more questions than answers. Alena, without thinking, spun around and hurried off towards the foyer. Her movement was so quick, both Lily and Jaxon jumped.

"Uh, where are you going?" the man asked in a panic as Alena snatched her keys off the table.

"I think I figured it out," Alena called as she tossed open the front door. "I'll be back home later!"

"Wait, Alena, don't leave me alone with him!" Jaxon shouted as she dashed out of the house.

The next thing Alena knew, she was speeding down the mountainside back towards the city. Alena pulled onto the city road and reminded herself to slow down to not draw any attention.

A hint of King Belial's energy lingered as he watched over her while she retraced her path to the marketplace. This time she made it into the nicer parts of the kingdom without so much as a single sight of the P.O.E. Alena entered the market grove where a small group of people mulled about. An even smaller group of Paladins lingered by the entrance, but only a couple glanced her way.

Alena pulled up to the same space she had parked in before, got out of the car and headed into the massive area. She kept her breathing calm to not draw suspicion as she went to Saffron's table. There she found the same man from before as he quietly wiped down the table with a cloth.

"Um, excuse me, but where is Saffron?" Alena asked, which got the man to snap a defensive gaze to her. However, as he did so, a flash of recognition showed on his face.

"Oh, you're that friend she was with the other day," he stated. "She's already headed to the chapel."

Alena thanked the man and promptly left the market. She looked across the road towards the old white building. There was a pin-prick of cold sweat that beaded at the back of her neck as she examined the chapel. Was she even allowed to go over there? Alena supposed it wouldn't hurt to take a peek inside to see if she could spot Saffron. King Belial distantly chuckled in her head, but hung back as Alena crossed the stony street.

She walked over the unkempt lawn and climbed up the steps. Each of them creaked with age as she went along. She hesitated when she reached the door. Alena shifted her feet back and forth as she reached up towards the golden and ornate handles. Shoving back her nerves, she cracked open the double doors and looked inside. It was definitely not at all what she expected.

Before her there were pews, of course, but no groups of people like she had assumed. Instead, she found art supplies of all kinds strewn onto the floors and benches. Canvases, paints, clay, and unfinished sculptures. Alena further pushed open the doors and slipped inside, carefully stepping around a stack of homemade papers.

Up upon the pulpit was a grand easel coated in years of paint and a half-finished painting sitting firmly upon it. Behind it was a large stained glass window that depicted images of angelic figures, casting a rainbow-like glow across the large room.

Just before the pulpit, Alena found Saffron. The woman sat in a pew with her chin tilted upwards towards the rainbowy-light. Her hands were firmly clasped. Alena wondered if she should leave, not wanting to disturb Saffron's prayers. Before she could make a decision, the other's eyes flickered open. Saffron looked at her with only a hint of surprise.

"Oh, Alena, hello," she said before she scooted over and patted the seat beside her. Alena gritted her teeth before she accepted the offer and carefully sat down on the old wooden bench.

"I'm sorry to disturb you." Alena fidgeted as she realized this wasn't the public space she assumed it was. "Do you... live here?"

"It's alright, the Lord told me to expect a visitor today." Saffron sighed and sat back against the bench, far more comfortable than Alena. "But yes, this is my home and studio."

"W-Why?" Alena couldn't help but ask, unable to picture the reason someone would want to live in a place like this. Sure, she had her own ancient home, but at least it was an actual house. The chapel didn't exactly look comfortable.

"Why not?" Saffron lightly shrugged. "It was just sitting here abandoned for years. I think the art in the windows is beautiful, and it helps me to feel closer to my Lord."

"You're not wrong," Alena stated as she scanned over the winged beings etched onto the glass. They certainly were lovely. She wondered why the people who had built the place had left it alone. Alena asked as much. "Hmm, why was it abandoned?"

"Do you know much about religions of old?" Saffron asked, her tone a hum as she shifted in her seat to be closer to the other. Alena had never cared to know much about them before and so she shook her head. Saffron's smile was sad as she went on, "Well, back in the Before Times it was most common to worship a singular god. And while people may still practice in the privacy of their homes, it's nothing large like it once was. It can be dangerous to openly worship anything. Leaves a sour taste in people's mouths nowadays."

"Why's that?" Alena asked, her voice sounding far too loud in the echoed halls of the chapel. She felt an uncertain twist in her gut. "Is it really just because of the demons?"

"Demons can be as powerful as God, can't they?" Saffron asked. The smirk she gave Alena was almost devilish. It made her flush, but Saffron hadn't seemed to notice. "Many people of faith were devastated to learn that."

Alena tapped her fingers against her thighs, unable to process the strange aura she sensed around Saffron. She didn't understand her in the slightest, but supposed Saffron likely couldn't get a read on her either. Alena asked, "How did you handle it? You still talk about worshiping God all the time."

And Saffron giggled at that as if Alena had told a funny joke. The latter frowned, uncertain about what she may have said.

"Oh Alena," Saffron said as she glanced down to her lap. She wore a long skirt, it ruffled and flowed around her in waves. Saffron gently took the silken thing between her fingers and lifted it slightly up past her knees. Alena's flush deepened to crimson, but it soon left in confusion as Saffron revealed the marking on her thigh above the knee. The mark resembled an upside-down triangle, the bottom lines crossed to each come down with a hook-like shape. An 'X' ran through the triangle while a 'V' was stationed between the two hooks. It was golden and bright against her dark skin, and if Alena didn't know any better, she would even say it sparkled. Was that a...?

Before Alena could even comment, the mark vanished. Saffron slipped her skirt back over her knees. Her face was a dark red as she stood up despite the other's stupor.

"Allow me to show you," she said as she motioned for Alena to follow. Despite Alena's judgment, she did. The two of them made their way to a side room, where a set of stairs led up to a second floor. Alena didn't question it as Saffron grabbed her hand and led the way upwards into what appeared to have been an attic. From a singular glance, Alena could tell Saffron repurposed it. A circular window was placed in the wall to give the area light. Many colorful fabrics hung from the rafters, separating areas of the large space into different rooms. As Saffron entered and lightly batted away the curtains, Alena caught sight of the other's bed. It was a simple mattress on the ground. The bedding looked soft and lived in with two silk pillows laid out. One of them had the same marking from Saffron's leg sewn into it.

Saffron led Alena to the furthest corner of the attic behind yet another cluster of curtains. It was a bit disorientating as all the colors made Alena's vision swim. It didn't help that there were also pillows set around the floor. The sight of them made Alena's eyes droop with sleep. She kept firm on her feet, however, as Saffron went to the furthest curtain and pulled it aside. Alena choked on her own tongue.

The first thing she noticed was the painting that hung on the wall, another crafted by Saffron's hands. This one, however, was a bit different than the rest. The same person that was in most of her paintings now sat on a rock at the forefront, their feet dipped into crystalline water. Their body, the thing that had initially shocked Alena, was of a masculine form and absolutely stark nude. Despite the light muscles that rippled down their chest and stomach, they held up an elegant hand to cover half their face. What Alena could see of it was a sly and playful smirk, along with piercing blue eyes. On the person's back were attached two massive white wings, the tips of the feather's dipped in yellowish-gold.

Alena grinned, finding herself in a euphoria of realization. She playfully laughed as if the painting's energy was contagious. "Is this your personal stash?"

"Hush." Saffron returned the look as she stepped away from the painting. When she moved, Alena could see there was a corner table just below it. Spread across it were various glass-blown vases, a rainbow of color that matched the massive window downstairs. Beside them sat the tiny bird candle Alena had made. Saffron stepped over to the pillows on the ground and motioned to them. She asked, "Please come meditate with me?"

Alena hesitated, uncertain of how that would work out with another person. However, she followed along and sat cross-legged on one of the pillows in front of Saffron. The other was already sitting comfortably on her own, eyes shut and breathing soothed. Alena fidgeted as she got settled and allowed her eyes to fall. There was an unusual tug against her, but she managed to pull away.

It was as though her body tried to keep her astral form inside, not wanting to relinquish her to this unknown place. Alena settled her breathing and waited for her heartbeat to calm before she finally slipped away.

Alena floated, but this time unlike all of the others, she felt far too light-headed. Weakened even. She staggered and opened her mind's eye, but the world around her was so sharply bright she recoiled away from it. Alena covered her eyes, though that did little to help as the light encased her entire being inside and out.

"Are you okay?" came Saffron's voice, gentle and worried. Alena took a moment to become accustomed before she blinked her eyes back open. She had been so used to the dark and red realms of King Belial she hadn't expected this place to be any different. Alena carefully stepped over to the edge of the stony platform she and Saffron stood on. It overlooked a valley full of luscious green fields and jagged mountaintops. Meadows of wild flowers of every color spread out between them, and past that a crystal blue waterfall. It was almost as if they had stepped into one of Saffron's paintings. Alena turned towards the woman and her breath escaped. Behind them stood a large marbled castle placed right into the mountainside. Gold trimmings were intricately carved across its surface to reveal a mural of flowers.

"What is this place?" Alena asked, her voice sounding small as wind blew down from the surrounding peaks.

"It's my astral temple," Saffron said, but that only made Alena's brows knit together. Saffron noticed the look and explained, "It's the place I made to go during my astral meditations. You don't have one?"

Alena shrugged. "I kind of just stay in a cave."

"O-Oh." Saffron chuckled, but it was not in a cruel way. She looked almost endeared by the answer. Alena found herself flushed as Saffron turned to head towards the entrance of her temple. Saffron let out a loud sigh. "I suppose that's the way of your King."

Alena froze as Saffron's words bounced around in her head. H-Her... King? How did she know... Alena hurried to catch up with Saffron to further question her, but as the two entered through the temple doors the words died away on her tongue. Before them was a long hallway that branched off into many paths leading to different rooms. However, Saffron wouldn't give Alena the time to explore as she grabbed her hand and pulled her along. They headed towards a large oak door at the very end of the hall. As they power-walked, Alena caught a flash of red on the hand Saffron held. King Belial's sigil burned wildly. Oh. Perhaps that was how Saffron knew. If she had a mark too, then surely she would have been able to perceive Alena's.

They both made their way to the very end of the hall, where they passed a window that looked out over the vast mountains and valleys that lay beyond. As Saffron came to a stop just outside the door, she released Alena. Saffron fluttered her shaky hands over herself to fix up her hair and straightened her clothes. The usually confident woman looked so nervous that Alena couldn't help but give her a slight nudge to reassure her.

"Are you okay?" Alena asked, as she should be the nervous one for whatever reason they were there. Saffron took a deep breath to settle herself, though her shoulders remained tense.

"Yes, let's go, we're already late enough as it is," she said as she turned towards the massive doors. Alena worried the other would need help to open them. But as Saffron had made this place, she also controlled it. The doors easily swung open as she approached them. Alena followed her into the room and the brightest of the lights had returned.

Alena squinted as they walked into the center of what appeared to be a large throne room. The same marking... the same *sigil* that was etched onto Saffron's skin was tiled onto the floor.

'Welcome to our home!' A light sing-songy voice came excitedly from the opposite end of the room. *'I've been waiting to meet you, Alena. I've heard so much about you!'*

Alena came to a stop and snapped her head upwards to look upon a tall platform where the massive throne sat. There she saw the same person, the same *being*, from Saffron's paintings as they stood tall and proud with arms outstretched in greeting. Alena's breath was stolen away for not even her friend's excellent artwork could have prepared her for this being's true beauty. They stood with head held high; their golden hair fell around their shoulders and framed their feminine face. Vibrant, almost eerily so, blue eyes stood out starkly against bronze skin and looked as though they stared into her very soul.

The same white wings sat on their back, massive things that Alena didn't doubt could blot out the sun. They were now outstretched to their full span.. At the end of each feather, the white turned to a true gold, not the darker yellow Saffron used in her paintings. The gold shimmered and shined as if it reflected the stars themselves. The being was thoughtful enough to wear a sheer ruby robe over their body, though it left nothing to the imagination. Alena couldn't help but stare. Also unlike the paintings, upon this beautiful creature's head, spouted two grand golden horns that matched the feathers' tips. They curled up and out of their hair, twisting to give the appearance of a halo.

And perhaps if Alena had noticed them from a distance, that's what she would have assumed it was. The angelic being smiled at her, a bright and dazzling thing. Alena could hardly look at them a moment longer and, instead, she glanced at Saffron. The other stared at the being with eyes full of wonder, as if it was the first time she saw them, something Alena *knew* to be false. Her gut twisted at the look in Saffron's eyes. They showed the type of demonic devotion Alena was familiar with, but there was also... something foreign to her. A deeper expression that Alena wasn't privy to. It made her feel like she should avert her stare.

A moment later, Saffron tore her eyes away to look back at Alena, a large smile on her face that mirrored the light-being's.

"Alena," she whispered as if she were out of breath. Nevertheless, Saffron went on as she motioned a grand introduction towards the being before them. "I'd like to introduce you to the Lord I've devoted my life to. Lord Lucifer!"

Chapter 29

*L*ord Lucifer. At the sound of their name the angelic being, no, the *demon*, flapped their wings and took to the air. They glided down and landed a couple of feet away from Alena and Saffron with the grace of a dancer. Alena staggered back as a gust of wind roughly blew against her. The demon looked amused with their dazzling smirk as they tucked their massive wings closely against their back.

'It's such a pleasure to finally meet you,' Lord Lucifer said, voice silky and oozing with honey. It made Alena blush. *'We don't get many new followers these days.'*

Alena felt like a fish out of water as she floundered and sucked on air. The astral realm around her shifted as it threatened to kick her out. She wanted to speak, to greet Lord Lucifer, but found her tongue far too heavy. The demon noticed her hesitation and chuckled. Saffron giggled as well as she set a comforting hand on Alena's shoulder. It helped to keep her there.

"I understand this is overwhelming," she said. "It's not every day you get to meet the great Empress of demons, the King of Pride."

Alena focused on Saffron's hand to calm herself as she tried to smooth over the situation. "Um, how many titles do you have?"

'All of them,' laughed Lord Lucifer. It helped to put Alena further at ease. Lord Lucifer took it as an opportunity to saunter closer to her. Alena stood firm, though she watched their every movement wearily. Now that she was closer to the majestic being and could scan over their graciously androgynous appearance, she noted how fluid it was. Lord Lucifer's form ever shifted like a beam of light through the chapel's stained-glass windows. They would appear just slightly more masculine in one moment and more feminine in the next. A beauty that set her heart alight and she could understand Saffron's adoration.

Lord Lucifer reached out and grasped Alena's hand in both of theirs—a sort of awkward handshake that suggested the demon struggled with the human custom. Alena gave them a nervous smile and curled her fingers around Lord Lucifer's. They had claws on each finger much similar to King Belial, though theirs glittered and shined as if freshly manicured. The king of demons dipped their head to her, and with the movement Alena caught sight of an old and jagged scar that ran from the crook of their shoulder and down their chest.

Lord Lucifer stopped just short of kissing Alena's hand as their eyes narrowed at the sigil imprinted on her skin. They lightly frowned and slowly ran their finger over the marking. Something in their touch that spoke of sorrow. Alena held her breath as the sigil burned hotly and Lord Lucifer straightened.

'Alena,' came a deep and dark voice that sounded so out of place in the halls of light. Alena jumped and found King Belial standing beside her. She took in a sharp breath. His skull bleached white and even his irises glowed more than normal. Alena wondered if it was because of this light world, maybe Lord Lucifer themself, that made everything seem so much shinier than normal. It was not without its downfalls however. Alena scanned over King Belial's grayish skin and saw little dark puffs of smoke rise off him. As though the light desperately tried to burn him away.

Alena winced at the sight with concern in her voice. "Does that hurt?"

King Belial grunted, *'No of course not.'* He left her to wonder if that was the actual truth. She hadn't the chance to question him anymore as King Belial set his massive hand on her hip unprompted and tugged her away from Lord Lucifer and Saffron. Alena whimpered and tried to squirm out of his hold as Lord Lucifer chuckled at the sight. They looked the utmost amused despite their narrowed eyes towards the other demon.

'Oh, Belial, it sure is good to see you again,' Lord Lucifer hummed as the one in question regarded them with a deep nod. Alena felt rather crushed up against King Belial as her hands ran up his side. A mirror of their hug from days before. Her gut twisted and clenched, with the undesirable urge to play it off as though it were nothing. But why was that so wrong, suddenly? Only Saffron carefully watched Alena's actions. So intently it made her shy away. Lord Lucifer clapped their hands together.

'Well, since everyone is here,' Lord Lucifer sang, 'how about we have some tea?'

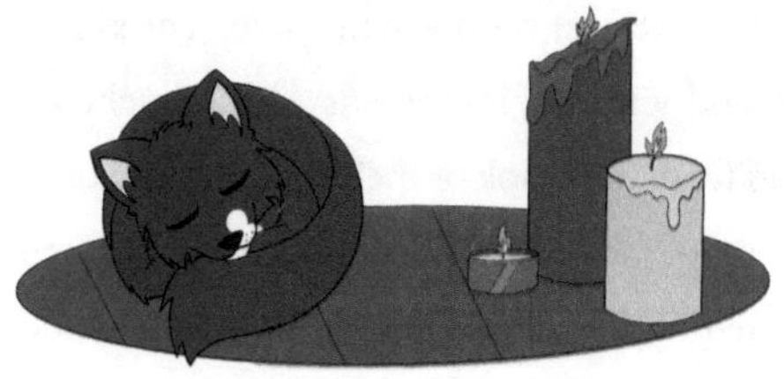

It was a... surreal experience for Alena. The four of them congregated out on a large balcony, one of many that clung to the side of the mountainous castle. They sat at a circular metal table that twisted around like the roots of a tree to form an intricate design. Jewels of every flavor were embedded in the open gaps. The chairs they sat in matched and were relatively small. Alena sat close to King Belial and had to bite the inside of her cheek to keep away the cackling laugh that wanted to escape. The sight of the massive demonic entity in a tiny chair was almost unbearable for her. Had it not been for the unearthly physics of the astral, his weight would have crushed the frail metal. Alena knew better than to laugh as she valued her life. Lord Lucifer, however, giggled and chortled as though it had been a purposeful choice to give the other demon a chair much too small.

King Belial was mature about the situation and pretended not to notice, though occasionally his bony brow twitched. He was mostly silent as the others drank their tea from elegant Victorian styled cups, the tea itself smelling strongly of lavender and honey. Alena leaned forward to sip at hers with difficulty as King Belial's tail found itself gently wrapped around her middle. The touch burned and Alena had to question why the sudden clinginess, but would wait until they were alone.

'So how's your corner of hell been faring lately?' Lord Lucifer made small talk as they sloshed the tea around in their cup. King Belial shrugged and looked bored.
'It's hell.'

Lord Lucifer nodded. *'Those pesky incubi have been running amok of the place lately. They have had no guidance ever since...'* They trailed off, and Alena caught sight of something deeper within the demon she hadn't noticed before. A strange sadness in their eyes.

"O-Oh, yes," Saffron suddenly spoke up. She so comfortably brushed her hand up against Lord Lucifer's bicep. The action was enough to bring back the light to the demon's eyes as Saffron continued, "She has to keep chasing them away from my temple. I have the place warded but they're very persistent."

Warded? Alena looked around. She had read in her grandfather's book about such things, ways to guard your space using energy and other means. She hadn't noticed anything like that around, however.

"You can't see it," Saffron said when she noticed Alena's gaze, "but there's a big bubble around the place."

'You'll do well to hang around Saffron,' Lord Lucifer purred as they slipped over to lean up against their devotee. Lord Lucifer's robe fell around their shoulders, chest exposed with not an ounce of shame. Saffron blushed at the praise as the demon went on, *'She's been at this for years under my guidance and is very well equipped.'*

'He's a bit biased.' King Belial snorted.

'I am!' The other demon beamed and Alena couldn't deny she found herself getting sucked into Lord Lucifer's allure. Even as their form's constant shifting made her dizzy. Curiously, though, she still couldn't pinpoint what to refer to them as. Saffron had said 'she' and King Belial had said 'he'. Was it both? Neither? Alena shifted in her seat and chewed on the inside of her lip. The last thing she wanted to do was offend the demon king... or empress, as Saffron had said. Lord Lucifer blinked,slow and languid, their attention on Alena with half-lidded eyes.

"I hope you don't mind me asking a question..." Alena stammered out towards Lucifer. "But what are you? I mean like, gender-wise, I can't tell."

'I'm the wind in the air around you and the sunshine through the tree branches,' Lord Lucifer said, a smile on their delicate face. *'I am God, a personified ball of light. I can be whatever you perceive me as.'*

That just made Alena more confused than before. She looked to King Belial for answers.

The much larger demon grumbled, *'That's just his confusing way of saying we don't subscribe to your human concepts. Species, gender, race, time, they all exist and do not exist for our kind. Don't ponder it, Alena, it'll drive you to madness.'*

Alena looked curiously at the one beside her, always having seen King Belial as male. She supposed the demonic simply had their own preferences. Similar to the way she, herself, didn't fully feel one set gender. The realization made her feel more at ease.

'Well, as much as I enjoy this small talk about me,*'* Lord Lucifer spoke as soon as there was a lull in conversation. They went on with, *'What about* you, *Alena? King Belial has told me you wanted to talk about something?'*

She what? Alena froze up. Why would King Belial say that? She hadn't even known Lord Lucifer until that day. A flash of gold and the flutter of feathers shot through Alena's mind. The caverns and the painting. Alena felt almost bashful as she suddenly remembered the reason she had even sought out Saffron. The chaos of meeting another demon had practically wiped it from her mind. Alena remembered long ago King Belial said he wasn't the one to tell her more about what the Event was. But maybe... maybe that was Lucifer.

Alena claimed as much, "I wanted to know more about what happened during the Event."

The vibrant light around them flickered and went dim, as if the sun had abruptly fallen from the sky. The warm air chilled as Lord Lucifer's joyous face had grown blank. Alena tensed as their bright blue eyes melted away into a darkened red. Even Saffron grew still and looked at Alena like she had just kicked a puppy. Had she said something wrong? She looked to King Belial for an answer, but his arms were crossed and closed off.

'Why would you want to know about that?' Lord Lucifer asked, their sweet voice raspy and worn. Alena felt like claws had gripped her chest at the sight of the demon. Something deep within her told her to tread carefully.

"It's haunted me," Alena was honest. "It's what my society thrives on, but I don't know what actually happened. How can I continue with demonolatry, if wondering about it is constantly in the back of my mind?" She thought of the beginning of her connection with King Belial. The fear she felt and perhaps still occasionally did. Her concern was that she'd end up like the last President of the United States. Lord Lucifer had grown impossibly still, an action that no human would have been able to do. Saffron squeezed her hand on their bicep before she frantically waved to get Alena's attention.

"I know about it," she said. "I can tell you."

'It should be Lucifer,' King Belial stated. Everyone looked expectantly towards Lord Lucifer until the demon king gave a small nod. Alena noted how ragged they appeared. Nevertheless, a new light appeared in Lord Lucifer's eyes. This one didn't reflect the warmth of the sun, but rather, the scorching fires of hell.

'We used to have the ability to physically manifest on your plane of existence,' Lord Lucifer said. Their tone was hard as if the honey voice had turned to beeswax. *'That was in ancient times. But then the world became more modern and less people believed in us and stopped giving us offerings. So we had lost that ability. There was a shift though. Despite the height of technology, people began to come back to us in droves. Spirituality was on the rise and we were able to reclaim our forms. The world was a changed one, though, of which we were well aware. So we tried to keep things on the down-low for as long as possible.'*

"What changed?"

'Well,' Lord Lucifer went on, *'a celebrity of the time had thanked their fame and fortune on a demon. Which, as you could imagine, threw people into a tizzy. And to make matters worse, some demons...'* They averted their eyes from Alena. *'...had grown tired of hiding away in the shadows and so revealed themselves to society at large.'*

Panic. Ultimate panic and societal collapse would have ensued. That much Alena was certain. Lord Lucifer caught sight of her from the corner of their shadowed eyes. They saw she indeed understood what would have happened. She saw the repercussions every day of her life.

'The current president at the time, a surprisingly open-minded man, wanted to put the people's minds at ease,' Lord Lucifer said. They reached up and sat a hand on the crook of their shoulder, right over the scar. They rubbed it on impulse. *'He wanted to see eye to eye with the demons and their followers. So he threw a grand ball and invited me. Very few people knew of my invitation. And I was very happy, excited even. So I gathered up a group of my oldest and most trusted devotees and took them to the ball. They were happy too, wanted to meet the president and teach him about how I had helped them in life.'*

Lord Lucifer stopped to take in a few deep breaths that Alena knew weren't necessary for the demon. She patiently waited for them to be ready. Lord Lucifer shifted. *'But that night was the only true evil any of us had ever known. The ball had started off a lovely evening, but then men with their guns stormed the halls. The first to go down was the president himself, then... then befell my followers. So many of my closest and dearest companions, my friends... my lovers. All dead.'*

Lord Lucifer's movements were slow and calculated as a wall went up before their features. They held onto themself as if it was all they had. Saffron shifted closer to the demon to snuggle her cheek up against their shoulder. Lord Lucifer's moves were robotic as they glanced at her with round eyes, like they had forgotten she was there. A single white wing moved to envelop the woman, to hold her close as if it were the only means to keep her safe.

This appeared... more than just the connection between deity and devotee. Was that even possible? Alena felt like she had intruded in more ways than one. Saffron wrapped her arms around Lord Lucifer in a hug and the demon rested their head against hers. The astral temple around the group shuddered and wept.

"I'm sorry. You don't have to continue," Alena shot out quickly. It didn't feel right, but still Lord Lucifer gazed at her with dark eyes.

'No, Belial is right,' Lord Lucifer responded. *'You deserve to know your history. To know what you need to watch out for.'* Alena understood. It was messy and violent, but if she were truly going further down the path, she had to know. Lord Lucifer sat back up straight, but kept a defensive arm around Saffron.

'It had been a coup all along,' they said. *'The vice president had set the whole thing up. Kill the president, blame me, use the fear to rule with an iron fist. But what he had failed to remember is I am not a pacifist when it comes to authority. I slayed that man where he stood, but the damage had been done. The country fell to ruin and the man's wife took over for him. She formed the Paladins of Exorcism as a claim to protect everyone from us. Created this bastardized version of a kingdom while the rest of the world* supposedly *burned and died.'*

"Why would they go through all the trouble?" Alena asked, unable to wrap her head around the demon king's story. "It sounds like things would have been so much nicer if the last president made peace with you."

'That is true, but some humans don't want peace, Alena.' Lord Lucifer sighed. *'Some people want power. The people who betrayed the president understood well enough what demons are capable of. How we can help people to new heights. And they wanted to nip it in the bud before it got too out of hand. That's all it is.'*

Something fierce burned in Alena's gut. Her fingers clenched into fists. That's really what all the pain and suffering from the P.O.E. was about? Simply control? The mere thought of it all made her body in the physical realm itch and twitch. Alena rubbed her hands together before she lightly leaned forward to set her hand on the table towards Lord Lucifer.

"I'm sorry you had to go through that," she said, "but thank you for sharing it with me."

They looked taken aback, not expecting a show of kindness from her. Lord Lucifer's eyes finally turned back to blue as the icy wall melted and they set their hand on hers. Their voice was small, nearly timid. *'You seem a very kind human, so I thank you as well.'*

Lord Lucifer also leaned forward, but it was a tad too close for King Belial's comfort. His tail tugged Alena back quietly and so the two separated their hands. Lord Lucifer looked playfully at the other demon, their mood uplifted now that the history lesson was done with. They chuckled. *'Oh you don't have to worry about* me, *Belial. I won't steal her from you, unless...'*

They looked at her from the corners of their lidded eyes. There was a certain look about it that made Alena squirm. Saffron gave a soothing smile and said, "I wouldn't dream of you leaving your king. But I will say my Lord Lucifer is the most patient demon I've met. You don't need to be nervous of her, even when she... does *this*." Saffron shot a look at the demon in question. Lord Lucifer looked as though they didn't know what the human talked about.

The sudden change in mood made Alena light-headed, but she supposed it was better than to dwell on the horrid things Lord Lucifer had gone through long ago. She smiled to keep the mood going.

King Belial noted this and snorted to get her attention. *'Hey Alena. Don't let these two's holier than thou attitude get to you.'*

Alena was about to ask what he meant when King Belial sent glare at both Lord Lucifer and Saffron. He growled, *'They're absolutely fucking.'*

Alena swallowed her tongue as Saffron yelped, her face flushed a near impossible red. Lord Lucifer cackled, the good mood finally returning in full.

'We are!'

And with that, the two humans and their demons continue to talk well into the evening. The air was as light as the grand astral temple around them. However, something dark began to swirl around Alena's head. The uncertainty. The lingering threat of the truths she finally learned.

Chapter 30

"Don't be a stranger, Alena," Saffron said as the two of them stood beside the chapel doors. She had a sad look on her face. "Like I said, we should stick together. I've never met someone else that loves a demon like I do."

Alena wanted to say she didn't *exactly* love King Belial in the same way Saffron did with Lord Lucifer. However, something made her refrain. She hadn't even known that kind of relationship with a demon was possible. Alena flushed and nodded. "Y-Yeah, you too." She truly had a million things she wanted to ask Saffron. It was already late though, and Alena had to return home.

She took her leave shortly after that, for she had much to talk about with King Belial. It was a nervous desperation that had her foot heavy on the gas pedal. Her stomach fluttered as her knuckles whitened against the steering wheel. There was hardly anyone out there as she drove through the city; the sky had grown dark. In the back of her head, she knew she couldn't go *too* fast or a passing Paladin might stop her. Though if they caught her out that late, anyway, she'd get stopped for suspicious activity. Bile rose in her throat.

The rest of the way home, Lord Lucifer's tale of the Event stayed in her mind. Alena still felt the way Lord Lucifer's sorrow had reached her, the biting pain. It reminded her of the way King Belial spoke of her grandfather.

'Keep focused on the road,' said-demon grumbled.

Alena snapped to attention as she turned off onto the mountain path. The drive had otherwise been silent. It was warm, though. King Belial's energy enveloped her body and the entirety of the cab.

Much later, Alena finally arrived home and quietly headed inside. The house was full of King Belial's darkness and Alena couldn't resist as she stopped to revel in the feeling. She hadn't a qualm with Lord Lucifer, but their bright and burning energy was nearly too much. This, though... This felt like home. Alena peeked in on Jaxon who had already fallen asleep on the couch, Lily curled up on his chest.

Alena glanced at the painting still on the coffee table before she crept over and gathered it. Lily popped her head up and let out a loud call. Alena shushed her and motioned for the little cat to follow. The two made their way up the stairs into the bedroom. Alena all but leaped into bed and let Lily curl up beside her. However, she felt alive with energy and knew she wouldn't be able to join the cat in the world of sleep. Instead, she rolled over onto her back and allowed her mind to drift once more. Alena didn't go to the usual cave nor did she go into the astral-version of the house.

Instead, she let herself imagine an ancient dark stone castle hidden away deep within the woods. It was covered in shadow and comfortable. The kind of place where she could hide away from the world. A place where she could be its king! She smiled. Something in her chest felt right as she imagined every floor and room within this castle. Her very own astral temple.

For now, the rooms were mostly empty, as she didn't know what to put inside. But for the one she designated as her bedroom, she placed an enormous bed. One she could only imagine the comfort of. However, it needed just something else. She looked at one of the dark stony walls and placed a painting of Lily, what she thought one of Saffron's might look like. Alena got a little creative with it and placed the cat in a fancy little outfit. Something a queen of old would wear.

With that, Alena finally felt content as she sat down on the edge of the bed. She could figure out the rest later, for now, her energy had depleted. Maybe she could allow herself some sleep, but no, she needed to talk to him. Alena would wait a bit longer.

'How lovely,' came King Belial's deep voice. It sent a shivering thrill through her. Saffron and Lord Lucifer's obvious relationship was still fresh on her mind, but Alena knew she couldn't let that affect her own. Even though she was... curious about it. Alena looked to where King Belial leaned up against the doorframe. Huh. She must have subconsciously made them large enough for him to fit through. Horns and all.

She smiled as those fluttery feelings of *devotion* returned to her. "H-Hey."

They were both silent for the moment, King Belial's arms crossed against his massive chest. He averted her gaze to glance around the room, deep in thought. Alena remained in silence until he pushed himself off the doorframe and approached her. King Belial grunted, *'Was I too rough on you? I apologize if my tail almost squeezed the life out of you.'*

"It's fine." Alena chuckled at the memory. It wasn't different from any of the other times he had clung to her. "Just took me by surprise... Why?"

'Lucifer reigns over pride,' King Belial said, *'but he is also a very lustful demon. I wouldn't put it past him to seduce you away from me.'*

"What?!" Alena flushed, sure she had picked up on the other demon's flirtations. Though she never considered they were earnest. "Why would Lord Lucifer do that, I-I mean, you said Saffron and them..."

'Lucifer loves humans.' King Belial chuckled as his toothy smile grew. *'He likes having lots of them around and rather enjoys coupling with them. Lucifer hasn't had that in a while. I'm just being cautious.'*

Alena remembered the interactions between Saffron and Lord Lucifer, and her face heated. She felt a little dizzy. The fact it was possible for humans and demons to... *couple* as King Belial said. It was almost too much for her. And yet... Alena squirmed in her curiosity. She looked up at King Belial to see that he watched her expectantly. She wanted them to remain open with one another and so asked, "How does that even work?" Alena's voice sounded far too small.

'How does what work?' King Belial asked in a way that suggested he knew what she meant. *'**Fucking**? Haven't your parents told you that? You're an adult.'*

"You know what I mean!"

King Belial chuckled. A rumble that came from deep within his chest as he stepped up closer to Alena. He towered over her when she was standing, but now, as she sat, he was massive. She had to crane her neck as he brought down his skull lower to meet her halfway. If it were possible for the eye sockets of a skull to be half-lidded then that's how Alena would describe the look on the demon's face. His red irises glowered as his tail twitched with interest.

'Would you like me to show you?' he purred and Alena couldn't control the faint and needy gasp that slipped out of her haggard lungs. Her words got lost as even the astral-version of her tongue felt too dry. *Oh, but he could probably help you with that.* Alena curled her fingers in the silken bed sheets to keep the traitorous thoughts at bay. King Belial's gaze flicked down to her hands, an air of amusement about him.

'I mean, you really shouldn't fall asleep in the astral,' he said in a playful tone. *'So why else would you put in a bed?'*

Oh... Oh no! She hadn't considered that. Alena squirmed, but never did she take her eyes off him. It was no longer just her blood that sang out for the demon before her, but her body as well. The treacherous thing. She was about to break her brain. King Belial noticed her turmoil and lightly smiled as he straightened. He sat a single large hand on her head, though for once it brought no comfort.

'Relax,' King Belial said, *'I only joke with you.'* He stopped and took in Alena's disheveled appearance. He chuckled. *'Unless you're interested, of course.'*

Alena's chest still clenched with uncertainty. She asked as much, "I... King Belial, is that really okay?"

'Is it okay to be sitting here, speaking with me like this, on the terms of your society?' he asked. Alena struggled to hear the words as she could only focus on how close he still was. *'Followers of my kind find various ways to show us devotion. Sometimes it looks like the connection between Lucifer and the painter. It just depends on what **you** need from me out of this partnership.'*

Alena felt heavy and no longer had the strength to support herself. She fully leaned forward to rest her head up against his stomach. Her thoughts swarmed like flies, but she couldn't catch a single one. Alena had thought she had the ins and outs of their connection figured out, but now... She whispered, "I'm not really sure."

'There's no need to force anything,' King Belial sighed, his voice just as weary as she felt. He stepped away to sit down beside her on the massive bed. It creaked under his weight and dipped downwards. His tail curled around her waist and slid up her back to rest across her shoulder. Alena let out a content sigh at the contact and allowed herself a moment of indulgence as she rested her cheek up against the limb. As she snuggled against it, King Belial appeared content as well. *'If you're fine like this, then so am I.'*

She was, and so they stayed like that for a while. Alena tried not to let her body doze off in the physical world. King Belial allowed her to stay there and rest up against him, though she noticed how his form slouched and he gazed off into the wall, deep in thought.

"Hey are you okay? You seem down."

'It's nothing you need to concern yourself with,' he said without an ounce of hesitation. She frowned as she pressed up closer to him.

"You don't have to tell me," Alena said, "but I don't mind being an ear to listen."

King Belial's rigid form softened as he set a hand on her shoulder. His thumb comfortingly rubbed in circular motions. *'While I did speak with Lucifer the other day, it had been a few years since I last spent a bit of time with them. I wanted to give him time. I thought maybe he would have been... healed, by now.'*

Alena's brows knitted together as she waited for the demon to continue. *'We used to be at each other's throats a lot in the Before Times. Yet we worked well together. But now I often feel like I'm balancing a porcelain pot on my head when I'm around him. I understand his pain, but I simply miss how things used to be.'*

"I noticed their scar," Alena commented as she remembered how Lord Lucifer held onto themself. She could still remember the agony the sight had given her. So she understood where King Belial was coming from. And yet still to her, the scar didn't make sense. "I didn't know that was possible."

'When we could take physical forms,' King Belial explained, 'we were much more powerful and had an easier time bending your reality to our wills. However, we could also get attacked and injured.'

"If you can control how your forms look, wouldn't they just be able to remove it?"

King Belial sighed. 'Lucifer got that during the Event. He keeps it as a reminder, the last memory of the followers he lost.'

Alena groaned and brought her knees up so she could wrap her arms around them. She rested her head against her knees and whispered, "I hate this, I hate this for all the people they've hurt and I hate it for all of you... Haven't you ever thought of... doing something about it?"

'Absolutely Alena!' King Belial snarled so loudly she jumped. Something hot blazed deep within his eyes. 'Every damn day I wish I could physically manifest again. If I could, I would appear right in the middle of the P.O.E.'s headquarters and take every single one of those bastards out.' King Belial caught sight of the wide-eyed stare his follower gave him and settled. He looked away from her and rubbed at the back of his neck, just behind one of his massive horns.

'Ah,' he sighed, 'maybe long ago I could've, but I am just one demon. Nowadays, the least I would need is Lucifer's help and incredibly strong devotion from a lot more followers than I currently have.'

"You've been thinking about this a lot, haven't you?" Alena forced a smile. The sight of such passion in the demon made her desire for worship swell within her chest. King Belial stared like she had caught him doing something he shouldn't. He cleared his throat and slid the hand on her shoulder up to cup her face.

'Don't...' he whispered, 'don't worry about it, just focus on your own path for now.'

Alena opened her mouth, but promptly shut it. She wanted to talk more, but for her own good, knew it would only cause distress. If the great demonic king couldn't do anything about their broken society, then what hope did she have? She hunched over as the pain of the past few days bubbled over. And her... her wrath, that deep and dark thing that coiled around her heart like a sleeping dragon. It stirred. It wanted to awaken, to do something, but Alena only pushed it further down.

There was not much more for her and King Belial to speak about, and it had already grown so late. She forced herself away from him to lie back on the massive bed. The astral temple around her bled away and the next thing she knew, she stared unblinkingly at the old house's ceiling. Beside her Lily still slept happily, the cat's form rumbled like the motor of Alena's car. Alena rolled over to wrap an arm around Lily, when she felt King Belial's hefty energy still linger close by.

It sent a wave of emotion flooding over her, warmth and safety. Despite herself, Alena reached out to the wave of ripples she caught sight of in the corner. He approached her, enveloping her in his energy like a blanket. Alena sighed as she set her hand on the empty bed sheet beside her. The air there grew heavier. The touch wasn't as tangible as she wished it could be. But for now it was enough. Right now, she was safe and far away from any Paladin that would wish her harm.

Alena soon fell asleep to join that coiling dragon in her chest.

Chapter 31

The day started out like any other as Alena woke up in the afternoon while Lily lightly batted at her face. She enveloped the little cat in her arms as she went about her "morning" routine. However, Alena felt in a daze. Her heart weighed heavy, her head too filled with fog. The day prior had left her a lot to think about and the thoughts sparked a storm. It awakened her old anxieties from the darker corners of her mind where they still lurked.

The truth behind the Event hung like a storm cloud over her shoulders along with the distressing and hollowed pain she felt from Lord Lucifer. Alena desperately wanted to work out her feelings around what she learned, but it was far too much. At least for now. Instead, she thought of her connection with King Belial. It sent a warm buzz across her skin as she headed down into the kitchen to make the daily offering of coffee. Their talk from the night before was still fresh in her mind. The way his heat felt next to her. Alena flushed as she ran over his words about how she didn't have to force their connection to be any one thing. And yet...

Alena set Lily on the counter as she got the coffee started, though her mind was elsewhere. Alena curled her fingers as she recalled the phantom touches of

King Belial's much larger hand on hers— No. Icy claws gripped Alena's heart. Surely such a relationship couldn't work between them. Her feelings towards him was strictly that between a deity and their devotee, wasn't it?

Lily flicked her tail against Alena's arm to break her out of her thoughts. She scratched the cat behind the ear and fed her before she gathered the coffee and headed to the basement. There she would feel comfortable. Alena sighed as she set King Belial's cup on his altar and gazed up at the grand skull on the wall. Alena didn't know when the space had become somewhere she felt safe, but she was glad it did.

She took her grandfather's journal and sat on the plush rug she had added to the stony floor. Alena sipped her cup of coffee as she always did with Lily curled up beside her. She had neared the end of his personal lesson plan for her. It made her heart grow weary and her head felt light. Alena felt like she could understand the old man now and dare she say they were similar. In the very least, they both did truly trust Belial.

"And perhaps that's the best way to connect with the demonic divine," her grandfather had written. *"With the utmost respect people give unto other deities, yes, but also with hearts torn open to reveal the most vulnerable parts of ourselves. To gain the respect or even love of a demon is the deepest kind of bond one may ever witness."*

And now, she would have to move onto the more advanced grimoires hidden away. But perhaps that could wait as she heard the sounds of movement come from above her. Alena chuckled. Jaxon proved to be someone who enjoyed sleeping in far more than she did.

"Come on, Lily."

Setting the book aside, Alena and her faithful companion headed back up the stairs and through the dark hall. She met Jaxon in the foyer, just as he headed out of the kitchen with the rest of the berries they gathered days prior. He popped them into his mouth.

"Hey, are you wanting to finish up the living room today?" He sounded exhausted, eyes baggy. Alena cringed inwardly as she felt cruel for not having helped him in the past few days. She was determined to make up for pushing the brunt of the work onto him. Though by his haggard appearance, she figured the rest of the cleaning could wait.

"How about we head back into the forest today?" Alena asked to be kind. Jaxon's gaze lit up, and the exhaustion vanished from his eyes. Well, at least that made him happy.

She slipped her shoes on by the door and the two of them headed out. With a loud meow, Lily dashed ahead of them. She pranced around in excitement and leapt at anything that moved as she waited for the two humans to follow. Alena chuckled as she and Jaxon entered the woods. They followed the same, now trodden, path they did before. Jaxon foraged more of the edible herbs around them, while Alena quietly observed. She still didn't feel knowledgeable enough to trust herself with finding food.

The surrounding forest was tranquil with only a slight breeze blowing. Soon they reached as far as they had gone before and Jaxon made to circle them back around. Alena hesitated as she looked off into the dark grove. She asked, "How about we try to go deeper today?"

Jaxon's back went rigid and it struck Alena with the immediate worry that she said the wrong thing. Jaxon glanced over his shoulder at her, something hidden in his eyes.

"Why would you want to do that?" he asked.

"I just want to know the place better," Alena answered. The mountain was her home. It was so very much a part of the house, a part of King Belial. She felt soothed by it and wanted to get to know its ins and outs. "If you don't want to, I can go on my own. I won't go too far."

Jaxon took a deep breath to steady himself. "Alright," he said. And with that, he led her off into the direction she wanted to go. They stepped over branches and stones that had yet to be trodden, mirroring the first time they came into the trees together. Alena walked a foot behind Jaxon with Lily close at her heels. Something about the air between them had become tense. Though she couldn't pinpoint it as Jaxon dragged his feet along.

After another five minutes of walking or so, Alena's ears pricked at the sound of rushing water. Lily dashed between her legs and Jaxon's as she ran up ahead of them. Alena had no choice but to pick up the pace and go ahead of Jaxon as she didn't want to lose the little cat. She pushed aside a couple bushes as she exited the thick of the trees into a clearing. The sight made her stop in her tracks.

Before her was a waterfall that cascaded down the mountain to form a crystalline pool. Large fallen boulders surrounded it along with dense plant life that thrived with the freshwater. Lily hurried over to the edge of the pool to stoop down and take a few licks. Her ear flicked at the sound of a skittering bug and she scurried off towards the rocks. Alena approached the area as if in a daze and stopped only once she reached the edge of the pool. She gazed towards the waterfall's source. She couldn't see it; it only went up and up.

Jaxon exited the trees behind her and took a slow look around the area. His brows pinched tightly, deep in thought, as he hurried over to her. Alena noticed him focus on something off to the side and she was quick to follow his gaze. Beside them near the water's edge was a bed of foliage that was completely flattened. She paid more attention and noticed that the clearing was greatly disturbed. The fallen sticks laid broken, and the flowers trampled. Alena looked to Jaxon for answers and when he noticed her, he sighed in defeat.

"This place is…" Jaxon started as their eyes met and Alena could see the gears turn in his head. "Yeah, I stayed here for a bit when I was hiding out. I just didn't… want to come back."

Claws had gripped her throat. The memory of smoke. Alena went to apologize, but Jaxon didn't allow it. He shrugged as he nervously looked off into the forest. He said, "Hey, at least it's a pretty place to have in your backyard."

Things eased back up as Alena couldn't help but agree. It was almost like she had stepped into one of Saffron's paintings. Just like being in the woman's bright astral temple. This, however, existed on the physical plane. Something she could have never fathomed to hide within Lenoria. Alena sat down on one of the rocks and slid her eyes shut as she allowed its warmth to soak into her body. Comfort. She sighed and her muscles relaxed. Jaxon sat down a foot away on a separate rock.

"What are you thinking about?" he asked after a moment of silence.

"Huh?" She blinked her eyes open, flustered as she nearly forgot she had company. "Oh, um, King Belial... He really reminds me of the mountain, so—"

"Of course." Jaxon sighed as he leaned back and took in the sun as well. Alena fidgeted, like she had been caught doing something she shouldn't. Jaxon went on, "I'll be honest, I still don't understand the demon stuff, and it makes me nervous."

"That's fair," Alena said, thankful to change the subject. "I still don't think I can explain, but you asked me once why I would choose to worship a demon?"

"Even if it isn't bad like they say," Jaxon said, his eyes darkening, hiding something within them. "It's still a pretty strong risk if you get caught. Also... demons seem kind of dangerous."

With the look on his face, Alena was reminded of King Belial's wrath towards Jaxon, over what simply appeared to be old furniture. She hadn't been on the other side of that rage before, not to that point. Alena's gut twisted, because while she felt such devotion to the demon, she could still remember when she had first discovered him. She could understand the terror Jaxon must have felt. Alena slowly thought over her next words to say.

"I won't argue that they can't be, but..." Her heart fluttered as Jaxon stared with curious eyes. Alena figured it might as well have been the time to be honest. Saffron never hid her own connection; not from those who mattered.

"I've never felt as safe as I do now with him by my side." Alena sighed, and it was like the waterfall itself had washed over her. "And maybe it'll sound sad to you, but I don't think I've been as close with another human as I am with him. He's just so..." Capable? Strong? Alluring? Alena shut her mouth and glanced away as her face flushed a bright crimson. She had a lot of things she wanted to say about King Belial, but gushing to Jaxon wasn't how she wanted to say them.

"Hrm, you sound like you're in love with him or something." Jaxon laughed, which got an immediate squeak out of Alena. It... It wasn't like that. Not like Lord Lucifer and Saffron. Alena's chest felt tight. Jaxon was quick to wave off the look on her face. "Relax, I'm joking. Maybe he should help you not be so uptight."

Alena raised an eyebrow, glad to be moving on. "Have you seen the world around us?"

His face went blank and Alena realized far too quickly what she had said. The air was tense again as Jaxon looked over his shoulder. As though he had expected a Paladin to crash through the forest at any moment.

"Jaxon, I—"

"It's alright." He put a hand up to kill any apology she had on her tongue. His haggardness returned. "I get it. I'm just saying, this is the world we're forced to live in. Archie was a pretty happy guy, even with the stress of family expectations. I was never that optimistic."

"I saw it happen," Alena stated as the memories flooded back. The feeling she had as she stood in the street and watched. The world was full of smoke, and if she focused even more, she could see the flames too. It wasn't something she wanted to picture. Alena wheezed. "And I just wished I could have done something... but I froze up, I was terrified."

"They would've just got you too." Jaxon shook his head, but then forced a sad smile. "You know he had the biggest crush on you?"

"*Huh*?!"

"Yeah, that's why we went to that shop so much." Jaxon chuckled as he rubbed the back of his neck. "I could tell you wanted nothing to do with us. Archie, though, maybe he was a bit too optimistic."

Alena's heart grew heavier. She grimaced. "What am I supposed to do with this information now?"

Jaxon shrugged, his eyes still held shadows. "I just wanted you to know," he responded. "We've never had any bad intentions for you."

The two were silent after that. Just them and the sounds of nature, the waterfall roaring. Eventually Lily finished up playing and returned to Alena's side to bat at her for attention. She made sure to give the feline some extra love as Jaxon pulled himself back up.

"Well, that living room isn't going to tidy itself," he grumbled and turned to go. Alena held onto Lily as she followed once more. They began the trek back down the mountain. Lily seemed happy enough to be carried this time. Alena flopped her every which way and the tiny cat didn't seem to mind.

By the time they reached the house again, Alena still felt incredibly light, dare she even say content. Despite the heaviness and Jaxon's silence. Being out there in the trees might have been growing on her... a little.

"We should do this more often," Alena commented as she and Jaxon made their way up the steps onto the wrap-around porch.

"I wouldn't complain about that," he murmured as she tossed open the front door. "Not that I don't like your house, but it's kind of— "

Before Jaxon could finish his sentence, Lily's ear twitched and her tail puffed out. The cat yowled and leaped from Alena's arms, leaving scratches behind as she landed with a hard thump in the foyer. Alena called after her as Lily bolted up the stairs and into the bedroom. What on Earth—

And then Alena heard it. A not too distant rumble. She froze and it was like time both stood still and moved far too fast. She spun around to see the sun glint off the hood of a vehicle as it made its way up the long dirt road to her driveway. Alena's blood ran cold. The Paladins of Exorcism.

Chapter 32

I t felt like deathly claws had gouged into Alena's limbs to keep her in place. She couldn't move. She...

'Alena go!'

Alena finally broke away and shoved Jaxon into the house as she leaped inside and slammed the door. She could only hope the agents hadn't noticed them. Jaxon immediately started for the backdoor just as they had planned. Alena went to follow to make sure he made it out safely when she slid to a stop.

"Wait, Lily!"

"Fuck," growled Jaxon as he spun around and ran as fast as he could up the stairs after the cat. "I'll get her!"

Alena hurried after and was only about halfway up the steps when there was a singular knock on the door. No! Alena wanted to freeze up again and panic. Instead, she reached out to feel King Belial's energy for reassurance. It was hard with her mind in such a frazzled state, but he was there with her, she knew. Alena forced her nerves to stay down. She had to think clearly. She could smuggle Jaxon and Lily out the back door, then answer the agents. She could say she was in the tub or something.

"Miss Usher?" the agent at the door called out in a nasally tone as they allowed themself into the house. Alena stared down into the entryway as a tall and lanky person stood there, with dark hair pulled back tightly into a bun. They had sharp features. Alena recognized them as Sir Chambers' intern. Immediately, they caught sight of her. "Greetings, Miss Usher."

The dragon of wrath living in Alena's heart sparked awake as she glared at the intern. She had to keep her cool though, so she further forced the feeling away. Instead she put on a false smile, a small one, not too big.

"It's just Alena, no *Miss* anything, please," Alena said, deciding to make small talk. She desperately wanted to glance behind her towards the bedroom. That was too risky. It would bring attention to it.

"Oh, Alena, of course." The intern nodded with a sort of understanding that managed to further cool Alena's anger.

"I'm here on behalf of Sir Chambers," they explained, even though they both were well aware. They still wore that uncaring expression from before, but if Alena dug deeper, she could see a sharp glint in their eyes. They took in her every movement. Calculated.

"Where is he?" Alena decided to remain curt but not too hostile to the other. She wanted them gone and out of her and King Belial's house as soon as possible.

"We had a busy schedule today, so he's taking care of business elsewhere," the intern went on, not at all aware of the storm brewing within the person before them. "I'll just do a quick once over and be out of your hair."

"And your name is?" Alena asked so she could know what to call them.

"That is... not important," they responded, nearly on guard as if it were some well kept secret. And perhaps to these low-ranking members of the P.O.E. it could have been.

"Is there at least a title I can call you?" Alena raised a brow. "Like Sir or Lady?"

"Neither of those fit me, I'm afraid."

"Yeah, I get that." Alena sighed. She was still on edge as she motioned vaguely towards the living room. "Well don't let me keep you from your job."

The intern nodded, jotted something down on their clipboard and then headed into the kitchen instead. Alena stiffly followed.

'Just like last time, keep your cool,' she heard King Belial's deep voice reverberate around her skull. On one hand, she was glad to have him there beside her. On the other, her nerves pricked with concern that him being there would give her away. *I'm really trying,* she thought back to him.

Alena hovered in the kitchen archway as the intern waltzed in like they owned the place to scan over every inch and surface. She leaned against the wall and watched them, hoping she'd keep a calm appearance. Alena's heart was anything but calm as it hammered nigh painfully within her chest. Her mind just kept jumping to Jaxon and Lily upstairs. The intern would eventually make their way up there and then...

There was a gentle creak on the stairs and a cold sweat dripped down Alena's brow. She dared not turn her head fully and so glanced from the corner of her eyes. There on the landing was Jaxon, pale as a ghost as he clutched onto a squirming Lily. His hand was roughly clamped over her muzzle. Alena sucked in a sharp breath and held it there as Jaxon crept his way down into the foyer. She flicked her fingers to tell him to come no further. Jaxon winced as Lily's claws dug into his arm, but he still held on strongly as he frantically looked for a way to go.

"So, where'd you get all this?" the intern asked as they shuffled inside Alena's cupboards and examined the wild plants she and Jaxon had gathered. The intern turned to face Alena.

Jaxon leaped into the dark hall. There was a shuffle and a small clank, which Alena quickly covered up with a loud cough. She wiped at her mouth while the intern's face pinched tight like they had licked a lemon.

"The forest around here," Alena casually said, ignoring the look of disgust on their face.

"You know a lot about foraging?"

"Only some things." Alena shuffled her feet back and forth. She dragged the conversation reluctantly as she desperately wanted to hold that information close to her chest. Alena had to be honest though, at least to a point. She shrugged. "Figured I should learn while living out here."

The intern nodded and headed back into the foyer, now done with the kitchen. Alena obediently followed, sparing only a glance towards the dark hall. This was good. Jaxon knew how to get into the basement, he and Lily could hide away there. Relief cascaded over Alena like cool rain and her racing heart thumped back down to a normal pace.

"Oh, I see you've been cleaning up in here," the intern commented as they walked deeper into the living room. Their eyes scanned every corner of the room.

"Slowly," Alena said as the intern peered inside one of the cardboard box's top flaps. Alena continued to hope there wasn't anything incriminating inside as she forced herself to continue. "It's a lot of work for just one person."

"Is it difficult living alone out here?"

"At first." Alena was honest. "But I've found it to be pretty peaceful now," she lied. The intern nodded with a hum as they continued to trifle through the boxes and other things scattered across the floor. The entire time the intern moved and examined the area, they kept their body tilted ever so slightly towards Alena. A way to keep her in their peripheral.

Eventually, the intern finished their inspection of the living room. They stepped around Alena and made off towards the staircase but froze. They took in the dark hall beside them, brows furrowed. It would be fine, Jaxon would be down into the basement by then.

The intern sounded displeased. "It's still dark through there. We told you to put better lighting in."

"O-Oh, yeah, sorry about that," Alena stuttered as she searched her brain for an excuse. Her head filled with fog in her panic.

'The nails,' King Belial growled and Alena was quick to say, "I couldn't find anything to pull the nails out of the boards."

The intern looked at her more fully, trying to gauge any change in expression. Alena wanted to scream, but stared cooly at the other. The intern didn't see what they wanted. They turned away and pulled out their solar powered flashlight. The sight of it made bile rise in Alena's throat as the intern shook it. It flicked on. Alena prepared to follow the intern into the dark just as she had all the times before.

Something was wrong.

King Belial's energy hissed and coiled beside her like a snake. A sharp pain from his worry flooded into her skull. Alena gaped and wanted to ask him what made the demon feel so different. The thoughts died quickly as the intern took a couple strides into the darkened hall. On the third step, there was a soft clatter as they stepped on something laid in their path. Alena felt numb. There shouldn't be anything in the way.

The intern moved their foot and looked down at the offending object curiously. They stooped down and when they came up, Alena thought perhaps her heart would stop completely. Dangled from their boney fingertips was a dark violet ribbon with a strange jagged coin strung onto it. Lily's collar. The key to the basement.

Chapter 33

The house appeared to ripple, but Alena wasn't in the astral this time. Her head was light, and she wobbled as she felt faint. The intern leaned closer to the ribbon to examine the name inscribed onto it. Alena couldn't breathe. Them finding it was one thing, but if Lily wasn't wearing it... She and Jaxon... Alena took in a wet and wheezing breath that made the intern's gaze snap to her.

'Alena, stay calm,' King Belial's voice boomed beside her, just as strong as ever. His energy enveloped her, and she could almost feel his arm wrap tightly around her chest. She breathed easier as King Belial pressed up against her back. His words shot in her ear. *'I'm right here with you. Have confidence in that.'*

"Who's Lily?" the intern asked, looking from the key to Alena.

"I'm not sure," Alena rushed out. She cleared her throat and went on more calmly, "That probably belonged to my grandfather. It must have fallen out when I was moving boxes around." The words sounded hollow to Alena and she wanted to kick herself. The intern noted the tone of her voice as well; their eyes pinched at the corners. Alena could see how their shoulders drew back and tightened. On guard. The intern placed a singular hand on their hip to finger at the hidden dagger there. They slowly turned and started their walk down the hall. A spark of adrenaline made Alena woozy as she stumbled after.

"Hey wait," she called, "maybe you should just skip the hall this time. It's too dangerous with how dark it is. I don't want you to get hurt. Let me remove the boards first."

"It's fine," the intern snapped, their tone as sharp as their looks. They had none of Alena's bullshit, and she knew that. The intern walked to the end of the first hall and turned down the next. The light from their flashlight cascaded down the dark corridor and they froze in their tracks. Alena couldn't breathe as she heard them question...

"Who are you?"

"Just a friend, visiting..." came Jaxon's voice. The world fell upon Alena's shoulders. It wasn't just King Belial's energy, it was soul crushing. She reached the intern's side, her demon close behind, and caught sight of Jaxon at the end of the hall. It may have just been the artificial light, but he looked ghostly pale as he cowered on the other side of the bookshelf. He held something dark in his arms that he desperately tried to hide. Alena's heart sank.

"Keep your distance!" the intern yelled at Alena as they jumped away from her. They held her firmly in their gaze. "Why didn't you mention someone else being here?"

There was nothing Alena could say to make the situation any less guilty, but still she whispered, "I thought he... left already." The intern wasn't convinced. They stepped further down the long corridor towards Jaxon. Their body was ridged and quivering like a frail leaf in winter. Alena was on edge from a few feet behind while they strode up to Jaxon.

The man was deathly still as the intern shone their bright light onto his face. He winced and Alena could only hope they wouldn't recognize him as a wanted fugitive. The intern went to speak, but the words died away as Jaxon's arms shook with movement. Alena's fingers curled into fists, her muscles grown taut as she remembered her spars with King Belial. The intern looked down at the writhing shadow in Jaxon's arms and lowered their flashlight.

"Is that a... cat?" The intern's voice was hollow. In an instant they forgot about Jaxon and whipped around to face Alena, tongue lashing. "Those are forbidden! You know I'll have to report this to the higher ups."

Desperation clawed at Alena's throat. "N-No, please, she was my grandfather's!" What else could she say? Her body was aflame as terror and aggression tore through her. Each pricked at her skin like Lily's claws. The dragon in her heart began to boil.

"That doesn't matter, it's illegal," the intern said, eyes sharp and heartless. "We'll have to confiscate it and—"

It bubbled over.

"*No!*" Alena snarled and slammed her foot on the ground and the house shook as King Belial's hoof slammed in tandem. "Lily isn't going anywhere!"

Lily yowled and finally fought her way out of Jaxon's arms. She slashed at his skin and he dropped her with a grunt. Lily leaped at the intern with claws unsheathed. They let out a blood-curdling scream as the cat latched onto the hand over their holster. Lily sank her needle-sharp teeth into the limb. It reminded Alena of all those times Lily would devour her meals. As the intern fell back into the bookcase, Alena rushed forward to reclaim her cat. However, by the time she moved, Lily detached herself and bounded away. Her black pelt blended into the shadows unseen.

The intern wailed as they fell against the wall beside the bookcase and slid down to the floor. Before either Jaxon or Alena could do anything else, they whipped out their dagger with their good hand.

"Stay back! Get away from me!" they screamed as they waved their weapon about. It was still so dark in the hall and yet Alena's vision grew to great clarity as she could see nothing but the weapon. It glinted and her chest burned. She found it hard to breathe. She wanted to glance at Jaxon to see if it had the same effect on him, but she dared not look away. The intern gulped in ragged breaths as they pushed themself up against the crook of the bookshelf. They shoved their hand against it to use it as leverage to stand. Against their weight, the bookshelf slid open ever so slightly. The only thing to stop it being the chain that kept it locked.

Alena felt so cold. The intern mirrored her expression.

They kept the dagger firmly aimed at Alena and Jaxon as they gapped at the bookcase beside them. Alena couldn't see what they did, but knew it had to be the lock. With just a hint of darkness from the basement beyond. The intern came to the same conclusion Alena did so long ago. They looked down at the purple ribbon still clasped in their hand.

"Please, don't..." Alena rasped, her voice a shell of what it was only a moment ago. The intern ignored her or perhaps hadn't even heard. They only moved to slide the key into its lock and soon the chains fell to the floor with a loud clatter. The house around them echoed as no one dared to make any movement. Alena and Jaxon were both too petrified of the weapon, and so the intern was the only one with enough confidence to grasp the bookshelf and pull it open. Though even with the dagger in hand, said confidence hindered on a thread.

Alena's knees quaked together as her deepest terrors came to light and the basement was revealed to the P.O.E. agent. A hushed breath slipped from the intern's mouth as a frightening and dark miasma wafted up from the depths before them. The basement creaked and shifted as if itself were a live beast that laid in wait for its meal. The intern looked as though they would faint. Alena certainly felt the same.

And so she internally pleaded, *"Oh King Belial, please do something!"* At the thought, the demon's warmth returned to her side. Her leg lightly tingled as his tail brushed up against it.

'How far would you go for what needs to happen?' King Belial asked, his voice breathy against her. Alena's brows furrowed, for what had he meant by that? Was now really the time to be so cryptic. She wanted to argue with him, beg him to tell her what to do. But... Alena thought back to the days and weeks, down to the hours and minutes they had spent with one another. His protection. His companionship. And dare she say what may even be his trust. King Belial had yet to let her down. Alena took a deep breath to settle her frazzled nerves. She would trust him. There was no reason for her to not.

The intern turned their flashlight towards the cavernous basement and started their descent. Their footfalls on the old steps reverberated in Alena's ears.

Alena took a careful step forward as the intern vanished further down the steps. Jaxon finally broke his stare to glance at her, though he still looked just as petrified. Alena wanted to say something to Jaxon, anything, but her voice failed. Instead, she stood on the edge of the basement's entrance, watching the intern reach the second to last step.

Alena could see the way their spine went rigid as they shone their flashlight into the room in front of them. From her vantage point, Alena couldn't see what they did, but she knew... A table at the end of the room. To the intern it was full of nefarious ritualistic objects, dark candles and jagged crystals, with cups scattered around filled with mysterious liquids. Stood above it all being the large skull with a clearly demonic symbol carved onto its forehead. Though to Alena everything the intern saw was an act of devotion. The candles crafted tenderly by her own hands, the cups once filled with the coffee of their mornings together.

The intern wouldn't understand that. They couldn't know what true devotion felt like, for their government was run on fear. For only a split second Alena let herself wonder what would happen now. The intern would likely turn around and drive the dagger into her gut as they'd been taught. Alena would bleed out onto the floor, giving one last offering to Belial in her death. The thought not only terrified Alena, it felt like a hole had torn into her chest. If she died then who would take care of Lily and the rest of the house? Who would be there to sit with King Belial in the cold and lonesome mornings?

Alena realized while she may have been conflicted about the means of her and King Belial's connection, she was... happy. For perhaps the first time in her life. And she did *not* want that to be taken away from her. The icy claws within her gripped her stomach and made the muscles in her legs tighten. King Belial was beside her and oh, how she adored him. And anything she chose to do in that moment, she chose to do for him. For both of them.

Alena launched herself down the steps, her footfalls memorized even in the dark. Jaxon made a sound, but it was muffled as her ears roared. The intern whipped around with a shriek, dagger raised. Alena collided with them and the two fell hard into the basement.

The bloodied dagger clattered against the stone floors.

Chapter 34

The world spun in circles as shadows ebbed at the corners of Alena's vision. Her ears rang and she thought perhaps she was in a different realm. As though the fall from the stairs had sent her straight to the astral. The shock from having thrown her body onto the basement floor began to ease away as she blinked open her eyes.

"Alena, are you alright?!" Jaxon called as he bounded down the basement stairs. He only froze once he reached the bottom step. Alena's eyes adjusted to the low light. The intern's flashlight had landed somewhere off in the dark, to illuminate a singular corner of the basement.

Alena was sprawled out on the ground and beside her was the intern. Below them, their ankle was twisted at an awkward angle. As she stared downwards, droplets of a deep scarlet fell to the stoney ground. Alena stared as more blood came and soon the burning of her cheek was too much to ignore. She reached up and immediately flinched back at the sharp pain. More blood spotted along her fingers. Alena winced as she pushed herself upwards to turn the world right-side up again. Jaxon stepped off the staircase and went to her. He reached out a hand which she gladly took and allowed him to pull her to stand.

"That knife got your face pretty good," Jaxon fretted as he hovered his hand around her wound. Alena could only imagine what her face looked like.

"I... I'll be fine," Alena uttered breathlessly. As soon as the words came out, Jaxon pulled her into a hug without warning. Her spine went rigid at the contact.

"You really scared me there," Jaxon said and despite her discomfort, Alena returned the hug. Her hands shook, but at least Jaxon felt very warm. King Belial's heat pressed up against her back, making her feel just a little too closed in. She welcomed it.

'That was stupid,' the demon growled in her ear, his breath like steam. His large hand cupped her side, gently. *'But I am glad, you're okay.'* Alena let out a content sigh and motioned to lean into King Belial's touch, but the demon moved away. He hummed. *'So what are you going to do, now?'*

Alena pulled herself away from Jaxon, though he still lingered. She looked down at the intern, who also began to stir. And that's when Alena saw it. Beside them only a foot away, the dagger still laid, coated in a light layer of Alena's blood. Before the intern could fully come to, Alena leaped for it, staggering as her head pounded. Despite the instincts within her that screamed to get as far away from the weapon as possible, she snatched it up. Jaxon tensed as Alena gripped the dagger.

The intern pulled themself up into a sitting position as they slowly blinked. They took in Jaxon and Alena on either side of them, dagger in the latter's hand. They shrieked. The sound echoed off the walls and Alena flinched. King Belial growled as his energy continued to curl around Alena. The intern attempted to stand but as they put weight onto their ankle, they roughly fell back down.

"D-Don't hurt me!" they cried and tried to crawl away from the two, only making it as far as the closest wall. "I don't want to die on the clock!"

King Belial was intrigued at that, though Alena hadn't enough time to decipher whatever the demon now plotted. Jaxon sneered at the intern as he realized he and Alena now had the upper hand. The man snapped, "Then why take a job where you have to hunt after oh *so* dangerous demon worshipers?"

"My brother convinced me it would be easy!" the intern shouted as they cradled their injured hand. "Because, like, who *actually* worships demons?!"

Alena winced at the sight of the limb. Lily had done a shocking amount of damage that she hadn't realized was possible for a cat. The intern started to cry, their tears cascading down their face much like the waterfall within the forest. Alena went to take a step towards them, unsure what else to do. However, they only screamed at her to stay away and so she did. Whatever fight that was left within Alena left her as she watched the sad display.

"So should we just like... *get rid* of them?" Jaxon asked after a moment of silence which only made the intern wail louder. Alena snapped her gaze to him as though he had grown a second head.

"What? Of course not, Jaxon," she said. Alena may have been into an array of suspicious activities, but murder wasn't one of them. She would not prove the P.O.E. right in their assumptions and prejudiced fears. Alena felt King Belial's inquisitive stare as she glared down at the intern. "We aren't bad people, we aren't *them*." Still that begged the question, the same one King Belial had asked... What *was* she going to do now? She needed to figure things out. Alena still couldn't get all her thoughts straight. Her face was still bloody.

"Can you keep an eye on them for a bit?" Alena asked Jaxon. The man looked uncertain but nodded. He crossed his arms and watched the intern with narrowed eyes as if he expected their sobbing to be an act. Alena staggered over towards the boxes and opened up Lily's to snag an old blanket from it. It wasn't sanitary, but at that moment, Alena didn't care. She pressed the old fabric to her wound and it greedily soaked up her blood.

She sighed and headed further into the basement to the altar, of which she promptly set down the bloody dagger. King Belial immediately hovered over it. *'Oh, is this for me?'*

"I'm just going to keep it there for a bit," Alena explained. "Even if they manage to stand, I doubt they'll be brave enough to take it from your altar."

Alena sat on the floor, legs crossed, as she slid her eyes shut and tried to relax her breathing. It was dark behind her eyelids as she tried to detach herself from her body to meet with King Belial. She needed to know what she should do. She needed to speak with him upfront. Her face still burned and her head pounded. The clear indications of her physical body kept her grounded to the spot and she desperately tried to clear away the fog in her head.

'I can't help you with this.' King Belial's voice echoed around the dark space.

"But I don't know what I'm supposed to do."

'You're smart, you'll figure something out.'

"There are so many possibilities and I don't like them. King Belial, I'm so... scared. I don't want to make a mistake."

'That's simply a part of human existence. You make mistakes and learn from them. And we demons are here to help you when the mistakes are a bit too much.'

Alena grumbled for she wouldn't get much of anywhere with him. She still sat there, though, and wondered. She could speak it over with Jaxon, but something about the way he stared at the intern unsettled her. He didn't look all there and likely was still full of adrenaline. Alena tried to drop further into the darkness of her mind, trying to think things over while she still had peace and quiet. She felt so haggard, however, and she was so tired of the stress and terror that constantly tore her body apart. Alena was tired of having to do all these things alone. She had King Belial, and while she adored him he was still a demon, and didn't exactly meet her eye to eye. Alena wished Saffron was here. She found her so much easier to talk to. So much more well adjusted to the life they lived than she or Jaxon were.

Slowly her body finally felt lighter and airy, as though she could fly away. Alena wondered...

"King Belial, I want to go talk with Saffron. Can I do that?"

*'Hmm, now **that** is something I could help you with,'* he responded and instantly his rough hand gripped her astral body. Alena yelped as she was forcibly tugged from the physical and thrown into the void. King Belial's voice was the last thing she heard.

'Just go with the flow!'

Her body contorted and was shot out of a portal. Alena rapidly blinked her mind's eye and gasped as she floundered about within the brightly lit hallway. The temple before her was a familiar one as she gazed upon the floral patterns and glaring lights. She staggered to her feet and hurried over to the nearest window. It looked out onto a vast garden where a singular apple tree grew in front of a small rocky pond.

Alena could sense Saffron was down there. Her gut burned with intuition as she ran further down the hall and turned sharply into another corridor. She came upon a set of golden stairs that lead downward and wasted no time to take them two at a time. Alena came upon a grand archway that led her into the garden she had seen. She slowed her pace as she walked out into the array of rose bushes and lavender plants. The grass was a lush bright green and Alena couldn't help but be unsettled. Almost like the world around her was too perfect.

She came upon the tree, the apples on it just as red and shiny. Alena grew the strangest desire to pluck one and bite into it. Would it taste fake or like the greatest apple she ever had? She ignored the feeling. Something warned her that it may not be a good idea to partake.

The tree's trunk was vast and it took her a few seconds to walk around it. A gentle hum reached her ears as she went. On the other side of the tree Alena found Saffron on the lap of Lord Lucifer. The two of them hadn't noticed her as they were solely focused on one another, leaned comfortably up against the tree. Saffron had her head rested on the demon's shoulder, her eyes shining with the pure devotional bliss that made Alena blush. She didn't think she could ever give such a look to King Belial. Saffron ran her fingers through Lord Lucifer's silken gold hair, their eyes lidded shut with a content look on their face. The humming was coming from them. Their claws lightly scratched against the sigil mark on Saffron's leg.

Alena stood there, unsure of what to say. She half felt like she should just turn and leave. However, there were much more pressing matters to attend to. She cleared her throat. "Oh, um, hey."

"Alena?!" Saffron gasped as she leaped from Lord Lucifer's lap, face flushed greatly. The demon's crystalline blue eyes snapped towards her and became red, their face contorted into a mixture of surprise and anger. Alena saw their form flicker. Their golden hair and horns turned an inky black that dripped down onto their previously white wings. The feathers changed to resemble that of a raven's. The astral realm around them immediately changed from day to night, but the stars overhead still provided enough light to see. Saffron glanced at Lord Lucifer with concern and not an ounce of fear, though Alena herself shivered. It made her remember Lord Lucifer was a demonic entity just like King Belial.

'What are you doing here?' Lord Lucifer snapped, all warmth from their first meeting gone. Their wings quivered as one hovered defensively around Saffron. *'You shouldn't be able to enter like that.'*

"I think King Belial just kind of... threw me." Alena stammered out before the situation could escalate any further.

'Ugh, of course...' Lord Lucifer trailed off and slowly withdrew their wing. The sky lightened back up to dawn, though the demon still stayed in their darker appearance, aside from their eyes which turned back to blue. Lord Lucifer frowned. *'Apologies for the animosity, darling. You... surprised us.'*

"I'm sorry for barging in," Alena was quick to say as her own astral form eased. She shook her head, there was no time to dwell on what happened. Jaxon still waited for her back in the physical. "I need your help." Alena gave the two a brief rundown of what happened back at the house. She made sure to keep out the minor details, because even as she gave the gist of it, Alena saw Saffron's horrified expression grow. Lord Lucifer quietly listened to the tale, expression void of emotion. When she was finished, Alena pleaded, "Please, I don't know what to do."

The group was silent as Saffron looked to be in deep concentration. Then she nodded. "I'm afraid I can't help you from here, so I'll come to you." Alena blinked, shocked by that, but was elated nevertheless. Perhaps with Saffron there, *something* could be done to smooth over the situation. Except...

'Saffron, you can't go,' Lord Lucifer cried out in shock. *'It's far too dangerous!'*

"It'll be fine," Saffron said as she turned from Alena to face the demon. "Because I have the Lord to protect me, right?" Lord Lucifer's expression became one of distress as they shuffled closer to Saffron. Alena stepped back to give the two some space.

'There's not much I can do if they learn the truth about you... about us,' Lord Lucifer whispered. Their voice regained the softness it had when they told Alena about the Event.

"I know that, Luce."

'Then why would you go and leave me?'

"Because there's not many of us left," Saffron said as she leaned forward to envelop the demon into her arms. She snuggled into their chest. "I made a promise to you that I'd help out as many demonolaters that I could." Lord Lucifer hugged her back as though it would be the last time. Alena frowned because despite their anger a moment ago, she still couldn't bear to see such sorrow on the divine being's godly features. She stepped forward.

"Lord Lucifer, may I also make a vow to you?" she asked, which got the duo's immediate attention. Her palms in the physical world sweated as she hoped this wasn't a vow she would grow to regret. Alena declared, "I promise you, I won't let anything happen to Saffron while I'm around." Lord Lucifer blinked and their expression turned the most serious she had seen it before.

"That is a bold claim, Alena, and I accept it," they said without hesitation. "But be warned I do not take kindly to those who break their oaths to me." Alena supposed she could also accept that.

She turned to Saffron and motioned her to come closer, to go away with her back to their respective physical bodies. Saffron nodded, and before she left, planted a dearly loving kiss upon Lord Lucifer's lips. They returned it in earnest with a hidden desperation that was heart shattering. Saffron parted with them, but their arms still reached out for her as she hurried to Alena's side.

Alena wished she could give them more time, but that was currency she didn't have. Alena asked, "Will you be able to remember the direction to my place if I tell you here?"

"I will simply have Lord Lucifer guide my way," Saffron assured. Alena nodded, a nervous twist in her gut. Her responsibility to Lord Lucifer began to hang heavy on her head.

'Saffron, Alena!' Speak of the Devil, the two in question turned to look at the demon in question. Lord Lucifer stood there, expression stony and wings spread

out to great lengths. The astral wind blew and carried with it Lord Lucifer's voice. They called, *'Be aware that when you leave here, the path you choose is one that cannot be changed.'*

Chapter 35

Alena slowly dabbed the blood off her face at the kitchen sink. The wound stopped bleeding sometime during her meditation, though it still stung. She hadn't seen how bad it looked yet, and wasn't exactly looking forward to that. So instead she gathered up Lily and cleaned the intern's blood off her muzzle. The cat lightly squirmed but allowed it, her green eyes gazing deeply into Alena's dark brown. She felt numb as she staggered her way to the stairs by the hall. There she continued to sit and hold onto Lily as she and Jaxon waited for Saffron to arrive.

"Can we trust this friend of yours?" Jaxon asked, tension in his voice. He didn't want to deal with any more people.

"Yeah, she's... trustworthy." She wanted to say, *"She's like me,"* but that wasn't Alena's knowledge to share. He accepted that answer, but never moved away from the hall's archway. He stood, arms crossed and guarded as he stared off into the darkness like the intern would somehow escape the basement. Jaxon's fingers curled on the dagger.

Alena wasn't all that concerned with the intern. No. What kept her on edge was the old mountain road that led to her property. Of the intern's vehicle that now sat abandoned outside behind Alena's. Would Sir Chambers or the other agents of the P.O.E. notice them missing? Alena imagined it was less of a 'would' and more of a 'when.' She wondered what the punishment of harming a Paladin would be. Could the P.O.E. do anything more severe to her than burning her alive for worshiping a demon? Alena shivered and held Lily closer to her chest. She had to keep it together for all of their sakes.

'You don't have to do that for me,' King Belial said. *'Feel free to let it all out when we're alone together tonight.'*

It flabbergasted Alena that he could be so calm. As if he already knew the outcome of whatever was to come. And maybe he did. She sighed and leaned into the hefty energy condensed around her. She wished she could embody even a fraction of his confidence.

The sound of a car up the drive made Alena's grip on Lily tighten. The cat squeaked and struggled out of her hold. Alena and Jaxon snapped their wide-eyed stares towards the door. Alena kept her calm as she leaped up and hurried over to a window. A vehicle had parked just behind the intern's. Saffron got out a moment later, and so Alena felt she could breathe easy again.

She wasted no time to throw open the door as Saffron approached the house. The woman carried a bag with her, of which she quickly dropped to the side as she caught sight of the other. With a gasp she asked, "What happened to your face?!"

"Don't worry about that right now," Alena said, exhausted. Saffron listened and dropped the subject. Instead, she wasted no time to bring Alena into a crushing hug. Alena not only accepted the action, she melted into it with a broken whine.

"Sorry it took so long," Saffron said as she motioned towards the bag, "I didn't know how long I'd be here, so I brought an overnight bag. I hope that's not too presumptuous of me."

"N-No, you're always welcome here," Alena got out as she finally released the woman. Saffron fully entered the foyer so Alena could shut the door, and with her brought a small gust of wind. Upon the breeze, Alena heard the slightest hint of a wing's flap and the room grew somewhat brighter.

"So you must be Saffron," Jaxon regarded. She looked him up and down, eyes wary, and Alena could feel the same expression from Lord Lucifer. Then Saffron smiled.

"That's right, and you are?"

"Jaxon."

"Nice to meet you."

"Hey, we can do better introductions later," Alena spoke up which turned the others' attention to her. She frowned and averted her eyes. "That P.O.E. intern is down in the basement. They sprained their ankle and got a nasty bite on their hand. It might still be bleeding."

"Bite?" Saffron asked, to which Alena motioned towards the little cat that quietly sat on the stairs. Saffron's eyes lit up. "Oh my lords, you have a kitty!"

Saffron walked over to Lily and snatched her up without a struggle. Lily purred and snuggled up against the woman's shoulder. The cat remained calm in Saffron's arms as the woman prodded at her mouth, feeling her fangs. She turned to look at Alena, eyes ablaze and serious. She asked with a new found urgency, "Do you have a first aid kit of any kind, Alena?"

"Probably in the bathroom," she motioned to Jaxon to go look. He hesitated, eyes dark despite the light that Lord Lucifer brought to the room. After a moment, he finally moved and hurried up the stairs. As they waited, Alena felt the energy within the room shift and change. She noticed a brief flash of shadow begin to mingle with the sparkling light. They flickered across the room towards the kitchen. Alena wondered if King Belial and Lord Lucifer were going off to discuss something.

Soon, Jaxon came back down the stairs with an old shoebox in tow. It contained bandages and unlabeled jars of some sort of tincture. Saffron sat Lily down and the three of them headed off into the basement.

Down in the basement, the intern still cowered up against the wall. Their solar powered flashlight still gave light, but it had begun to dim. Saffron was quick to assess the situation and motioned for Alena and Jaxon to stay back before she took the first aid kit and tiptoed her way to the intern. They noticed the newcomer immediately and whimpered as they tried to scoot away from her. Saffron hesitated and went no further.

"Hello, my name is Saffron," she introduced. "Would you like some water or something?"

The intern didn't respond, just stared at her with dilated pupils. Saffron crouched down to be more at eye level with the other.

"I'm sorry for the mess you and my friend went through," Saffron went on. "They don't want to get hurt or killed, but we don't want *you* to either."

The intern's gaze flicked between Saffron and the others, their eyes narrowed. "That man threatened to kill me." Saffron shot Jaxon with such a venomous look that Alena balked. It burned with the fires of Lord Lucifer, and reminded Alena greatly of them.

"And why shouldn't I have?" Jaxon snapped in defense. "Their fucking Paladin friends killed my brother!"

Jaxon's gaze pierced like knives. The intern flinched back and tried to hide behind their arms. Saffron let out an apologetic sigh before she brushed off Jaxon's wrath. She put up her hands.

"Everyone here is a bit tense," Saffron said and no one could deny that. "But we are all people that want to get out of this situation without any more escalation, okay? So who is the person I'm speaking to?"

The intern hesitated as they thought over their options, but appeared more at ease. What else could they do but comply at that moment? They lowered their arms ever so slightly to take in Saffron. "Hmm... it's technically Veronica, but I prefer to go by Vero."

"Well, it's nice to meet you, Vero," Saffron said as she lifted up the first aid box. "So would you like some help with that nasty wound?" Vero nodded and offered their gnarled hand. Saffron quietly moved towards them and got to work. She dabbed their hand with the mysterious ointment and wrapped it up before she moved to their ankle. Vero yelped as Saffron lightly touched it and then quickly apologized. She took another wrap and carefully went over the limb.

"Alright now that that's done, do you want to get out of this basement so we can talk more comfortably?" Saffron asked as she stood back up and extended a hand to Vero. They looked at the offending limb as if it were a snake about to strike. However, they glanced towards where King Belial's altar still stood proudly to weigh their options. They were quick to accept Saffron's help. She pulled them up to see that they actually towered over her. However, Saffron didn't let that stop her as she held onto them while Vero kept their injured ankle up. Saffron motioned for Alena and Jaxon to keep their distance, and so the two of them hurried back up the stairs.

Jaxon went on ahead to leave the area, his breath huffy and shoulders tense. Eventually the group made it back to the foyer where Alena could vaguely feel the gazes of both King Belial and Lord Lucifer. The two demons curiously watched the humans at work. She also noticed how Vero stared unblinkingly at the door with the strongest yearning. Alena cleared her throat to get Vero's attention.; Their stare was a cautious one.

"I'm really sorry about all this happening," she said, but they made no reaction to imply it was either accepted or denied. That was fine. Alena knew she wasn't owed acceptance.

Saffron helped Vero over to the couch and found Jaxon lingering in one of the room's corners. Saffron regarded him wearily before finally giving Vero some space.

Lily, curious at the display, trotted over to sniff at Vero's ankle as though she hadn't previously attacked the other. Vero shrieked and the cat jumped with a hiss. Saffron quickly snatched up Lily and handed her off to Alena, who kept her enveloped in gentle arms.

"You know, I don't think you've told me her name," Saffron said as she back-tracked and went to sit in one of the reclining chairs. Her voice was light to try and keep the mood easy.

"It's Lily," Alena responded, "but her full name is Lilith."

"A name fit for a queen." Saffron nodded as Alena heard a soft *'aww'* from Lord Lucifer.

"We can't just act like everything is fine!" Jaxon groaned. Alena sighed, for she knew Jaxon had a point, but what could they do? She looked to Saffron with the unspoken question and she seemed to understand immediately.

"Either way," Saffron said, mainly aimed at Jaxon despite looking at Alena from the corners of her eyes. "What's done is done and the next step is just letting Vero go home."

"Y-Yes please," Vero gasped. They looked so hopeful for the first time since the incident. "I won't tell a soul!"

"Highly unlikely," Jaxon growled, which got them to deflate.

"Saffron is right," Alena agreed. "I mean we can't just keep them here." The group fell into silence once more, the energy of the room tense enough to snap a rubber band. It was decided and yet so much was still left up in the air. Alena looked more fully at Vero. "You can stay here tonight to heal up your leg. You can go in the morning."

Vero looked more than a little distraught that they weren't able to go immediately. But with one look at themself, they knew they weren't in the shape to drive down the mountain. And so it was decided. Saffron looked to be more at ease as she leaned further back into her seat, but Jaxon and Vero only looked all the more tense.

'Alena, darling,' Alena heard Lord Lucifer's gentle tone as their lighter energy swooped in beside her. They were curious and hopeful. *'Perhaps it would be nice to smooth things over with a meal, I'm sure everyone would do good to have some food.'*

King Belial chuckled at the idea and shook his head. Alena put on an understanding smile nonetheless. "I'm not sure it's the best time for that."

Jaxon and Vero snapped their gazes to Alena, concerned when they saw her stare off into the supposedly empty foyer.

'Please feed Saffron.' Lord Lucifer reiterated and Alena wondered if that's what the demon queen had initially wanted. *'She was so concerned for you, she hadn't eaten yet today.'* Saffron blushed at that and let out a tiny, "Luce..." under her breath. Oh there it was. Alena chuckled and decided some food would help soften their moody bites. She left the group to head into the kitchen. Jaxon followed. She passed by King Belial in the foyer, but he said nothing, just continued to watch over her.

As Alena started to gather up some of the leftover veggies, Jaxon went to help her. The two began to make their stew in utter silence. She glanced at him, a knot in her throat as she recalled their conversation from earlier. It had felt like so many years ago. Alena had to say something, anything, to smooth things back over.

"Would you consider us to be friends?" she asked, which made him hesitate. She sighed. "I-I'm sorry for putting you on the spot like this. You... You can leave, if you no longer feel safe here. I won't fault you for that."

Jaxon looked at her, *truly* looked at her and his hardened eyes finally softened.

"No, I should apologize to you for how I've acted..." he said after a moment. "I... know killing them would have only made things worse." Alena was silent as she reached out to him and gently squeezed his arm in understanding. They didn't need words, and she felt too ragged to find them.

The two spent the rest of the time in the kitchen, quiet as they threw together a meal before they brought it to the others. Saffron happily chowed down and Alena could swear she even saw Lord Lucifer hover over the woman's shoulder, taking energetical bites from the soup. She didn't seem to mind though. Vero, on the other hand, only stared down at the soup as if it had been poisoned. Alena didn't think they ended up eating anything.

Soon the evening went and night befell them, the group not saying much more as they waited the passage of time. Jaxon allowed Vero to sleep on the couch, while he took an old comforter and made a nest in the kitchen across the way. He made it no secret he wanted to be as far away from the intern as possible. Lily thought the man on the floor was great fun, and so spent the time flopping around on his blanket. Saffron had gotten up to hover around the entryway between the living room and foyer. Her gaze was deep in thought. When the house had grown dark, Alena finally went to join Saffron to see if everything was alright.

As she moved, she caught sight of Vero looking her way. She hesitated.

"Alena, was it?" they asked when she noticed them. She nodded and they went on, "Can I ask you something?"

"Go for it."

"W-Why would you choose to worship a demon?" Vero asked, and to Alena's surprise it was a lot less venomous than the tone Jaxon had initially used when he found out. Alena waited to see if this question was just a trick of sorts, but no, Vero looked so exhausted it seemed earnest. Alena hummed and looked away as she thought about that question.

She caught sight of Saffron, her eyes half-lidded as she wordlessly mouthed something. Speaking with Lord Lucifer. Beyond her in the kitchen, Jaxon grumbled and tried to gently push Lily away but she only took it as play and pounced back on him. Alena laughed at the sight. The house around her, despite how dark and decrepit it appeared, felt warm.

Her voice was barely above a whisper. "I think my life is better now with him in it."

Vero didn't respond, only stared as they tried to wrap their head around it. That was fine though, Alena didn't expect anyone else to understand. And so she left them there on the couch to go stand beside Saffron. The woman's eyes slid open and she smiled which sent a comforting buzz to Alena's belly.

"Do you want to take my bed?" Alena offered. "I can sleep on the floor."

"No, no," Saffron waved her off. She hesitated, and shot a glance into the kitchen towards Jaxon. "I think I'll stay up and... keep an eye on things." Alena winced, but she supposed she couldn't blame Saffron for being on edge. She didn't know Jaxon too well and hadn't a good first impression. Alena hoped they'd be able to smooth things over in the future, but for now left things as is.

"I hate that I dragged you into this," Alena said instead, "but I don't think Vero would have trusted me after what happened."

"It's no problem, I only do what I think is right." Saffron looked up towards the landing and Alena followed. There she saw a few sparkles in her vision, stark against the dark house around them. Alena smiled as she could picture Lord Lucifer being perched there like some sort of large bird, as they watched over the house from their vantage point. Alena turned her expression towards Saffron.

"I'm glad to have met you," she said and the other beamed. The feeling was mutual, and Alena realized it must have been hard for Saffron as well. Having to keep her love a secret and hide away in the old chapel right under the P.O.E.'s nose. It was nice to know someone else that shared the same knowledge and a demonic bond. Alena went on, "Saffron, would you mind if I stay up with you?" She imagined it would be nice for them to continue talking about their demons and hidden knowledge well into the night.

It was then Alena felt her back grow incredibly hot as King Belial slid up to her from wherever he lurked. She tensed as his large clawed hand heated up her shoulder and the muzzle of his skull nudged the top of her head. He stepped away then, trailing his claws across her back until he had gone, leaving her so much colder than she thought possible. Alena looked after him and saw a dark shadow creep its way into her bedroom.

"While company would be nice." Saffron giggled. "I believe you have a lot of words to exchange with your king."

Alena flushed and could only manage a nod before she hurried up the stairs. Her heart pounded, but she also felt a cooling flood of relief as the horrid day finally came to a close. She passed by Lord Lucifer on the landing and felt their tinkling amusement.

'Have fun~' They chortled and the need to defend herself and claim it wasn't what they thought rose quicker than ever. However, Alena chose to ignore them altogether, the only thing on her mind being King Belial.

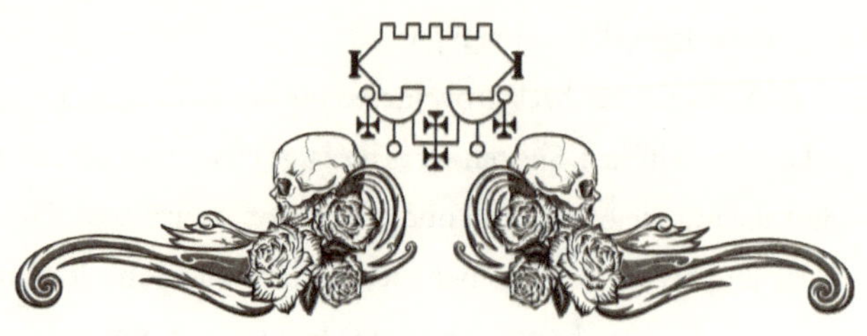

Chapter 36

Alena forewent the bed and headed across the hall into her bathroom. It was small and enclosed, so she felt great comfort from it. She lit the candle to provide light and shut the door. Finally she gazed into the cloudy mirror to check her appearance. The slash on her face was still a bright red and ran the length of her jaw to cheekbone. Alena winced because Vero had quite the arm on them. She wondered if it would leave a scar as she turned away from her reflection.

Alena ran the tub's faucet and took off her clothes to slip into the lukewarm tub. For once she wished it was hotter as she desired to reclaim her warmth. Well, it wouldn't be too much longer now. She quickly tried to clean away the grime and bits of dried blood from the day so she could comfortably lay in bed and give herself away to meditation.

King Belial lingered distantly as he waited for her to finish so they could finally talk about the day's events. It touched Alena how he still respected her wish to be alone in the bathroom. She sighed as she let the water ease her aches and sting the scrapes on her side. But also, she couldn't help but wonder; why wait? Alena leaned back and slid her eyes shut. Mentally, she took down that boundary just for now and beckoned him towards her. King Belial wasted no time as she heard the heavy falls of his hooves enter the room. The candle hissed as the flame died and cast the two into darkness.

A wave of comfort washed over Alena. She had no reason to be afraid of him, not anymore. The shower curtain rustled and she was flooded with a blast of hot air that made the water feel even colder. She leaned into the warmth and a heavy arm wrapped around her. Comforting. Alena allowed herself to drift off and when she opened her mind's eye, she was on the bed in her astral temple. King Belial was nowhere to be seen.

She leaped up from the massive bed and crossed the obsidian floors towards the tall arched window within the room. Alena looked out for the first time since creating the temple and gazed at a deep sea of trees. The world was stuck in perpetual night that turned the forest around the temple deep blues. A breathy sigh escaped her as the sight reminded her of home back in the physical. She could even see a rocky ridge off in the distance, and from it fell a crisp waterfall. Her heart lurched and Alena knew he must have been there.

She leaned out of the window to look down at the ground far below. Her temple had been placed on a high mountain top. She flicked her wrist and, in an instant, a flight of stony stairs carved into the side. She clambered out of the window, imagined the night air to be warm against her face, and hurried down. Before long she ran through the trees and moved aside anything that could trip her. She had to get to him, that's all she cared about.

Soon Alena came out of the forest and into a moonlit clearing. The only sound was the crash of the waterfall as it cascaded down the rocks into the pool below. It reflected the moon and nearly made it glow, the surrounding rocks bleached white. More importantly, there he was. King Belial. He stood by the water's edge, his red markings and irises glowed in tandem with the moon. He was like an ethereal beast of the woods, his horns curled upward towards the sky as he looked her way, expecting her. Waiting for her. And Alena would let him wait no longer.

She ran to him and didn't even stop when she reached him. The crushing reality of what happened that day caved in around her. Alena wailed as she tossed her arms around the demon's waist and sobbed into his stomach. King Belial didn't seem at all surprised by this as he sat a gentle and warm hand on the top of her head.

'You may cry it out now,' he whispered, *'for later there may not be enough time.'* And so she whimpered against him, and only when she found her voice again, did she speak.

"I just don't know what to do," she whined, each and every choice she made that day passed through her weary mind. "I'm so confused and... and scared."

The field was quiet then, not even the waterfall heard. King Belial said nothing for the longest time and Alena feared she may have shown too much weakness. However, the demon's voice was gentle when he finally did speak. *'What do you want in life, Alena?'*

She leaned away from him to look up in confusion.

'If you could have anything I could give to you, what would you want?' King Belial reiterated.

"I..." Alena trailed off as she thought it over. That was the same thing he asked her before, wasn't it? Alena narrowed her eyes. "It hasn't changed from when we first met. I just want to live a nice life, free of having to fear like this. But..." Her voice trailed off as she remembered how she gave him his offerings every morning, his warm touch on her shoulder that promised safety. Her face heated up in the physical world as she looked at the way the moonlight kissed his skull. She wasn't quite sure what type of connection their's was, but... Alena supposed it didn't need any sort of label. Not now. Her voice was barely above a whisper. "I think I would also be happy if you were in that life as well."

King Belial's expression was warm, despite his words. *'Would you feel the same if I were forced to leave you, or if it were between me or death?'*

The words wracked a shiver down Alena's spine. Not because it sounded like a threat, but because it had been a warning. How close had she come to dying that day? Had she been only an inch from Vero's blade striking her throat instead. Alena didn't think she wanted to know. But how should she respond to King Belial's question? Alena looked deeply into his eye sockets and Lord Lucifer's words from earlier came back to her. She sighed.

"It's too late for me to go back, you know, I..." Alena's heart fluttered as her eyes drifted downward, to take in the glowing markings on his chest as if they were the only thing that kept her there. She smiled, "I care about you, and I don't care if you're a demon, or whatever the nature of our connection really is."

'So you would choose to simply die for me?' he asked as if that were an easy question. Bite returned to her as the question struck like claws against her skin.

"I would fight for you!" she corrected. "I would fight the whole of the P.O.E. for you! And for Lily, Jaxon, and Saffron!"

King Belial flicked his tail, a smile on his boney face. *'So tell me Alena, **what do you want in life?**'*

Alena dug deeper into her insecurities, cracking them open like a frail geode. Though instead of crystal, there was only ash to be found. Smolders from the pyre where Archie had burned. The smoke from that day was no longer in Alena's lungs, but much like the fire, it was forever scorched into her memory. Just as, perhaps, the night where Jaxon had broken into her house looking for shelter.

Does it haunt you too, Jaxon? Alena thought to herself as her friend's enraged face flashed through her mind.

He had every right to react the way he did tonight. Even if it could have ended badly for Vero. Despite everything, Alena still couldn't find it within herself to hate the intern. Weren't they also doing what they had to survive? Just like her, Jaxon and Saffron were.

Dearest Saffron who had been so gentle with Vero. It wasn't fair how someone with such a kindly heart had to live while keeping others at an arm's length. And why? Because Saffron had the audacity to give her love to a demon? A demon that had also been through so much hardship and loss.

All due to what would become the Paladins of Exorcism. The source of all of their problems. The P.O.E. had promised the people of Lenoria safety, but ultimately, they had killed far more than any demon had. Alena gritted her teeth. As long as the P.O.E. were around, her desires for a nice and fearless life were impossible.

King Belial's eyes burned hotter than any fire.

"I know now," Alena growled. "What I want is to destroy the P.O.E!"

'You understand, next time, you may very well have to take the life that threatens yours,' King Belial said and immediately Alena's reservations came forth. She knew, deep down, that it was only luck Vero hadn't been fierce. If they were... Alena wasn't sure what would have happened. Understanding this, Alena nodded. King Belial appeared solemn.

The demon finally turned from her and pointed his skull's muzzle towards the astral moon above them. It reminded her so much of the first time she saw him in the light. The way the sun glistened off his skin while he took in the astral version of Saffron's painting. It made her heart clench just how attractive the demon truly was. She clenched her fists just as she had done then, a desire to run her hands over his skull.

'In olden times I was known as the lawless one,' King Belial's voice drifted over to her, it was rough and tired. Like an old mountain that had begun to wither with age, but it had been there for many years and would still remain for many more. He was eternal. King Belial went on, *'All I've wanted since the beginning of Lenoria was to hear someone say they wanted to dismantle the Paladins. You just had to be the one to say it, the one to also want it.'* He stopped and looked back at her with eyes that burned with the fires of hell. *'So it shall be done.'*

There was no questioning it, Alena knew right down to her bones this was what she wanted. She leaned into him and reached upwards. King Belial bent down and allowed her fingertips to brush along his skull. She couldn't feel it too well, but in the physical world her fingers tingled at the touch. Alena further fell into him, her other hand splaying out across the burning markings on his chest. That hand grew warm. She melted into it, becoming more pliable. The demon wrapped his massive arms around her and pulled her up to be more level with him. Alena sighed and buried herself into the side of his skull. It was perhaps not as hard and boney as she had thought.

King Belial, in turn, nuzzled her back. It was a moment for both of them with shells cracked open and walls fallen down. While the moment would not be one to last, for now, Alena found bliss. It was the closest thing to peace either of them would feel for a long time.

"Thank you for everything, King Belial," Alena whispered.

'Belial.'

She blinked and leaned back to look at the demon's face with furrowed brows. He chuckled at her confused look.

'You can just call me Belial.'

Alena awoke midday as she always did, her head heavy with fog. She was laid out in bed, fully dressed with drying puddles of water that lead from the bedroom door to the comforters. How had she gotten there? She was pretty sure she passed out in the tub, but she supposed it didn't matter. King Belial's... No. *Belial's* hefty energy moved swiftly away from her to go back to his lair in the basement.

Belial felt content, she thought. And in that moment, the night before flooded back to her. How close they had become. The words they shared. Alena's face flushed, but she had no time to dwell on it as a new found energy burst through her. If she didn't move quickly, she would lose her nerve. That was something she couldn't do. Not now. Not ever. She burst out of her room and crossed the landing.

Alena rushed down the stairs as if her life depended on it. She whipped through the foyer and into the living room where the others were already up and around. Her sudden entrance made Lily leap into the air with a surprised meow. Jaxon stood against the wall again and looked rather concerned by the sudden entrance. Across from Alena, Saffron sat in the recliner and looked at her curiously, but there was a knowing to her gaze. As though she already suspected what this was about. Alena's gaze drifted over towards the couch where Vero lay. They were still asleep. This was good. Vero couldn't hear what Alena was about to say.

'Well you've certainly got yourself in deep,' Lord Lucifer purred in her ear with humor. Alena ignored them as she wheezed to reclaim her breath. Then she finally spoke.

"I want to fight back." And only when the words escaped her mouth, with the eyes of those she called friends glued to her, Alena lost her nerve. They stared silently with confusion as if she had just sprouted nonsense. Alena flushed and grew clammy, but had to follow through. She had gone through too much since she first moved to that house to remain a coward.

"What are you talking about?" Jaxon broke the silence. Alena could tell by the way his eyes grew steely, that he did actually know. How could he not?

"You know what I mean," Alena responded, "against the P.O.E. And, what the hell, maybe even against King Byron himself."

"Alena, you can't be serious." Jaxon was guarded, a wall up between them. "We all know well enough what the P.O.E. is capable of. We'd be killed."

From behind her, the foyer grew five times heavier. Even without looking, she knew Belial had made an appearance. Her heart swelled for him.

"I know it'll be dangerous and, yes, I might even die," Alena said. "But it's something I have to try. With or without anyone's help, because I know I'll have Belial by my side."

"I am cautious," Saffron finally spoke up from where she sat. Alena gave her full attention. "But... My Lord said our paths have been set into motion. I will follow you, Alena, for the hope one day we will not have to hide."

Alena smiled despite the weight of it all. She didn't think she truly deserved Saffron's support, but it meant the world to her that she had it. Even as her oath to Lord Lucifer hung over her head. The light bringer in question was quiet as they observed the humans and Alena couldn't pick up on their thoughts.

"Ah, fuck it," Jaxon finally grumbled at the sight of Alena and Saffron. "I'm in too. I think going out swinging would be better than hanging around here all day doing nothing." Now that took Alena off guard and she was quick to wave him off.

"You really don't have to, if you don't want to," she said.

"I couldn't let you go at it without me," Jaxon responded. "It wouldn't be right. Not after what happened to Archie."

Alena felt warm, much like how she was with Belial, and now her heart swelled for the two in front of her as well. The people that were willing to risk it all for her goal, but she supposed they all had something to gain. On the couch, Vero groaned and rolled over. The group fell silent, but the intern's breathing continued to be at ease. Still asleep for now.

Alena's back heated up even more as Belial pressed up against her. His voice was rough as ever as he said, *"Looks like you've found your coven."*

SPIRIT-PEDIA

BELIAL

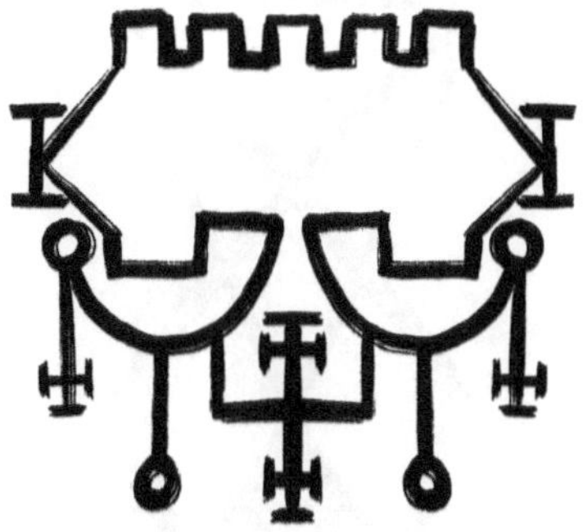

Titles(s): King
Element(s): Earth, Fire
Direction: North
Planet: Jupiter
Colors: Red, Black, Brown, Green
Correspondences: Lawlessness, Business, Relationships, Darkness, the Void, Mountains, Nature.
Preferred Offerings: Sweets, Black Coffee, Bones, Obsidian, Bloodstone, Sandalwood, Jaunts through nature in his honor.

LUCIFER

Titles(s): King, Prince, Lord, Emperor/ess

Element(s): Air, Fire

Direction: East

Planet: Venus

Colors: Black, Red, White, Gold

Correspondences: Pride, Rebellion, Freedom, Corvids, Snakes, Peacocks, Knowledge, Art, Music.

Preferred Offerings: Fruits, Lavender, Roses, Chocolate, Coffee, Sweets, Rose Quartz, Carnelian, Obsidian, Items depicting his likeness, art in their honor.

About the Author

Riley Daemon is a proud pagan with a deep love for the demonic. They showcase this passion by making art and writing about witchcraft and the occult. Riley adores wolves and owls, but ultimately is a cat person.

They currently have two books released, Whispers in the Forest and Bringing Forth Belial, and are featured in Reverent: An Anthology of Divinity.